Escape Artist

Books by Ed Ifkovic

Lone Star
Escape Artist

Escape Artist

An Edna Ferber Mystery

Ed Ifkovic

Poisoned Pen Press

Poisoned Pen Press
6962 E. First Ave., Ste. 103
Scottsdale, AZ 85251
www.poisonedpenpress.com
info@poisonedpenpress.com

Printed in the United States of America

For my grandkids,
Christopher and Emily,
With love

Chapter One

I was getting ready to leave the city room when Sam Ryan mentioned Harry Houdini. Curious, I dawdled at the pinewood table that served as my desk, fiddled with the ancient Oliver typewriter, and shifted some papers.

"Last time he was in town, some years back, he performed at the Opera House." The old man, publisher of the *Appleton Crescent*, leaned back in his chair.

I had no interest in showy carnival antics, too slapdash Circus Maximus for my taste, but Houdini, whose early boyhood had been spent on Appleton streets, always made for good copy. My parents often talked about the escape artist whose father at one time had been rabbi at Zion Congregation.

"The great Houdini." That was Matthias Boon, the new city editor. "The celebrated handcuff king himself."

Miss Ivy, Sam's sister, looked up. "I hear he is staying for a week with David Baum."

Matthias Boon looked surprised. "Who's that?"

"A childhood friend."

Boon sneered. "You know, I don't understand this malarkey he spouts. Tied up, imprisoned, boasting about escaping. What kind of an act is that?"

Byron Beveridge, the beat reporter, broke in, a bit of awe in his voice. "He does this Metamorphosis act with his wife. She ties him up and puts him into a box, and in three seconds he changes places with her."

Boon grunted. "Impossible. Trickery."

Bryon shook his head. "Of course it is. So what? Barnum was right." He beamed. "But a real showman."

"Foolish, really, such stunts." Miss Ivy yawned.

I kept still, just listened.

Sam skimmed the sheets before him. "You know, suddenly he's all the rage in Europe. He can extricate himself from the most complicated set of handcuffs. He's escaped jails in Russian Siberia, in London. He can free himself from a straitjacket…"

Miss Ivy spoke over his words. "My brother is a loyal follower."

"He can trick innocent souls into forking over hard-earned dollars for some obvious chicanery," Boon sneered.

"Mr. Boon, you're new here in old Appleton. You don't understand the appeal of a man like Houdini in this town." Sam's voice rose, excited. "A real home-grown hero."

Boon frowned. "A grown man strutting around publicly in his BVDs, jumping into nailed boxes, taunting the police."

Byron Beveridge drummed his fingers on his typewriter. "I've seen him perform. In his early days, starting out, when I worked in Chicago. He was with a dime museum, real shabby, with snake charmers and bearded ladies. Then he reinvented himself. Impressive, I must say."

Boon would have none of it. "Seems to me you small-town folks are easily impressed by circus acts."

"He's one of our own. Small-town boy who made it big." Sam's spectacles slipped down his nose and he readjusted them.

"Just proves that the world is nuts," Boon concluded. He glanced my way but looked through me. Since he arrived from Milwaukee a few months back, he'd decided that girl reporters shouldn't exist.

Sam pointed to typed pages on his desk. "Houdini's provided us with press sheets, including an interview he gave in London. He expects us to publish them verbatim." He tapped the sheets with his index finger. "With his curiously ungrammatical quotes."

"What are you saying? We can't interview him, we small-town hicks?" Boon guffawed. "Now the question of the hour is this: How *do* we get an interview with the man?"

Sam grinned. "It seems we don't. He and his brother are here socializing with old buddies, though he's performing a one-shot benefit for the Children's Home on Platt. The man may crave publicity, but no one's seen him around." He shrugged. "No interviews, I guess."

"The obnoxious little Jew," Boon muttered.

I sat up, iron-backed. There it was.

Sam glanced at me while Boon refused to look at me. "Maybe our little Jewess can convince him otherwise."

"Maybe this little Jewess will respect a man's privacy." I glared.

"I mean no insult, Miss Ferber." Boon spoke with obvious calculation. "I just assume you people all know each other."

My voice was chilly. "The Weiss family—he was Ehrich Weiss here, though you probably don't know that—left before the Ferbers came to town." I stopped, my throat dry, my head swimming. Appleton was kind to its small Jewish population. Indeed, the popular former mayor, David Hammel, was a Jew and lived across the street from the Ferbers. I'd not felt the sting of discrimination, not since my family had fled bigoted, ugly Ottumwa, Iowa, where I'd been routinely mocked. But now, again—here it was. "His father was the first rabbi of our temple."

The room got cold all of a sudden; glances shifted, eyes averted. "All the more reason." Boon, the willful baiter, the bigot. Suddenly I wondered how much his undisguised dislike of me stemmed, not from my being a young girl and a reporter, but my being a Jew.

"I mean no harm." Boon sucked in his cheeks. He was lighting his pipe and watched me, over the blazing match.

"Then you harm inadvertently."

"Meaning?"

I turned away.

"We have a paper to get out." Sam stood, stretched his back. "Maybe we should get busy."

I picked up my notebook—"Always carry it with you," Sam Ryan often reminded me— and wrapped my blue chiffon wrap around my shoulders, drawing it close around the high-neck lace collar of my dress. I slipped on my kid gloves. I dreaded climbing the five weathered cement steps that led from our subterranean city room up to the street level. After a year as a girl reporter for the Democratic afternoon daily, I'd come to gauge my level of fatigue by my approach to those five steps—from the rare exuberance of a rich, vital day of reporting to the familiar exhaustion after a day of disappointment, false starts, emptiness. Lately, I approached those steps with the reluctance of Sisyphus pushing that dreadful stone up a redundant hill.

As I moved past Matthias Boon, he leaned back in his swivel chair and boasted, "You know, I like a good challenge. I think I'll interview the great Houdini. It's all in the manner of approach. What stage performer lacks an ego? And his is overweening, I've heard. Self-love makes a man vulnerable."

Good Lord.

Boon was still crowing. "I once convinced a reluctant Tommaso Salvini to talk about his life. 'I have nothing to say,' and then he couldn't shut up. And he was a crowing sort of buffoon."

"I don't know…" Sam began.

"Houdini is a vain exhibitionist. He's mine." He started to choke on his pipe tobacco.

Up on College Avenue, I headed to the courthouse, but stopped walking. I didn't want to do my job. I wanted to stay in motion, strolling aimlessly down the avenue, lost among the stragglers making their late-afternoon purchases. I stared in the window of Schiebler and Schwante. Hmm, Japonette handkerchiefs on sale for three cents. Yes, I'd buy myself a set from the wages of a job I'd soon be losing.

Only recently I'd lingered for hours down in the city room, dreamily staring up at the half-windows, contemplating the lower extremities of Appleton citizens wandering past. Yes, Mamie Tellis' ample bottom, awash in a pale lavender crepe de chine go-to-tea dress under a Persian lamb coat. Mayor Linsome's bow-legged waddle. Caroline Tippler, in her perennial crinoline smock, headed to her waitressing job at the Sherman House, her stride lively. Mildred Dunne, the high school librarian, with her shuffling baby steps. Principal Jones, lumbering past, his gait slower since his wife died last year. I knew them all and loved the panorama.

And then—then Matthias Boon arrived from Milwaukee.

The splendid human comedy out in the street now metamorphosed into a dark *danse macabre*, the march of the doomed. Inside my tiny space, under the large shadow of that small man, despair gripped me. I wasn't happy.

"Edna." A voice startled me out of my gloom.

"Hello, Mollie." I nodded to the salesgirl at Pettibone-Peabody's Department Store in charge of the woolens and long johns aisle—and one of my "informers," as I termed them, gatherers of gossipy bits and pieces that I typed into my reports. *Mr. and Mrs. Boris Leyendecker are in Little Chute for the weekend, visiting Mr. Leyendecker's sister, who has returned from Rome.* Mollie Seagrum, buxom and matronly, a spinster with a light-hearted wit.

Joshua Hutt has returned from a term at the University in Madison to attend to his late father's estate...

Mrs. John Boyesen will be making her annual pilgrimage to...

Yet I'd relished my job, thrived on it, actually. A year back, fresh from Ryan High School, class of 1903, I'd battled my family over my desire to attend the Northwestern School of Elocution in Evanston, Illinois. In my heart I knew it was my circuitous road to ending up on the New York stage and becoming the next Sarah Bernhardt. But my family had vociferously fought me, what with spending money in short supply, my father ailing, my mother imperious, my older sister Fannie spiteful—this excuse, that one, hundreds of them. Innocent girls leaving home, lost in big cities, horribly tempted, gaslight encounters, strangers in the dark rainy alleys, a drain on the pennies needed back home, on and on, wearying me.

So I'd stormed down into Sam Ryan's *Crescent* office and pleaded for a job. "I can write." Said simply, declarative. Sam recalled my high-school essay about Passover at the Appleton synagogue, which he'd printed. He hired me on the spot. Three dollars a week.

It had been a wonderful year, bizarre and at times freakish. I was a novelty: a girl reporter on the streets of little Appleton, population 12,000, give or take a dozen wandering souls on the outskirts, including the shabby, dispirited Oneidas who knocked on back doors selling baskets of huckleberries.

I cared little that the stalwart citizens viewed me as strange, unseemly, perhaps a little maddened. A progressive town, Appleton was, with Lawrence University and an opera house. But still and all…a *girl* asking untoward questions? And of men? A girl in a sensible straight-boned bodice worn over a black miroir velvet skirt that sometimes got caught in the pinewood planks of the sidewalks as I trudged up and down bustling College Avenue, storming in here or there, dropping in at Kamp's and Sacksteder's Department Store, at the Wae Kee Laundry on Oneida, at the Ladies Aid Society on Superior Street.

What have you heard?

Do you know if…?

Why? Really? Tell me.

Tell me. I'm here to listen. Really. I…

My mother was horrified when I got the job, though she ran the family novelty store on College and was also subject to disapproving glances. Nice little Jewish girls, with spectacles and a high-school class pin, in decent Midwestern towns, acting like brazen New York City reporters; unsettling, truly. Whispered about. I cared not a whit. I was tackling life head on, albeit a small-time version as bland as thin broth. To me it was the pulse of life. My beat was the nondescript, routine social register, largely women's doings, society musings, endless teas and church socials. *Professor Meyers of Lawrence University will*

speak on horticulture in the Bible Tuesday at the Masonic Hall.
The public is…

I loved it.

I felt *important*…I, the plumpish, plain girl.

The only time I didn't feel insecure, homely, awkward—invisible, frankly—was when I marched on College Avenue with my pad and pencil, headed to the courthouse. Heads turned, eyes narrowed.

The old city editor John Meyer had trumpeted my writing, had praised my embellished, adjective-laden prose, my quirky insertion of local-color dialogue into a prosaic piece about the Knights of Pythias spring flower show. Each morning when he handed me the daily assignment, he nudged me to be…creative.

"Flower it up," he advised. "Go for the bedraggled orphans and the weepy widows."

A student of Dickens melodrama and the bathetic effusions in the romances of the Duchess, I need not have been so encouraged. I'd learned the power of sentimental thrusts, purple prose, the beautiful sweep of sentences that rose like spring flooding on the Fox River.

Sam Ryan, the septuagenarian—or was it octogenarian?—owner, the little old bald man with the jaunty walk, just winked. He knew a good thing when he saw it. For three dollars a week.

When I'd started out I was a chubby, round-faced cherub of a young girl, eyeglasses resting precariously on my high-bridged nose, showing up that first day in a homemade walking dress of dark green broadcloth and wearing an outlandish hat fashioned by sister Fannie—round as a saucer, with papier-mâché red cherries cascading off it, accented with purple-dyed ostrich plumes, and a nun's veil netting that looked like ocean mist.

Sam Ryan's eyes had widened with alarm. "The hat has to go. You look like some scary grande dame in a Puccini opera. You look like you've been exploded." The hat came off. "And wear your hair up."

My hair was unmanageable, a wild thicket of deepest black, wiry impossibility, tumbleweed untrainable with ribbons and stays and seashell clasps and mother-of-pearl barrettes. So the next day I wore my hair up, decorous, with a sensible hat. I was learning. People didn't take you seriously if you looked like an act in a vaudeville revue. Fannie, told of the slight to her creation, fumed.

My beat included the courthouse at the other end of College Avenue, a mile and a half away, at the Chute. It was hardly an exciting place. All the meaty news happened closer to downtown at the Elks Club, Moriarity's Pool Hall, the Sherman House, Little's Drug Store, the jail, the fire station—places where Matthias Boon and Byron Beveridge did their snooping around. But I prowled the marble, echoey hallways, gleaning this tidbit and that. Transfers of property, liens, writs. The rickety streetcar up College cost five cents, too big a dent in my meager budget, so I walked and walked and walked. At the end of the year I'd lost that plumpness, that young girl baby fat; and now, in blissful June, I was slender and tough. Nobody's fool. The Appleton girl reporter, sleek as a greyhound, and as wily, with smart-aleck vinegar in the blood.

But magnificently unhappy.

Matthias "Matt" Boon, the new man recently arrived from Milwaukee—just why had he left that cosmopolitan city for our little town?—was a tiny rubicund man built like a tree stump, with that beet red face and those bushy Chester Arthur muttonchops.

My nemesis.

Chapter Two

I paused in front of Pfaff's Mortuary, adjusting a sleeve and checking my reflection in the window. My eye caught something. Across the street, Harry Houdini was standing outside Volker's Drug Store, arms folded, immobile. A cigar-store Indian without the cigar. I'd seen photographs of him flexing his muscles, wrapped in chains; he was clothed now like a drummer, yet the face was unmistakable. I scurried across the street, allowing a horse-drawn carriage to pass—Miss Fotherwell, headed with her Negro servant to examine fabrics at Myron's Clothiers, something she did daily—and stood dumbly in front of Houdini.

"Mr. Houdini," I began, breathless, then stopped. I'd interrupted him in some trance because he was staring, unblinking, into space. "Mr. Houdini," I began again, but again the small intense face didn't register my presence. I felt foolish—and intrusive. I took a step backward, looked toward the *Crescent* office and the small-canopied window of the law offices that were above the city room, and waited, deliberate. An image of the insolent Matthias Boon, that Napoleon who came up to the world's hip, came to me. "Mr. Houdini."

The head turned, the eyes nearly shut. "What?"

I didn't like his voice: small, hoarse, oddly bell-like. Even that one word—so blunt: *What?*—carried a hint of a foreign accent, a guttural Hungarian inflection. His father's son, the rabbi's boy, carried from some Budapest shtetl.

"I'm bothering you, I know."

He held up his hand. "You are?"

The small, calloused hand remained in front of my face. I noticed a scar across his palm, a pale pink lightning bolt that contrasted with the nut-brown flesh. Appleton's homespun celebrity who grandly announced himself the world's greatest entertainer. Brash, and a little presumptuous. I hugged my reporter's pad to my chest. He watched me, a faint smile on those thin, dried-up lips. A staring contest between us, Houdini and me. The great Houdini himself. A smallish man whose physical strength seeped, sap-like, through the rumpled summer suit he wore: sinew and muscle and tendon, a compact body with a thick neck. Blue-gray eyes, as deep as lake water, purposely holding you, mesmerizing, a snake charmer.

Feeling oddly calm in his presence, I decided I could outlast this overgrown yeshiva boy in the poorly assembled flowing tie, his diamond shirt stud gleaming in the sunlight. On his head an incongruous sailor's cap.

I broke the silence. "My name is Edna Ferber and I'm a reporter at the *Appleton Crescent.*" I actually pointed across the street to the sign. But Houdini refused to follow my hand. His eyes never left my face. "And," I beamed, "I've been told you're not granting interviews."

"So why are you talking to me? I ain't a man to change my mind." Said with that thickly accented voice. There was something else there now—a real humor.

"Because I assume entertainers *want* publicity."

His eyes smiled. "You sound like my wife Bess." He still hadn't moved a muscle.

"Is she in town with you?" Bess was his stage partner, the fearless woman sealed in boxes behind curtains.

"No, she's in New York."

"You're just here with your brother?"

"Are you conducting an interview?"

I waited a bit. "Seems like it."

"Ferber." He squinted his eyes. "Your father is Jacob?" His face relaxed a bit.

That startled me. "Yes. How…"

"I'm staying with David Baum, over on Oriental. David mentioned your father…"

"Why?"

"Is this part of the interview?"

"I'm curious."

"We were talking of the Jewish families of Appleton. The old days when I was here. The new families."

"Yes, I'm his daughter." I rushed my words.

"I know."

"You know?"

"Ah, Miss Ferber, another question but an easy one to answer. I spent my young years in Appleton. I got friends here. I visit. People *talk*."

"But your family left before the Ferbers arrived."

"David likes your father and mentioned him. They used to go to concerts together. He also mentioned the young daughter who rushes around town like a crazy chipmunk writing her stories and…"

I pursed my lips. "Are you saying I'm odd?"

Now he chuckled. "No, Miss Ferber, I'm the oddity. I let people tie me up, chain me, lock me in dark containers. I'm the odd one. You're the town scandal."

I could see he wasn't being serious, so I relaxed. "Sir, I get three dollars a week running up the streets of the town."

"Handcuffs pay better."

"I'll stay with my flowery accounts of afternoon teas with the Ladies Benevolent Society, sir. Less wearing on the wrists."

He crossed his arms. "A secret, Miss Ferber, though not a big one. Two days ago, my dear, David pointed you out to me as you interviewed a visiting lecturer at Lawrence. You were in the library, and David and I were meeting a friend there."

"You watched me?" I did not like this.

"Fascinating. A girl reporter. A young Jewish girl, at that."

"And?"

"You're…unrelenting."

"Meaning?"

"You have a lot of energy. You overwhelmed the man."

"What?" I was not happy.

"You were a delight to watch, Miss Ferber."

"Meaning?"

"I mean that you are a spunky girl. You tackle the trivial as if you was having dinner at the White House."

"I take my job seriously, sir."

"But it's Appleton, Miss Ferber."

"It's important to me."

Houdini ran his tongue over his upper lip. "Of course it is. Everything is important to you. But Appleton's routines are a lot more boring than your life should be."

"My job is less dangerous than handcuffs and sealed coffins, sir."

He got serious. "Safer is not good for the soul."

"What?"

He looked up and down the street. "Are these the boundaries you set for yourself, Miss Ferber? You're a bright, clever girl. That's obvious. Look around you. You don't take no risks. Where would I be if I didn't tackle the world out *there*?"

"Sir, if you don't think being a girl reporter in Appleton is a risk, then…" I waved my hand in the air.

He tipped his hat. "Ah, point taken, Miss Ferber."

"Thank you."

"So you and I are alike then." He bowed dramatically. "As I suspected. Two souls running after the horizon."

"I'm not saying that. I *like* my job here. Appleton can be lively, filled with…" My voice trailed off.

"But you're young. Don't be bound by College Avenue. It's easy to be trapped by what's easy." He pointed his hand across the street.

What were we talking about? Strangely, I felt as though he were interviewing *me*, for I deliberated, weighed my responses, felt the need to satisfy *him*…to provide *him* with information from my unheralded biography. Mine was an uneventful life story. Houdini seemed bigger than life, a mountain of a man, the world's adventurer. Me? Nineteen years old, and…what? An Appleton scourge, peeping Tom, prier into peoples' mundane lives. *Tillie Eisenhower will display her embroidery at the Masonic Hall beginning…*

I needed to refocus. "So I can interview you, Mr. Houdini?"

He laughed out loud, clearly enjoying our exchange. "You already are."

Something had just happened here. We liked each other. He was flattering me, I could tell, but more so—yes, he was flirting with me, innocently, trying to charm me. And I felt pleased, a little intoxicated. Men didn't flirt with me, the drab, plain girl with the bushel-basket pompadour and the round nosy face. And certainly not older men…and famous ones at that. Was it that easy for young provincial girls to fall prey to such idle flattery? Obviously it was; I was ready to follow Harry Houdini to the ends of his handcuffed universe. Well, maybe not.

For the next fifteen minutes or so we chatted like old friends, Houdini wanting to help me, this young intense girl, and a good measure of our talk was silly and frivolous. I'd been training myself to remember conversations, word for word, believing that a notepad suddenly thrust into the space between me and the soul being interviewed served as a wall. So, instead, I listened to his boisterous anecdotes and made mental notes.

Yes, he was in town to visit old school chums, David Baum especially, the boy he hung out with as a child, the two of them stealing peaches and crabapples from the farms out by Little Chute. Yes, he was here for a week, enjoying his hometown, traveling with his brother Theodore, and he'd try out his new show at the Lyceum—a "few surprises," he hinted—as he prepared to head back to Europe later that summer. He described his fascination with handcuffs, leg irons, ropes, and nailed boxes. He was animated, twitching, nervous, and he spoke loudly, boasting of his stupendous salary. "I make sometimes two grand a week." He got a little sentimental when I asked him about his boyhood, his embryonic magic shows, what he recalled from the old fields across the tracks in the Sixth Ward, a contortionist act, three silly performances managed by buddy Jack Hoeffler, who paid him exactly thirty-five cents.

"What was your most difficult feat, the most difficult escape you ever made?"

"I think my escape from the Siberian Transport. I was placed in the great vault intended for political prisoners, and when the massive door was shut, I had the hardest time of my life, perhaps, in releasing myself." He confided, "Eighteen minutes it took me. But, after all, I am Houdini. In Germany they called me *König der Handschellen*. You speak German?"

"Of course. King of the Handcuffs."

"Very good, young lady."

I got him to talk about his life as little Ehrich Weiss, and he got teary-eyed talking about his mother. What was he doing in front of the drug store? Well, his father the rabbi rented rooms on College Avenue between Oneida and Morrison. He pointed to a building. "Right there. Over the Heckert Saloon. Where I used to get my spanking."

"A sentimental journey?"

He ignored that. "But now I'm the master of chains and handcuffs, all made of the strongest iron." He made a bicep and told me to feel his upper arm. I hesitated, but he insisted. "Go ahead."

Feeling foolish, I let my fingers feel the hard muscle, which he flexed. Red faced, unsure, I dropped my hand back to my side. He was grinning, enjoying my discomfort.

Suddenly, as though slamming a book shut, he stopped talking. The interview was over. I backed away, thanking him, but he leaned forward. "Let me tell you a secret."

"To what?" A child's wide-eyed wonder.

"To your future. Because I sense you are like me—hungry to leave this small city, hungry for something out *there*. You have a *heimweh* for it. You know that word?"

"A talent, I suppose."

"You are hungry..."

"Oh, no," I protested, "I'm content…"

He hushed me. "No, you ain't. Stop this…this talk. Otherwise you wouldn't be assaulting strange men in front of drug stores. You'd be home, the dutiful Jewish daughter, serving your father and mother."

I closed my eyes and thought of my blind father, lonely on the front porch of our home. "Mr. Houdini, I…"

He held up his hand. "I'm not saying this is a bad thing, young woman. But you must let me finish talking."

"But…but…I'm content…"

"No, you're not. Contentment is for the baby in a cradle. All over the world I spot it, identify it. You—I see it. Keep in mind that I come from these streets. There's a hunger in some souls…"

I needed to get away, miserable now. How had this man, a stranger talking about himself, guessed my unhappiness?

"I'll tell you something. Just two things. Two things that lead you to success in the world. In fact, why I am the world famous Houdini and not little Ehrich Weiss picnicking on the Fox River. Houdini, one of the great people of the earth right now. Why people all over know me." He puffed up his chest, face flushed. I waited, breathless. "Can you tell me what they are?"

I panicked. What? What? Finally, I stabbed, "Imagination."

He slapped one fist into the other. "Good for you, Miss Ferber. But that you knew all along. The other?"

I was at a loss.

"Let me tell you then. Concentration. Imagination ain't nothing good without concentration. How do you think I get out of deadly bolts and chains? It takes imagination, true, the leap of fancy, maybe, but, you know, concentration shapes the edges of the fancy." Then he closed up again. "I expect to read your interview in the *Crescent*. I'll cut it out and paste it in my scrapbook."

The interview was over. But my mind spun like a child's top. My God, an interview with Harry Houdini! How would my revelations be greeted across the street, down in the office? I, the distaff interloper, the snooping girl, sashaying in with the scoop of the week. A bead of sweat formed on my brow. One more battle to wage.

Houdini kept talking. "You're a delightful young woman, Miss Ferber. And, I think, a brave one. I hope our paths cross again before I leave Appleton." That struck me as impossible. "Are you coming to my performance at the Lyceum?"

I hadn't planned to. Beer hall pyrotechnics; vaudeville buffoonery. "Yes. Of course."

"Would you like to have me tie you up and secret you in a box—and then change places with you?"

"No, sir. Coffins have no appeal for me."

He laughed then, uproariously and full-throated. I turned to go. "Ah, Miss Ferber." I swung back. He was handing me something. Two padlocks rested in his palm. In front of the drug store were two candy machines, glass-bowed containers of penny candy, set up against the white clapboards. Somehow, deftly, while we spoke, he'd undone the simple padlocks and now deposited them into my palm. "You'd better return these to the shopkeeper. Otherwise he'll have no candy left for the youngsters of Appleton to buy." He walked away.

I hadn't seen him touch the two dispensers in all the time I'd spoken with him.

Back at the city room, reached in a fury, I pecked out a two-page interview on my Oliver. No one there paid me any mind nor wondered at my sudden return to the city room. Within the half hour I was through, a rambling but nonetheless faithful account of my conversation with Houdini. As I typed, I felt euphoric. Still, his advice locked itself neatly in my brain. "Concentration and imagination," the secret code to *something*. There was a whiff of arrogance in his telling me how to succeed, which bothered me, a hint of his own self-congratulation. Frankly, I already possessed both qualities. I was a young woman of purpose, clearly. So be it. Ego is the province of an entertainer. Satisfied, I slipped the final page from the machine, read it over again, penciled in some changes, and sat back, triumphant.

Sam Ryan, nodding off in the late-afternoon warm room, roused himself. "You got the look of a fox raiding a hen house."

I gleamed, handing him the two typed sheets. Silently, he reached for them, sat up, and read the headline I'd provided: "Houdini is Master of Locks and Bolts." He shot me a look, shaking his head. "How?"

I shrugged.

He read on, a smile seeping into the creases of his mouth. "Good job." Then, getting the attention of Matthias Boon who'd been ignoring our brief exchange, he waved the sheets. "Here, Mr. Boon. This will run tomorrow."

Boon probably expected to read of some boating mishap on the Fox River or, maybe, the wife of the President of Lawrence University spilling tea on a visiting dignitary. He read the sheets rapidly, his small, stolid body hard, tense, the tendons in his neck purple and prominent. His stubby fingers drummed the pages, his nails so bitten to the quick that a line of dried blood seemed permanent scars. He eyed me. I expected censure or anger at my usurping his planned thunder. Instead, his voice was buttery. "A tad flowery and syrupy, no?"

I fumed.

He drew a red pencil across lines, editing, shifting, truncating my prose. He slid it back to me and half of my words had disappeared, blotted out, including my last mesmerizing paragraph about the trickery with the drug-store candy machines. Gone—all of that. Where I'd mentioned the *London Times,* he'd added a phrase: "the most conservative paper in the world." Why? Where I'd said how successful Houdini was, he'd added to my "poor fatherless boy" the phrase "wealth and ease." He'd brutalized my work, but I said nothing.

"Quite the coup, Miss Ferber." Sam saluted me.

When I looked at Matthias Boon, his expression could only be called hatred. "I guess it helps to be Jewish."

"No," I cut the silence, "it helps to be a reporter on the prowl."

Houdini's praise—his *celebration* of my spirit—flooded me, lifting me beyond the cramped city room. Something of

Houdini's energy or golden dust covered me, even as I realized that Matthias Boon would punish me for what I'd just done.

The stump-like city editor sat with his pipe in hand, his feet up, munching on the hardtack biscuits he kept in a brown bag in his drawer. The muscles in his neck looked like taut rope.

Well, one more nail to my own coffin. Which, I knew, I couldn't escape as seamlessly as did Houdini.

Chapter Three

Daylight was fading as I finally turned onto North Street, four blocks north of the *Crescent* office. There was my home, the white clapboard house with the gingerbread lattice, the floor-to-ceiling casement windows, and the generous wraparound porch on three sides of the house. Flower boxes, planted with Sweet William and marjoram, lined the porch, along with wicker baskets filled with cascading ferns. I loved the house, considered it modern and grand.

But I dreaded what I'd find there.

I dawdled, my long dress sweeping the dirt lane, dust swirling. From a distance in the faltering twilight, I could see my father behind the floral boxes and baskets tucked into the Adirondack chair he lived in these days. Sitting there, impeccably dressed in his black suit with knitted tie. Waiting for me. My heart raced.

Distracted, I nearly crossed into the path of Mr. Cyrus P. Powell passing by in his plum-colored Victoria. He ignored my raised hand of greeting as he maneuvered his horses into a brisk clip. There was always something about the severe man that made me shiver. I'd never seen the prosperous Mr. Powell smile at anyone. In seconds he disappeared around a corner.

All was quiet. Staring down the street, across that expanse of neat and mannerly homes, I was gripped by a wave of panic; my throat tightened. My father was bent over, his head nodding. Flickering gaslights started popping on, a syncopated rhythm that turned the street into a fuzzy, drifting landscape, a dark-laced panorama that made me think of Gray's "Elegy Written in a Country Churchyard," all that heavy gloom, that slate-gray mist, that…that sense of ending.

For a moment I closed my eyes. Stop this. No! But I couldn't shake the gnawing fear. I knew in that awful moment, paralyzed in the street, that my father would soon die—that this shadowy tableau of a slender man huddled outside his home would be something I'd have to flee.

I swallowed, roused myself, kept walking up the pathway, past the untrimmed lilacs already finishing their shrill spring-time bloom.

"Is that you, Pete?" He leaned forward, expectant, a little irritation in his voice.

"Yes, Bill. Appleton's Nelly Bly reporting home."

It was our private joke. For years he'd affectionately called me Pete, though he couldn't remember why. Then a few years back the Elks Convention met in Appleton, and the noisy, rollicking lodge members, bustling with cheer (and beer), hailed one another as "Bill" as they crossed paths downtown. So my father became Bill to me. Pete and Bill cemented a union that excluded my mother Julia and my older sister Fannie, sensible women who had little time for silly nicknames. Edna and Jacob Ferber, daughter and father, I'd long told myself, were the poets in the household, though I kept that news from the others.

Sitting with my father, I talked excitedly of my interview with Houdini, regaling him with anecdotes, imitating Houdini's voice.

When I finished, he clapped his hands. "Sam Ryan will give you a raise. I'm sure of it."

I got quiet. Not only were my days at the *Crescent* numbered, but, worse, I didn't know what to do with my life. I liked being on the Appleton streets, ferreting out news. I liked being away from the house. I liked being away from, well…my father's awful pain. For he was nearly totally blind now, only able to distinguish shadows, a hint of brilliant color or sunlight, maybe a dash of flashing movement as a horse trotted by. That was all. Save for the long harsh Wisconsin winter, he sat on the front porch day after day, losing interest in life, sometimes docile, other times irritable, and waited for me to return home—to take him for an afternoon walk or, at the end of my work day, to sit with him. At times a horrible debilitating pain would seize him, and though numb with fatigue, I would stand behind him, my fingers pushing into his tender temples, the nape of the neck, the center of his forehead, until, sighing, his skin grayish, clammy and wet, he closed his eyes, at peace.

I watched him staring straight into the darkening street. A handsome man with a high, intelligent brow shielding dreamy, half-closed hickory-colored eyes; a man always dressed in his immaculate black broadloom suit with a gold watch fob, and the silk cravat one of the women in the household expertly tied each morning. To me, he looked East European sitting there; old world, son of a shopkeeper from Eperye, a village outside Budapest, a market town; a man now without a country, or, more horribly, in a country of no light, no hope. His dark complexion, a gypsy's pallor as soft as vellum, suggested a man who hid from day-to-day rigor, but that was only now when blindness had marched its cancerous way into our home. The long slender fingers, a musician's hands, had been intended for violins or lyric poetry, not the housewares he tried to peddle in the emporium downtown—My Store. The name always made me wince. My Store. Of course, now it wasn't—my mother ran it. *Her* store.

All he did was sit—the porch, the parlor, waiting for supper. Or summer. Or winter. Or the end of day. For me. He used to smoke pungent cigars but that had stopped. "I need to see the trail of smoke. Smell means nothing by itself."

I understood.

In the long hot days of July and August, while the rest of Appleton sailed up and down the Fox River or strolled through Lovers Lane or picnicked at Brighton Beach on Lake Winnebago, I sat reading the *Appleton Crescent* to him. "The Lawrence Varsity Football team anticipates a successful fall program with the addition of Josiah Hunter, transferred from…" He'd yawn.

"Tired, Bill?"

"No. Keep reading, Pete."

"The Congregational Church will hold its missionary food drive on…"

I wanted to talk that evening about Matthias Boon, about the silences in the city room, but I couldn't. Houdini's splendid shadow covered me, though Matthias Boon's shadow kept intruding. I choked back a sob. In the gathering dark I reached out and touched my father's wrist. It was cold and clammy, dead. I tightened my hold, but said nothing.

Suddenly the silence was shattered by my mother's booming voice from an upstairs window. "Ed, are you just going to sit there? The kitchen is in chaos. When did you get home?"

"In a minute, Mother."

The window slammed down. I didn't move.

"You better go in, Pete."

"In a minute." I didn't want to move.

"Your mother's been in a mood since getting back from the store. And Fannie's giving her trouble."

I sighed. "Now what?" My mother and Fannie, two strong, fierce souls; demonstrative, hard-nosed. Stubborn, I fought them daily. Julia Ferber, wiry and severe, moved in short, halting steps, tackling a world she thought cruel and random. And Fannie, the homebody, pretty and lithe, belle of the ball, dizzy with boyfriends—and the modish clothing she spent hours whipping up. And the apricot and plum preserves she conjured up in the kitchen. And there I was, the third woman of the household: also strong, but tiny; the ugly duckling in a house where Cinderella made her own Parisian finery and banquet delicacies and danced the night away. The plain sister sat by firelight reading *Bleak House* or *The House of the Seven Gables* for the eighth time.

The window opened again. "For Heaven's sake, Ed. Do something. Fan can't deal with Kathe." My mother's voice was higher now, more frantic.

My father was shaking his head. "Kathe, I gather, burned the roast." Kathe was a high-school girl who helped with cleaning and cooking and was Fannie's helper in fashioning the clothing she craved. She was always at war with Fan, who supervised with an iron hand.

"In a minute," I yelled. The window smashed down.

A downstairs window opened. "Edna." This time it was Fannie, frustrated.

My father struggled to his feet, fell back into the chair. Though he turned to face me, he was staring over my shoulder, his clouded eyes scrunched in some feeble attempt at sight. "You're in trouble, Pete."

I jumped. "What?"

His face assumed its handsome proportions: the high cheekbones, the sliver of a moustache, the gentle jaw line. A beautiful man, my father. The flicker of a smile, seen so seldom now, with its curious power—it shifted the contours of his face until, well, I was reminded of a romantic stage hero, Edwin Booth maybe. Or James O'Neill.

"I can read your silence." He spoke quietly, the smile gone. "You talk of Houdini, but even in your excitement I can hear sadness."

I lied. I had to. I thought of Matthias Boon. "Just tired, Father."

Inside my mother banged something in the dining room, slammed a cabinet door. Kathe's whiny voice apologized to Fannie.

"And now your mother is angry with you."

These days my mother had little patience, especially with me. "Ed, do this. Ed, do that. Ed. Ed. Ed." The truncated name made me tremble, cringe. I wanted to scream at my mother: My name is Edna, horrible though it is. The name of the ugly stepsister in, say, a Marie Corelli romance. After all, my mother had told me more than once that they had been expecting—they *wanted*—a boy. They planned to name him Edward Charles.

Let Ed do it. Why is Ed late again? Ed, you...

My father stood and carefully opened the door, but I didn't move. I lingered out in the brisk night air. Inside was shrill gaslight; the clatter of ladle against soup tureen, the tinkling of silverware brushed and placed on the large mahogany table, the platter of roasted potatoes slathered with sour cream plunked down in the center of the table. And the ruined roast…My father had stepped through the door but now stepped back, closed it.

"Edna," he whispered, using my name and leaning down. "Sometimes your mother has no time for kindness." He bit his lip. "And sometimes a blind man has only kindness to offer."

"What?"

Again, the enigmatic smile, shadowy, oddly elegant. The impeccably dressed man who could not see his fingertips. "Well, the first can make a person hard and bitter. Be understanding, please."

"I don't understand."

"Of course you do." He squinted. "And the second—kindness all the time—blurs the edges, blunts life. Neither person can see what he's doing to other people."

He disappeared into the house.

I sat there too long and stared across the dark yard, trembling.

Fannie, confusion in her eyes, rapped on the window, her face tight. "Do you think you could join us, Edna?"

At supper my mother looked harried because she had to return to My Store. The stock clerk Arthur Howe, a wisecracking Irish lad, had agreed to unpack a new hogshead of figurines just arrived from a Chicago warehouse, and she had to supervise. "Never a moment's rest."

"Julia." My father was ready to protest but changed his mind. Tonight, like most nights at our six o'clock supper, he mechanically spooned his beef marrow soup, nibbled at his vegetables, bit into a slice of buttered homemade bread, each movement deliberate, tentative; a man afraid to slip, afraid of catastrophe.

At meal's end my mother folded the clean black sateen apron she'd carry to the store, nodded to us, and headed off. Kathe, who'd been cutting dress patterns in the back room, hurried to clear the dishes and mumbled that the burning of the pot roast was the stove's fault, not hers. As I carried the soup tureen from the dining room, trailing after her, I got annoyed. She stood in the kitchen, hands on hips, lips tight, and pouted.

I didn't care for the pretty Kathe Schmidt, a girl in her last year at Ryan High School. A red-faced girl with blond, straw-like hair worn in little-girl ringlets, periwinkle blue eyes, a cupid's bow mouth, and a curvaceous girl's body, a little thick in the waist; a pretty girl, the daughter of August Schmidt, the shy janitor at the high school. I considered Kathe both vain and simple—two deadly sins, though being boring was the worst—even though she was a friend of my closest friend Esther Leitner, a relationship I could never fathom. Esther was bright, dimensional, witty, a stunning beauty herself; Kathe was plodding as a workhorse, as empty as an upturned butter churn. A girl with coarse good looks. Hired by my mother at Fan's recommendation, Kathe had little use for me.

The two of us alone in the kitchen, Kathe narrowed her eyes. "I ain't to blame, Edna."

"You didn't hear me open my mouth to accuse."

Kathe grunted and hurried with the dishes. "I need to be somewhere."

Fannie walked in, for some reason having changed her dress— the workaday Empire house shift with the gray shirtwaist and flounced skirt replaced with a black satin tea dance dress with narrow black velvet ribbons and a red-taffeta Dutch square neck. A dress for a cotillion. Her newest creation, on display. She was showing off. "Did you forget something, Edna?"

Kathe was mumbling something about leaving as she dipped dishes in soapy water. I needed to go to my room to change for the theater, but paused. "On the table?" All the dishes were carried in. I was sure of it.

"No," Fannie yelled. "You were supposed to bring home the dress patterns I ordered from *The Delineator*." She adjusted the ribbons on her left sleeve.

"Oh Lord, I did pick them up, Fan. I purposely stopped at Taylor's Millinery, but forgot them at the city room."

"How *like* you," Fannie hissed. "I asked a favor of you and…"

Kathe dried her hands on her apron and watched, a hint of a smile on her rosy face. She'd seen these moments before, of course, but never seemed to tire of the fitful bickering of the Ferber sisters. Fire in her eyes, Fannie moved back and forth in the kitchen, banging the chairs, knocking a cupboard door, while I stood still, gripping a chair rail, implacable. We screamed at each other until from somewhere in the house the raspy sound of my father's voice stopped us. "Girls! Peace." A momentary pause; then Fannie and I, both breathing in, exploded. At that moment our mother walked in from the back porch.

"I forgot my..." She stopped, her eyes darting from one daughter to the other. "Not a moment's peace you two give me."

Fannie whined. "She forgot..."

"I don't care." My mother's voice broke.

"Edna, perhaps if you weren't traipsing up and down College Avenue," Fannie snarled.

I'd heard it before. "I don't traipse, Fannie. I'm not a traipser. I *walk*. Do you hear me? I'm a reporter."

My mother closed her eyes. "A reporter," she echoed.

"That's what I *do*."

"A young girl out *there*...in the world of men..."

"Like you, Mother." I breathed in. "Why do you always take *her* side? You're a woman out *there* running a store by yourself."

My mother lifted the account book off a shelf, held it to her chest, and glanced at the back door. "It's your father's store, Edna. I have no choice. You know that. We have to eat, you know. Your father can't do it. He just sits."

I looked to the parlor where my father sat. "Mother, please..."

Fannie stormed out of the kitchen, slamming a hand against a wall. I closed my eyes and held onto the chair to keep from falling. My temples throbbed. Yes, we'd always fought, we two hardheaded sisters, coming at the world from different camps. Fannie, the easily bruised child, temperamental, a tongue-lasher; me, the tomboy, the battler, the bull in the novelty shop. But something *had* changed this past year. Since I'd started working at the *Crescent*, a note of real resentment, even anger—sometimes

I even used the word *poison*—had entered our exchanges. My sister would never want the life on the Appleton streets, but she resented that I owned it. The night my first by-line appeared, she'd whispered, "It should say Edward Ferber. They wanted a *boy*." So our battles became volcanic. Frowning on my new role, my mother at first had screamed her disapproval, but now she was slowly drifting into a silence that was, peculiarly, more frightening. Under the sway of an imperious mother, Fannie often felt trapped at home. I *always* felt trapped at home, but I left in the morning, enjoying the illusion of freedom.

Kathe stifled a giggle.

"You can leave now, Kathe. Thank you," my mother said, annoyed.

"I'm not finished, Mrs. Ferber."

"I say you are. Good night."

Kathe smirked at me.

"Kathe," I began.

"No," my mother said. "Edna, no."

Chapter Four

Upstairs on the edge of my bed, hands folded into my lap, I swallowed a sob. I flashed to my moment in the street with Houdini—it seemed ages ago and unreal, the sense of new possibilities an illusion like his escapes.

We fought over nothing because that was all we had to fight about. The bloody wars of headstrong sisters. Fannie the Pre-Raphaelite flower girl; Edna the Hogarth crone by the woodstove. Once again Kathe Schmidt would gossip to everyone that the Ferber household was filled with screaming women. The witches out of *Macbeth*, she'd whispered to Esther. My snide remark when the story got back to me, "I'm surprised she's heard of the play."

I hurriedly dressed for the theater in a Persian silk dress with an Arab burnoose hood lined with red velvet. I dabbed powder on my blotchy face.

I had to rush or I'd be late. One of the pleasures of the job was my blue-coated cardboard pass to the Appleton Theater and Bertsehy's Hall, the opera house on Appleton and College. But my favorite theater was the old Lyceum on College near the university. Appleton saw a wealth of touring drama and musicals and circuses—like Negro glee clubs, Swiss bell ringers, P. T. Barnum's circus, and Wild Bill's western extravaganza. I loved theater most of all. I saw Rosa Coughlin in *Forget-Me-Not*. Blanche Walsh in Tolstoi's *Resurrection*. Mary Allibone in *The Spendthrift*. Alex Warden in *The Fire Brigade*.

Tonight I was meeting Esther to see Hazel Wilde in *A Taste of Winter*, straight from Broadway, via Kalamazoo and Peoria. I scurried out, whispering a quick good night to my father who was slumped in his chair, dozing, and walked briskly to the Lyceum. Once again, Esther was late. I fumed in front of the theater with its magnificent white columns and its ivied red brick façade. I refused to walk in after a play began.

On edge, craning my neck, I thought I saw Esther crossing College near the Masonic Hall, but realized, to my surprise, that it was Kathe Schmidt rushing past, turning onto Drew Street, her arms linked with her strapping hulk of a boyfriend. Hadn't Kathe said she had to rush home? No, what she'd said was: *I have to be somewhere*. Somewhere was obviously the arm of the brawny Jake Smuddie, a boy happily placed into the freshman class at nearby Lawrence University. His enrollment, rumor had it, was the result of an intervention by his powerful professor father and not Jake's scholarship. Jake pointed in my direction, but an uncharacteristically bashful Kathe grabbed his arm as they slipped out of sight down Drew Street.

Curious.

Esther touched me on the shoulder, and I jumped. "Father kept me. One of his lectures on female deportment in the new century." She giggled. "Rabbi Leitner on the Gibson Girl on the tennis court."

I mentioned seeing Kathe and Jake.

Esther shook her head. "Kathe thinks the world is trying to steal Jake from her clutches."

"She treats him like he's an over-stamped library book that she's decided to keep."

"Oh, Edna, Kathe's all right, you know. You just don't like Kathe because she's…frivolous."

No, you were going to say…because she's *pretty*. A hothouse tulip, all glossy and crisp and blatant.

I steered Esther inside the lobby of the old Lyceum, flashing the blue pass at the usher. Wearing a new dress, a pale green silk with wide puffy sleeves and a high-neck lace collar ruffle, Esther looked captivating in the way that some young girls always did, girls who never thought about their beauty. Esther never *considered* herself beautiful. Tall and willowy, dark complexioned with riveting hazel eyes, an oval cameo-struck face surrounded by lush, black cascading hair, she was a natural beauty. In high school a year or so back, she'd ignored the gasping swains, turning away from the breathless attention of the pimply, stuttering boys who dared approach her. She was waiting, I'd concluded, for a matinee idol. Such specimens—Arrow Shirt men, all square jawed and cobalt blue eyes—were in short supply in the Fox River Valley, land of chubby Teutonic boys, rarer at Temple Zion, where the watchful eye of her severe rabbi father followed her every movement. Quite simply, Esther turned heads. I got tongues wagging. Sometimes I wondered, flummoxed, at God's unfair treatment of my own sex. Beauty and…well, not quite the beast. Perhaps beauty and the bleak.

I breathed in the musty atmosphere of the old Lyceum Theater, a ramshackle mausoleum of nooks and crannies, vaulted ceiling, arabesques and curlicues, faded yet still gilt trimming, and a threadbare curtain. Worn red-velvet plank seats wobbled. Echoey walls, paint flecked and mildewed, whispered of legions of performers on that narrow stage. To me, this was Theater, capitalized. I thought of the old melodramas I'd seen there, widows tied to railroad tracks, maidens lured by black-clad curs under shadowy willows. *The Drunkard. Tempest and Sunshine. Ten Nights in a Barroom. Father, dear Father, come home with me now, the clock in the steeple struck one*— I'd seen them all. The histrionic gesture, the stentorian voice resounding to the rafters, the icy stare, the maudlin death scenes. The theater kept me alive. It kept my family alive—the Ferbers all enjoyed the stage. There was something about a curtain going up and the rush of piano crescendo. The shock of splendid scenery, a movement of bodies, the gripping plots.

"Well, well," a voice said from behind me. I turned. "Miss Ferber."

Mildred Dunne stood by the ticket window, staring at me with half-closed eyes. A stern disciplinarian in her mid-thirties, slender if not bony as a starved pullet, Miss Dunne was a dreadful woman, a school librarian who despised books and cherished silence. The only daughter of Amos Dunne, one of the rich landowners of the town and the proprietor of the feed store on Drew, she was famously a spinster, to use her own redundant phrase, until the arrival of Gustave Timm, the theater manager. Suddenly the woman remembered solely for admonishing us to be quiet was seen on the arm of the dashing Gustave Timm at church socials, at dances at the Masonic Hall, on the river excursions. Miss Dunne, I supposed, was pretty enough for such a handsome man—but there was something off about the giggled confidences and whispered intimacies the two engaged in, often right on Appleton sidewalks. She seemed ill matched to the effusive Gustave. My mother once nodded to a neighbor, "Why do women always choose the wrong men?"

Next to Miss Dunne stood the brothers Timm. In my mind, of course, they were the brothers Grimm.

"Good evening, Mr. Timm," Esther said to Gustave.

I sometimes found myself fluttering foolishly in Gustave's presence. Like his brother Homer, Gustave was tall and square-jawed, but he was dashing and Byronic, a man out of one of the melodramas he mounted on the Lyceum stage: deep violet eyes, a hero's swagger, and a deferential manner. He was just too close to a world I dreamed of, my life as an actress. Footlights and fantasy, star billing, bouquets of roses hurled my way.

Smiling, Esther spoke to the other brother, "And you, too, Mr. Timm."

Gustave's older brother Homer, standing at his side, cleared his throat. "Evening." He spoke too loudly.

Homer Timm, Gustave's older brother by at least a decade, was the Vice-Principal at Ryan High School. I'd never liked him, though such dislike, I'd often told myself, was irrational. Homer Timm kept order, and had once admonished me for "unladylike bustling" in the hallways, a charge I spurned. Friendly enough to all, he still struck me as a man not to be trusted with that smile that always appeared too quickly, and as quickly disappeared. He'd been a fixture in town for a decade, my mother told me, coming out of the East—Baltimore, or was it Philadelphia?—with a wispy wife and three small children, each one as pale as its mother.

The genetic power that produced a good-looking Gustave had missed the dress rehearsal where Homer was concerned; the eyes too sunken in a sallow cheek, the eyebrows too bushy, the brow too narrow, the nose too sloping and pointed—he seemed, oddly, the negative to the dazzling photograph to arrive years later.

Everyone in Appleton gossiped about the brothers Timm.

Just last week the *Crescent* published a notice of the upcoming September nuptials of Gustave and Mildred Dunne. That got tongues wagging. People talked of nothing else: the dashing interloper now wedding the staid librarian.

People also gossiped about Homer. He lived *without* his family. A consumptive Sophie Timm had been sent to convalesce at an East Coast sanitarium. The children lived with grandparents. Homer Timm, living the life of a bachelor in Mrs. Zeller's rooming house on Jackson Street, just up from the River Lock, ventured East during summer vacations but always returned ashen and morose. I knew my mother *tsk*ed about it: "A man too comfortable being apart from his family…"

As I watched, Homer Timm knocked on the door of his brother Gustave's small office just behind the box office. Waiting a second, his ear turned to the door, he opened it and walked in, though he hesitated at the threshold. From where I stood, I could glimpse Cyrus P. Powell, the owner of the Lyceum, sitting at Gustave's desk.

Cyrus P. Powell had fascinated me ever since the day he replied to Sam Ryan's request for an interview. Just four words scribbled on thick creamy linen stationery. "A preposterous request, sir." That was it. That day everyone in the *Crescent* office had roared, a tide of humor that kept bubbling to the surface as we went about our business. Of course, that was a day long before Matthias Boon joined the staff.

Cyrus P. Powell knew very little about Appleton, or Appleton of him, though he owned a good part of the real estate, including the storied Lyceum Theater. The son of the president of the Appleton Central Bank on Oneida, he'd been living in New York until last year, moving back to Appleton after his father died of a stroke. He lived alone in the mansion at the end of Drew.

A man always dressed in a severe black suit, a look he never varied, just as he never varied the stern expression on his face. Perhaps forty years old, tall and angular, sporting a Roman nose over a manicured moustache and a gray-white goatee, he was handsome enough to enflame a few widows. He became everyone's excited story for a week, largely because of his refusal to acknowledge anyone. Therefore, it was assumed, he was superior to us all. After a week, he was ignored and idly catalogued as a rich albeit handsome man who had little time or inclination for democracy.

His only acquaintance was Homer Timm, whom he'd known, years back, when both were students at Boston Latin. Once a month, no more no less, both men could be found at supper at Alter's on Main, a bizarre rite where each ate his meal quietly, seemingly without conversation, and both looked relieved when they parted company.

Appleton assumed it was Homer's influence that got his brother Gustave the job of Lyceum manager.

As I watched, Cyrus P. Powell scowled, muttered something to Homer who looked ready to apologize for intruding. Homer's back was rigid, his neck stiff, that eerie smile still plastered to his face. They didn't move, statues, and nothing about them suggested they were old friends. Gustave suddenly bustled in, a little too bubbly, but he stopped short. He shifted his body, ready to flee. Gustave always got quiet in Cyrus P. Powell's presence. It was clear to all—that is, to me—that Gustave was terrified of his boss. Now Powell dismissed him with a flick of his wrist, and Gustave, looking around at what was his own office, backed out, bumping into a wall. His brother Homer was rolling his head back and forth, disapproving. When Gustave stepped back into the lobby, he caught my inquisitive eye. The man looked ready to sob. As Esther and I shuffled past, headed to our seats, I glanced back into the office: Homer and Cyrus P. Powell were leaning into each other, their heads almost touching, both men looking as if they were sharing some dark secret.

Esther and I settled in our seats. Esther whispered, "Did you see how *menacingly* Homer Timm glowered at us?"

But I was not thinking of the elder Timm. I was bothered by the scene I'd witnessed in Gustave's office. What had just happened there? Secrets, I told myself. Appleton was filled with secrets. Everyone had secrets.

The curtain rose, nosily. Hazel Wilde appeared from the wings. Applause. My heart jumped, thrilled. A night of theater, magical.

We were the last to leave the theater because I lingered long after the final curtain call. I loved the stillness of the vast room, the usher sweeping the aisles, the stage crew bustling behind the dropped curtain. One by one the gaslights darkened. I savored it all—and the romantic image of myself backstage in a dressing room, aglow in makeup and accolades, smelling the red roses I'd accepted from fawning and handsome swains.

There was no one in the lobby by the time we left and we strolled out the front doors, up College Avenue, nearly empty of carriages and walkers. Gaslight gave the wide street a fairy-tale feel, with its vaguely Italianate buildings, the sagging store awnings, and the line of telephone poles strung up and down the avenue. The night was cool, the leafy sugar maples and white oaks rustled with a slight balmy breeze from the Fox River. In the distance church spires posed against a painter's blue sky, hazy white at the horizon; and a crescent moon appeared and disappeared behind wispy, stringy clouds. I rarely left the theater in anything but a rapturous mood: heart pounding, head spinning, fingers trembling.

Esther was rattling on about her father entertaining a family of prosperous Jews from Kaukauna who had a marriageable son Esther had purposely ignored, though the vapid boy never took his eyes off her. A wave of loneliness came over me. A beautiful night, and I was there with Esther, admittedly my best friend, yet something was missing. I'd been seeing Clarence Maxon last summer, a fellow lover of Thackeray, but he'd gone off to Notre Dame; we'd had a silly spat, and during his holiday visit back home, he'd failed to stop in to see me. Soon he'd return for the summer and I'd bump into him on College Avenue. Oddly, thoughts of Clarence led me to think of Jake Smuddie, that striking footballer who earlier had run off into the shadows with Kathe. I tried not to dwell on him, though I often did. I couldn't help it.

We wandered into City Park under the cool maples. At that moment I heard rustling on the dirt path that led back to the street. Both of us started, and some feet away a tall, barrel-chested man strode into view and as quickly disappeared behind a bank of arborvitae. He didn't notice us sheltered under a shady willow, but I recognized him. It was Mac, the printer from the *Appleton Crescent* offices. Just Mac—a man whose surname I'd never learned. Mac, a dark, mysterious wanderer, a printing wizard, a dervish with linotype and ink; a man who spent long days and nights in the press room just beyond the room where the others and I pecked away at our typewriters. Mac, the itinerant tramp who'd wandered in one day, took the job, and lost himself in that back room.

"Someday," Sam Ryan told me, "I'll turn around and he'll be gone. It's the nature of the beast."

Laconic, moody, Max had not said one word to me in over a year, though often I'd spotted him staring at me, a look I had trouble understanding. He rented a room at Mrs. Zeller's rooming house. Strange, how the single men of town gravitated to Mrs. Zeller's huge home: Mac, Homer Timm, and even new city editor Matthias Boon. You rarely saw Mac in town. A man with a flat pancake face, unlovely, pocked and dented, he had a cruel scar that led from his left eye down into the tremendous drooping walrus moustache that he lacquered so thoroughly it shone like polished wood. In the morning when I arrived at the city room, he was already in back, clamoring away at the presses, hauling trays of type, banging and knocking, and sometimes cursing so profanely I blushed. At night when I left, he'd still be there.

Now, seeing him disappear into the midnight woods, I trembled. I wasn't afraid. I walked the night streets of Appleton alone all the time. It was the way he looked at me in the city room, a look so hard and steely that I always wanted to confess. But to what? I hardly knew.

City Park closed in around me now.

"Home," I muttered to Esther. "I want to go home."

Chapter Five

At eight o'clock the next morning, a brisk shiny Thursday, I pushed open the heavy oak door of the city room, stepped down those five stairs. Matthias Boon huddled at his desk, face nearly touching the blotter, a green-tinted lamp casting an eerie glow over his block-like head. He didn't say a word as I sat a few feet away in my chair, but he coughed—loudly and sloppily, pretending consumptive, I assumed—and squinted at me. He stood, stretched out his arms, and disappeared into the back printing room, where I could see the giant Mac, glistening moustache on that beefy face, pausing a second, staring back at me. I heard him make a smacking sound as he spat chewing tobacco into a spittoon.

Boon thrust some copy at him, hardly civil, stepped back into the city room, and regarded me silently.

"Miss Ferber." He returned to his seat.

I rifled through some news clippings, shuffled them on the wobbly pine table that served as my desk, pushed into a corner where the smell of decaying wall mice seemed never to dissipate. As correspondent to the *Milwaukee Journal*, I rewrote copy to send on. The cramped, cluttered room was too ghastly, early mornings, so I reached over to switch on another lamp. Five pushed-together tables or desks, and a chicken wire mesh fence surrounded Sam Ryan's cubicle with the roll-top desk—God knew why! Chicken wire! And beyond the room Mac's domain,

where he churned out copy, handbills, flyers, notices, and ultimately the afternoon edition of the *Crescent*.

I pecked at the ancient Oliver typewriter, clacking and pinging.

The image of Harry Houdini shadowed the room, though
Boon would never mention his name…or my interview. But I
waited for my punishment.

Boon stood, let loose a phlegmatic spasm so loud that the
tomcat, luxuriating in the pressroom doorway, yipped and fled.
He approached my table, grunted something. Purposely, I looked
down, steely eyed, at the keys of the Oliver as he dropped a slip
of paper onto my table: my daily assignment sheet. I scanned
it rapidly and noted that my allotment of stories had been dramatically—cruelly?—diminished. This had been the pattern
for weeks, almost as though I'd show up one morning to find a
blank sheet facing me, a piece of unadulterated white paper that
signaled my departure from the Fourth Estate. Low man on the
totem pole, I already received the detritus of newsworthy runs.
When Boon was hired, Sam told me the veteran editor would
serve as mentor to me. What he didn't know was Boon's intense
dislike of women in the newsroom.

"Mr. Boon, there's a scant day's reporting here." I thumbed
the sheet. "You've even removed the county courthouse from
my route."

"Unnecessary."

"Unnecessary?" I echoed. "I've been doing…"

He cut me off. "Miss Ferber, your embellished account of
real-estate transactions strike many as a little too fanciful for
something so…prosaic."

I sputtered. "Embellishment?"

"Is there an echo in the room?" His lips curled up.

I stood, tired of this nonsense. "You seem, sir, to be purposely
reducing me to…"

"What? Miss Ferber? Tears? Reducing you to tears?"

I found my voice, waved the sheet at him. "I doubt, sir, if
any woman would allow you to reduce her to tears. That would
give you too much…value."

"You don't report news, Miss Ferber. You tell stories." He weighed his words carefully. "You like to describe people, Miss Ferber."

"And you have a problem with that?"

"Yes, when you're writing about Samuel Gottlieb arguing a property line with his neighbor Josiah Pholner. Lord, you dealt with Harry Houdini as if he were a character in a novel." He looked away. "Enough. Just attend to the items on that sheet and all will be happy." He pointed to the sheet I was still waving at him and turned his back on me. I smashed my fist down on the table. He flinched, but he busied himself with some papers. At that moment I glanced toward the pressroom: Mac, giant-like, arms folded, towered in the doorway, silent, severe, watching Matthias Boon. When I caught his eye he turned and disappeared behind his linotype machine and boilerplate.

My throat was dry.

Within minutes, the other members of the city room drifted in. Matthias Boon left the office without a word to anyone, off for breakfast at Platz's. He'd be back in a half hour, doubtless with a smear of clotted cream on his bushy moustache or a trace of strawberry marmalade on a sleeve cuff. Certainly with an array of poppy seeds speckling his protruding front teeth.

Still seething, I surveyed my office mates. Sam Ryan, owner and proprietor, had arrived with his sister Ivy, and as they unbuttoned their jackets, they were mumbling about some domestic travail. A man in poor health, Sam would drift in and out of the office, often losing his temper, swearing a blue streak, then apologizing to no one in particular. Sam was really old, a wiry sparrow of a man, a rabble-rousing Democrat from pre-Civil War days, a fiercely political soul. With his wire Ben Franklin eyeglasses and his dimpled chin and his flaky bald head, he seemed genial, a soft touch, but I knew he harbored a fierce and fishwife temper. He'd thunder at any mishap in the city room, the spotting, say, of a typographical error in some trivial copy, crumpling up paper balls and hurling them willy-nilly over ducking heads. He'd fought for the Union and on the Fourth of July wore his tattered blue uniform, decorated with ribbons of the Grand Old Army, marching behind the off-key fife and drum corps.

He was watching me, doubtless puzzled by my flushed face.

"Morning, Edna," Miss Ivy said. Sam's sister was a plump roly-poly spinster, older than her brother, with a duck's ungainly waddle, pebbly-bright gray eyes lost in folds of strudel-flaky skin, salt-and-pepper hair pulled into a gigantic knot. Her head struck me as a doorknob waiting to be turned. Terribly efficient as the *Crescent's* bookkeeper and solicitor of advertisements from the likes of the Woodsmen of the World and the Knights of Columbus, she occasionally proffered homespun wisdom, delivered in a twittering voice, about the happenstance irritability of men. "You know how men are," she'd say. Now and then she advised me to find a job more suitable for a young woman in the new world. "This," she'd point to the city room, "is no man's land." Then she'd laugh. "I mean no *woman's* land."

"Miss Ivy. Morning."

"Loved your interview with Houdini."

Byron Beveridge, sitting across from me with his malodorous cigar, puffed away while reading copy. Debonair, tall, lanky, a local Company G Spanish-American War veteran, he customarily threw his legs across his desk so that I faced the patched soles of his boots. He fancied himself a man about town, some dandy or bon vivant. Arriving late, he made a big to-do about removing his fashionable three-button cutaway frock coat and bowler hat. Blond and pink cheeked, he adopted a rugged, blustery demeanor and liked to brag about female conquest.

Nodding to Miss Ivy, I left the city room, notebook in hand. As I walked on the wide-planked sidewalks of College Avenue, I began my routine stops. Before long, I stood in front of the poster announcing Houdini's appearance at the Lyceum. Those massive chains around his body; those piercing eyes, challenging. What would he think of my interview when it appeared? Gripping my notebook, I headed up College Avenue.

Later that afternoon, already finished typing my morning copy, I met Esther for a sarsaparilla at Neumeister's Drug Store. Esther would tag along on my weekly stop at the high school to gather information about drama productions, oratory contests, the honor society, athletic meets. As we walked, I buzzed about my interview with Houdini, and Esther, wide-eyed, told me I was the luckiest girl in Appleton. I beamed.

Both of us liked to drop in at the old *Clarion* office, where I'd been the Local and Personal Editor. The four years spent at Ryan High School had been happy ones, filled with chatter, laughter, achievement, friendships. Good, good days. A boat ride on the Fox, a picnic at Aloah Beach at Lake Winnebago. In winter an ice-numbing sleigh ride across the pond beyond the high school. Life in those high-school years was spent rushing in the hallways, rehearsing school plays, dancing at the Masonic Hall. Summer days were spent lounging, carefree, in the hammock under the backyard cherry tree, devouring a Robert W. Chambers romance. Life only became serious when I left those strong walls.

I loved the old school. On the wide auditorium stage where the school's amateur theatrical society still mounted bowdlerized Shakespeare and creaky classics like Anna Mowett's *Fashion*, I'd excelled at oratory and dramaturgy; my thunderous rendition of "The Man Without a Country" sailed over the acoustical heaven until I was woefully intoxicated with my own performance. Up *there* on that high school stage, up *there*, the lead role in *A Scrap of Paper* no less, the embryonic actress; and now, down *there* in the subterranean vault of the *Crescent* office. To the depths.

We walked into the building, greeted Miss Hepplewhyte, the secretary, who sat eagle-eyed by the front door, chronicler of tardiness and noise levels; errand runner, mistress of the moral accusation, finger pointer at any mischievous lad. "Perhaps, Miss Ferber, your hat is a little too showy for civics," she'd suggested during my freshman year, a line I enjoyed repeating. She nodded at us.

But before Esther and I could maneuver past this unofficial sentry to Principal Hippolyte Jones' office where we'd be welcomed by the overflowing man who looked like Santa Claus with his enormous belly and his white whiskers—St. Nicholas with a *pince-nez*, my mother described him once—we met Homer Timm, barreling out of his side office.

"Well, well, well. Fresh from a scintillating night at the Lyceum." He bowed to Esther but not to me.

Homer Timm was dressed in the same shiny black broadloom suit he'd worn to the theater. While Principal Jones cared not a jot that I roamed the corridors during class time, Vice-Principal Timm cared a little too much, though he often masked his displeasure with his mechanical smile. He shared that smile with me now.

"I'm afraid Principal Jones is in a meeting with the mayor." He slipped back into his office and returned with some scribbled sheets. "Here. The cast of the graduation production of *The College Widow*. Performance dates." He frowned. "Satire should be off limits for school students."

"And why is that?" I asked. He didn't answer. "Next year, perhaps, Weber and Fields doing *Hoity-Toity*."

He bowed slightly. "Only if you return as our star."

He turned away, leaving us standing there. I looked at Esther who was suppressing a fit of giggles, so we hurried out of the building.

We sat on a bench outside the front entrance, with me scribbling some notes about the Ladies Temperance Society Silver Medal Contest to be held at the Company G Armory. Esther nudged me and pointed. I looked up. "What?"

"Look."

An ungainly man lumbered up the sidewalk toward the front entrance of the school. He paused to catch his breath, adjusting the coat that fit him poorly, and checked a watch fob. He shuffled with a pronounced limp, dragging a deadened leg as though pulling a stubborn tree trunk. Esther shrank back, hunched her shoulders, birdlike. The man slumped by, his leaden foot thudding on the wooden stairs.

"Tell me," I whispered. "Why is he here?"

Because, of course, I recognized Christ Lempke, a German immigrant who'd been wounded in the Spanish-American War. He'd been a farmer and mill worker living in a ramshackle homestead out on Bay Road, a genial man, friendly even. But the brief, splendid war had changed that. Returned home with a shattered leg and a dull, spiritless heart, he became a bitter man who hid away on the bleak farm. At the Fourth of July parade he looked unhappy, unresponsive to all the flag waving and firecrackers and hip-hip-hurrah. I always thought it odd that he even showed up.

Esther leaned in. "He brings Frana to school in the morning and collects her in the afternoon. He's like her…warden. She can't leave the school grounds, even for midday meal."

Frana Lempke, like Kathe Schmidt, was another casual friend of Esther—and another pretty girl that I had little use for. Frana had a small speaking part in *A Scrap of Paper*, and, to my horror, garnered slavish attention from the giddy, applauding boys. Only rarely did Frana join Esther and other young people for boating excursions on the Fox because her family kept a close eye on her. Most times when Esther organized these breezy outings I chose not to go along, for I felt too much radiance coming off Frana and Esther, even off the annoying Kathe. Three beauties, and me. So I stayed home with a book.

Frana, a senior, sometimes worked for Esther's mother during spring housecleaning or during the late-summer canning season. Frankly, I thought her too pretty and flighty to be allowed near pressure-cooked fruit and vegetables. Frana strolled down College Avenue warbling "I'm Only a Bird in a Gilded Cage" in a shrill soprano, which turned heads. She told perfect strangers that she intended to become a famous actress, an obvious ploy to get attention from the simpering, foolish men of the town who gazed long at her buxom farm-girl body, too mature for such a young girl. And one so ethereally fair-haired and blue-eyed. A girl, I felt, destined to collect dirty dishes in the dining rooms of the Sherman House.

"For Heaven's sake, why is her uncle escorting her?"

"Well," Esther confided, "I only just learned this. But you know how old-fashioned the Lempkes are. They're German Puritans or something."

"There's no such thing, Esther."

"Like Mennonites maybe."

I got impatient. "So what? They're strict Catholics. Does it matter?"

"Well, I guess someone told Frana's father that Frana has been *seeing* someone."

"For land's sake, Esther, we aren't living in the Dark Ages."

"No, no. She's been sneaking out after dark. And it's an *older* man." Esther waited, delirious.

I sat up. "Who?"

"Frana won't say. *No* one knows. She told her father—so I heard—that she's gonna marry him. He's gonna take her to New York."

"But who is it?"

"I told you, she won't say, but someone said she was chatting with one of those annoying drummers staying at the Sherman House."

I understood. How many times I'd sauntered by the popular hotel where itinerant salesmen, bored from their travels, abandoned their worn sample cases and lingered on the veranda, cigar smoke circling their heads, heads swiveling back and forth as they watched the town girls. Or wandered outside after a leisurely massage at the Turkish baths, flushed and friendly, brazenly flirting with the maidens of the town. Innocent enough perhaps, but annoying. And most were genteel, proper sorts, these lonely men missing wives or girlfriends. Now and then one of them, sloshy with foamy beer or an extra whiskey in the belly, muttered some indiscreet remark. Even a bold invitation. But seldom. The hosteller was too rigid to allow loose and lascivious behavior; any condemned drummer, cardboard suitcase in hand, samples tucked under armpits, was booted out.

"But surely she can't be interested in any of those men," I insisted. "I mean, no one takes them seriously."

"Smooth talkers, they are. And glib."

"Well, Frana *is* a foolish sort…"

"An innocent." Esther looked at me. "I know you don't care for her."

"She's vain and empty-headed," I blurted out. "She draws *attention* to herself. I saw her singing…"

"Just because she's so pretty." Esther had a malicious twinkle in her eye.

"Prettiness has nothing to do with it, Esther." I was hot now. "She shakes those blond tresses and expects the earth to stop its rotation."

"Anyway, Edna, her puritan family has imprisoned her. Locked her *up*. I mean, the uncle walks her to school in the morning and is there"—she pointed to the empty doorway—"in the afternoon."

"I wouldn't stand for it."

"You're not Frana, Edna. What can she do? My mother said…" The door opened and the students started to file out.

Though I glanced at them, I focused on Esther. "Tell me, what does Frana say about this?"

"She's not allowed to talk to her friends outside of school. For four days now this has been going on."

"And you didn't tell me?"

"I thought you knew."

"Maybe someone should talk to the drummer."

Boys and girls we knew waved hello, chattered, strolled by. One girl, to be married that summer, told me she'd be having a china shower and expected a notice in the *Crescent*. When she left, I muttered, "Crockery for the crass at heart." I was getting impatient; I had to get back to the city room. Yet Esther's gossip intrigued me. Frana, always the giggly, vacuous girl, suddenly had become interesting—the captive maiden squired to and from school by her crippled uncle, who admittedly looked none too pleased with his task. I lingered on the bench, if only to watch the inglorious departure.

A noisy gaggle of girls rushed by and suddenly, emerging from the crowd, an animated Kathe Schmidt slipped onto the bench beside Esther. I frowned and thought of burnt roast beef.

Kathe was laughing as she spoke. "Esther, you should have seen Mr. Timm's face when Mr. Lempke opened the front door."

"What happened?"

Kathe spoke to Esther in a manufactured lisp. "He yelled, 'Sir, you storm in here like Teddy Roosevelt charging up San Juan Hill.'"

"That's not funny," Esther said. "He doesn't have a lisp."

I shook my head. "Did he really say that, Kathe?"

Kathe smirked. "It was something like that. He wasn't pleased." The young girl rattled on and on, more drivel about Frana's plight, driving me to distraction. I stood. Out of here. I was in the presence of a hot air balloon.

At that moment Frana and her uncle appeared in the empty doorway, the two of them standing there, frozen; and I felt sorry for the girl I'd never liked. For Frana, caught in the flickering shafts of sunlight, looked scared, her face pale and drawn. Dressed in a drab gray dress, with a bunch of lace ruffles gathered about her neck and the incongruous ribbons she always wore in her hair, she seemed a cadaver, her uncle's fingers grasping her shoulder.

Then the tableau unfroze and Christ Lempke hobbled down the stairs, dragging the girl. Frana's eyes moved left and right, caught sight of the three of us on the bench, and her body stiffened. Her uncle tugging her along, Frana attempted to move gracefully; but Lempke's clumsy walk, the dragging of that bum foot, threw off her stride, and she kept stumbling.

When she neared us, she suddenly became defiant, twisting to face her uncle. He loosened his hold and seemed to spin, ready to topple.

"You're embarrassing me," she sputtered.

He followed her glance to Esther, Kathe and me. "You disgrace us, Liebchen." A hoarse whisper.

For some reason, Kathe was amused, a low whistle escaping her throat as she watched the squirming Frana, a fragile rag doll, loose-limbed and buckling.

"I ain't." Frana then muttered something in German that I didn't catch.

"The behavior of a whore," he hollered.

Frana's face turned scarlet and she tried to break away. Christ Lempke, furious, slapped her across the face. Frana screamed and burst into tears.

Lempke maneuvered the sobbing girl away from the school grounds until they were out of sight.

Kathe was laughing out loud.

"What, Kathe?" I snapped. "What's so amusing?"

Kathe pouted. "Nothing. He called her a whore."

I stood to walk away, but spoke directly into her face. "Doubtless it's a word you've heard before."

I sat in Pfefferle's Elm Tree Bakery sipping thick black *kaffee* with rich cream and munching on a piece of *Apfelkuchen* that Greta, the plump German waitress, just served me. Late afternoon, the small room quiet, I'd settled myself into an alcove under a print of a helmeted and mustachioed Bismarck in regal uniform, his face perpetually at war. I was writing an account of a social tea given by the Ladies Auxiliary of the Knights of Pythias, at which the Reverend Mr. Bronson Peck spoke of missionary work he'd accomplished in Jaffa, near Jerusalem. What I *wanted* to write about was that one of the lodge members, ninety-year-old Ezra Platt, had slipped into a noisy slumber and kept blurting out the word "balderdash" at odd moments. I wasn't convinced he was really asleep.

But my mind kept wandering to Frana and her abusive uncle—the *awfulness* of that scene. The fear in Frana's face. The slap...

High-pitched laughter snapped me out of my reverie. Kathe Schmidt had walked in and took a small table by the front door.

Was she laughing to herself? No, Kathe had said something to Greta. Not wanting to be seen, I pushed my chair back, blocked by the thick velour draperies, and sipped my coffee. The pastry was warm to the touch, perfect. The room had a few late-afternoon stragglers: two businessmen at one table, one of them deftly rolling a cigarette; two women at another, both reading the ads in the *Post*. Within seconds the door opened and Kathe looked up, expectant. She looked disappointed when she saw it was Mr. McCaslin, the drama coach and English teacher from the high school, who coldly nodded to her as he took a table at the back of the bakery where, unfortunately, he caught my eye. He dropped his eyes to his table. Within seconds he seemed fascinated by the strudel before him. An unpopular teacher, Mr. McCaslin made a point of not acknowledging students he saw outside school halls. He also famously liked Pfefferle's legendary strudel.

A moment later Kathe's boyfriend Jake Smuddie joined her, and the two huddled together. Loudly, in German, Kathe ordered a cherry-studded *Schaumtorte*. Jake said no, nothing for him. A glass of spring water, maybe.

Ignoring Jake's plea that she lower her voice, Kathe breezily exaggerated the episode of Frana and her uncle, her voice loud and rich with laughter. Did she want everyone to hear? Frana, oddly, was Kathe's friend. Supposedly they were *best* friends. Annoyed by the shrill young girl, the businessmen glanced over.

Jake Smuddie was a good-looking boy. On rare, vagrant occasions, I acknowledged to myself that I found him appealing. He was a footballer with wide shoulders and a broad chest. He wasn't a bookish boy, an irony, given the fact that his father was the severe Herr Professor, Solomon Smuddie, lecturer on Biblical Archeology—or some such yawner—and also the man with the first automobile on Appleton streets, notorious for scaring the poor horses in town.

Now, with Kathe tucking her head into his neck, Jake stopped her flow of chatter. "Why are you always making fun of poor Frana? It ain't nice."

Kathe, jerking back, accused him. "I thought you were *over* her." The brazen Kathe, oblivious of her surroundings, informed me plus the startled businessmen, the two women, and the frowning Mr. McCaslin that Jake had, indeed, seen Frana last year, had taken her to the Women's Christian Temperance Union Dance at the Masonic Hall. "You obviously *long* for that girl who abandoned you."

Frana and Kathe were alike in looks: the same Germanic fair hair, oval faces, cornflower blue eyes. Frana was delicate, doll-like, breakable. Kathe was coarse, rough mannered, and blunt, her pretty features unfinished, as though God had forgotten to tidy up the edges.

"I don't," Jake stammered. "It's just that you're always mean about Frana."

Her German accent grew prominent now. "Because her very name makes you act so…so…strange."

"Not true!" But listening, I understood that Jake Smuddie still had feelings for Frana Lempke. His whole voice shifted, the timbre softened. His voice was low-key and almost feminine with wistfulness, even hurt, in his tone.

"Well," Kathe summed up, "she's obviously playing with fire. She has that forbidden lover." She said the last two words with bold capitalization fit for a stage melodrama. "I already told you some old man wants to take her away and *marry* her, no less."

Jake shrugged. "She's always wanted to leave Appleton and go to New York to be an actress."

"Ha!" Kathe crowed. "She ain't an actress. You know, one time she even dragged me along while she followed that actress Mary Allibone as she headed for rehearsals at the Lyceum. Kept *talking* to her. I mean, Mary Allibone—world *famous*. Mary said, 'Leave me alone.' At the theater she demanded that Gustave Timm shoo Frana away, but Frana started wailing about being an actress, going onstage at the Lyceum, mind you. Mr. Timm tried to be kind to her but then he got angry and said go away. He almost called the police. He caught me rolling my eyes and shot *me* a look. Like I was part of her craziness. I got scared but

Frana kept pleading. One of the ushers came and led us out. Humiliating, I tell you." She grumbled. "An actress. Really!"

"She was in *A Scrap of Paper*."

"And she read her lines like…like reading the alphabet backwards." She made a smacking sound with her lips, doubtless enjoying her doughnut. "And you think that her family will allow that. Some sick old drummer dragging her off to New York. Jake, you are so simple. Her uncle will club her to death first. Her brothers will…You should see how he *slapped* her."

Jake finally raised his voice. "That ain't right."

Kathe launched into a new assault on him. "I saw you talking to her last week, you know. Outside the post office. You didn't know I saw but…"

Silence. Then, "I bump into folks, Kathe."

The door to the bakery opened suddenly. Solomon Smuddie was standing there, a massive man dressed in what townsfolk called his automobile gear: grotesque goggles resting on a funny corduroy cap, a severe-cut muddy brown waist coat, and knee-high black Prussian war boots.

I hadn't heard an automobile pull up, which surprised me. There were so few vehicles in town, and the drivers, propelling them like winged chariots, sailed through, leaning on horns, stomping on brakes, careening around corners. He may have been an erudite professor at Lawrence—I'd once heard him deliver a somnolent lecture on Aramaic pottery—but on the dusty though macadamized roads of Appleton he was Ben Hur distancing himself from an invisible Masala.

"Jacob!" he roared. "You are late!"

Jake jumped, knocked over a cup, the little boy reprimanded. "Father, I…"

"I told you the steps of the Tyler House." He pointed outside, aiming a finger one block up the street. "Does this look like the Tyler House?" It obviously didn't, though Jake, stymied, glanced around the room, as if to make sure. He muttered an apology and rustled past a glowering Kathe, past his rigid father, and out the door. With a glacial stare, the professor acknowledged the girl. I watched the exchange between the two. Kathe, hardly the winsome shrinking violet, fixed him in a contemptuous glare, daring; very unseemly for a high school girl with so venerable a professor. What fascinated me was his utter dismissal of Kathe, a gaze that suggested her unworthiness for his son, a look that suggested she was some brazen siren seducing the ivory-pure boy into gaslight abandon. His polar look suggested the very same thing that Christ Lempke had said to Frana: whore.

Good Lord! And I had to go back to the office and type up my notes about the Brown Betty Festival at the Order of Venus Lodge.

Chapter Six

The following afternoon, anxious, I hurried home from the city room because my father was expecting a doctor's visit, some specialist newly relocated to Milwaukee from back East. Dr. Alex Cooper was One Last Hope, capitalized. But they all were, these doctors who were often itinerant physicians making monthly circuits to towns across the state. My mother had orchestrated this new visit, as she had innumerable others over the past few years, from charlatan quacks dispensing miracle cure-alls of Indian tonic and soothing balms and restorative salts—to university men with degrees, oculists and physicians and visiting surgeons and…It didn't matter. A chance notice in the *Appleton Crescent* or *Post* or the *Milwaukee Journal* or even in the *Appleton Volksfreund*, the German language paper my mother read and where she'd once located the insane homeopathic doctor visiting from Bavaria—and Julia Ferber would dash off a note, a plea. *My husband Jacob Ferber has a shrinking optic nerve so please…*

They came, sometimes hesitantly, sometimes filled with false bravado, usually extending their sweaty palms for crisp dollar bills; but even the charlatans, dressed like dapper Dans with phony Yale class pins, even these slick, officious men were sometimes shaken by the sight and acquaintance with the gentle, handsome man. Jacob Ferber, resigned to a fate his wife and daughters refused, was a man sublime in his silences, his serenity curiously infectious.

Each visit left him weaker and sometimes more irascible, difficult. We talked quietly of the Pain, the fifth boarder in the house, the one that sat with us in the still rooms. One Last Hope. Again. Dr. Cooper, transported from Boston, a renowned specialist. But of what? I asked. Of what? The man was attending a meeting in nearby Neenah and agreed to visit the stoic, guarded Jacob Ferber.

One Last Hope.

My mother would pull on the man's shirtsleeves, imploring.

"Edna, don't bother coming home. I'll be there," she'd told me that morning.

No, I had to be there.

I crossed lanes, skirted by City Park, rushed up North Street, but already my father sat next to an old man, white-whiskered and heavy as a satiated field mouse, bursting out of a Prince Albert coat, a homburg on his lap, leaning in toward my father, chatting like an old friend. But my father stared straight ahead, and as I neared, out of breath, I heard him say, over the mumbled conversation of the monumental doctor, "Is that you, Pete?"

The doctor stopped, looked at me strangely, as though expecting the household son to appear. Smiling, I answered, "Yes, Bill." I pulled up a chair. "I'm sorry I'm late."

The doctor had a squeaky voice, out of sync with his tremendous girth and his ancient sequoia face. "I was very early, my dear." His voice reminded me of a winter sleigh ride, crisp and thin on a cold icy night.

The Pain. The awful Pain. Tell us how to stop the Pain. The blindness, well, that was fact now. But the Pain, excruciating, crippling, numbing.

At that moment my mother and Fannie, breathless, rushed up the steps. We three Ferber women stood there in a line, a hesitant link of blood, frozen before a dying father. Silence. We waited. The doctor made a rumbling noise, swallowed, and said that there was nothing he could do because the shrinkage of the optic nerve created the Pain. Perhaps an elixir, a tonic. But there was nothing that he…

My mother fluttered around the porch like a sun-mad fly, out of character. Usually she was matter-of-fact and logical; severe, humorless. And Fannie, her eyes following our mother's swooping, helpless movements, was on the verge of weeping. How much more futile optimism could we allow? It made me furious. I hated the doctor, that rotting mound of flesh, the buttons of his silk vest ready to pop.

I stared into my father's passive, resigned face, realizing that he didn't care any more. These were gratuitous moments for his wife, his daughters. He sat there staring, but that was the wrong word: *staring*. You can only stare if you have sight, I thought, horribly. No. Suddenly I had no word, no vocabulary for the scene. Helpless, I panicked: these were the limits of lexicography. There was something beyond language that mattered more.

I wanted to cry.

Later, the doctor gone after being given a thick slice of poppy seed *kuchen* and a glass of root beer, as well as his generous, if unwarranted, fee, I sat alone outside with my father, quiet. Inside my mother banged the cupboards. I understood the signs. It would be a long night. After each lame visit from a doctor my mother acted like a maddened caged animal. Sometimes she struck out at her husband, as though his blindness and his Pain were a personal quirkiness he could control, conditions he created to get at her, ruin her life, destroy her days. Those nights Julia Ferber sat in the kitchen playing solitaire on the oak table, game after game, the sound of cards being slapped down enough to drive me mad. There were times she was unable to speak to my father for hours afterwards, as though for her to utter a kind word would betray the resentment she harbored. My father, who understood, hid in the corners of the house.

We never talked about it because I didn't want to acknowledge that my mother, whom I loved, could blame a hapless man for being…hapless.

"I'm sorry, Bill," I whispered into the silence.

He reached out and found my hand, held it.

"Tell me about your day." A lazy grin. "Mr. Ryan must be overjoyed with your Houdini piece, no?"

I thought of Matthias Boon's coldness all day long. The intimidating Mac had left the back room and wordlessly dropped a sheet on my desk, my printed Houdini piece, his grimy thumbprint on the corner. He'd never done such a thing before, and I had no idea what it was all about. Now and then he'd step into the front room and address some concern with Sam, but rarely to Matthias Boon. This morning he'd given me a preview of my article, which would appear in the afternoon paper. When I started to thank him, he was already leaving, his hulking back to me.

I withdrew the galley sheet from my pocket and read my own words to my father. I wanted him to hear my interview before it appeared that afternoon. He leaned in, intent. I read well, dramatic, with flair, the product of Ryan High School's rigorous elocution regimen. When I got to the end, my father was smiling.

"Well?"

"You have a news nose."

I glowed. "You think so? So you like it, Father?"

"All Jews are escape artists."

"What does that mean?" I was startled.

"You know the history of our people. Think about it, Pete. Escape from shackles, bondage, struggles to survive. To escape endless persecution." He was now grinning. "Houdini is simply the first to make a spectacle out of it…to make others pay for the privilege of watching. The immigrant who broke free."

"But that's not the point."

"Of course, it is."

I'd always considered my mother the shrewd, intelligent force in the family: domineering, pessimistic, logical. A rigid woman, horribly unhappy. I'd inherited my mother's acumen, her perceptiveness. My father—well, I'd long ago labeled the handsome, dreamy man as the vagabond poet, the helpless businessman, the sad wanderer out of Budapest into America, the man who'd played, feebly, a few strains of Mozart on the violin that now rested in the dining room hutch. Listening to his careful words, I feared I didn't know my own father.

A voice from inside broke the quiet conversation. "Ed, did you see Kathe Schmidt today? I hope she remembers to come tomorrow morning to help Fannie with the dress patterns."

I called back. "No, I haven't seen her since yesterday." At the Elm Tree Bakery, wooing (and abusing) Jake Smuddie, fluttering those eyelids and spewing venom toward Frana Lempke, who still held a place in the footballer's heart. "Don't worry. She'll be here."

"How do you know?" My mother loomed in the doorway. "God, I wish these people had a telephone like civilized people." She didn't look at my father.

"Her mother wants her money. I've met the woman. She's greedy."

"That's cruel," my father whispered to me.

"No, it's true. You know that Kathe doesn't like coming here. She's made that clear. She'd rather run around town but she has no choice."

"Still and all…" I could hear displeasure in his tone.

"I don't mean anything bad."

My father tapped my wrist. "Of course you do."

Esther was running down the street, cutting across a lawn, even stepping over a bed of iris. Her long dress got caught on a protruding root of an old oak tree, and she grabbed at the fabric to rip it free. "Edna, Edna."

My father answered. "Esther, what is it?"

Esther caught her breath on the lower steps, so winded she couldn't speak, her face flushed and sweaty. I rushed to her. "News." Esther threw her hands up into the air. "I have news."

Esther, the town crier with the innocent face. I was the notorious town reporter, the town snoop, yet Esther, popular and garrulous, with a multitude of casual friends, always joining this clique or that, a social bumblebee, really reported the scintillating gossip or puerile revelations. People readily shared confidences with Esther, things they'd never reveal to me. She knew about secret engagements, hasty weddings, abandonments, even hush-hush pregnancies long before such news became commonplace; in her quiet, demure way, she often informed me of *sub rosa* life in quaint Appleton. Errant girls squired out of town in disgrace, drunken remarks spilled at a beer tavern, the dangerous behavior of the blacksmith's youngest daughter; even, shockingly, the lewd suggestions made to her and other girls by Seymour Weiser as they walked by him after Friday night services. She had no need of a printing press. I—for three dollars a week—was the ho-hum chronicler of social teas and church bazaars and honeymoon couples catching the 7:52 morning train to Milwaukee on their way to Niagara Falls.

Fannie and my mother joined us, and Esther, finally making it to the top step with my arm on her elbow, blurted out, "Frana Lempke. Gone."

"Gone where?"

"We think—Milwaukee." She swallowed. "Chicago. New York."

I was irritated. "All of them?"

Esther shot me a look before mumbling, "Gone."

My mother settled into a chair and sighed. "Esther dear, just what are you talking about?"

"Frana has run off with a man." One word, almost: "Franahas-runoffwithaman." She slowed down, breathed in, repeated the line. "Frana has run off with a man."

"Good God." My mother glanced at Fannie. "What is this all about?"

Fannie was puzzled. "Are you sure? I thought she was still seeing that football player, you know, the good looking…"

"What did you hear?" I broke in.

Esther took a couple of deep breaths. "Well, everyone *knew* she was secretly seeing an older man. I mean, her friends *talked*. There were rumors it was some drummer staying at the Sherman House. She was seen spending time around there…"

"But who?" From Fannie, interrupting.

"When did this happen?" I touched Esther on the sleeve.

"I bet it's that Calvin Steiner," my mother said. "Forty-odd years old, a drinker, that one, and always his eyes on the young girls. He comes into My Store, huffing and puffing, and if a farm girl is sifting through the pottery, he loses his train of thought and sputters like an old fool. Trying to sell me those mousetraps that wouldn't so much as catch an elephant passing by…"

"Was it him?" I demanded.

"No one knows. But I heard that the afternoon train leaving for Milwaukee had the usual bunch of drummers, and one man was accompanied by a young girl who hid her face." Esther let the drama settle on the porch.

"So how do you know it was Frana?" I wondered.

"Well, she's disappeared. When her uncle went to get her at the high school this afternoon, she was gone. She'd left early. She snuck out, it seems. She wasn't *there*."

"But that's impossible." I knew how severely the high school was run. If Frana's uncle was scheduled to collect her at school's end, there was no way Principal Jones or Vice-Principal Timm would allow her to simply stroll out, especially not with Miss Hepplewhyte, that authoritarian sentry, guarding the doors. It was not done.

"She lied, I guess."

"How did you learn this?"

"I was with my father at Pettibone's just now, and Mollie heard it from Kathe Schmidt, who said Chief Stone had been called to the high school. He was out of town but is just back and…"

"What's happening now?" Impatient, my words rushed.

"Well, everyone is rushing there. To the high school. The chief even called the teachers back for a meeting. Right now. Frana's uncle's raising Cain, it seems. He's at the school yelling and cursing. He refused to leave the building. And…"

We all started to talk at once, speculating, guessing, my mother *tsk*ing and talking about wayward girls, too pretty for their own good. She glared at the baffled Fannie, who, meeting our mother's iron gaze, was stupefied, homebody that she certainly was. Julia Ferber, daughter of fatalistic East European sensibility, always expected disaster, rainy days on her already-dark parade, flooding her beleaguered soul. Me, the younger daughter, already had defied her, becoming the subject of wagging town tongues. Fannie, pretty as a daisy, a fluttering girl, susceptible to flattery, well, that girl needed watching. My mother was a worried mother hen.

Esther then joined the noisy chorus and our four voices were at counterpoint: "Imagine…her poor family…didn't you just…I knew something like this would happen…just too pretty…traveling salesmen, you know how…not trusted…roving eyes…a girl too man crazy…an actress, you say?…glory be to God… because she had a part in some high school production? . . too pretty…I always say a young girl…not safe any more…You'd think…I think…I think…I really think…think…"

In the swelling babble of squawking, overlapping voices my father spoke, and, like a factory siren blast, there was sudden silence on the porch. We turned to him.

"What?" My mother was peevish. I realized it was the first word she'd spoken to him since the afternoon visit from Dr. Cooper.

"She's just a little girl." His voice was filled with sadness.

Chapter Seven

Esther and I wanted to rush downtown. Ignoring my mother ("Ed, this is not your business"), we headed toward the high school where we spotted Amos Moss, the deputy chief, huffing along in huge strides, headed up the stairs. We caught up with him as he opened the front door.

Amos Moss was the number-two man in a town that sustained two full-time law officers and a receptionist, an old widow named Tessa Monger. Three part-time constables filled the ranks. Occasionally, I stopped at the police station, though Byron Beveridge regularly covered that beat. I never cared for such visits. No one there took me seriously. Tessa was the least offensive, a shaky, twitchy woman always on the verge of crying, though she wore a constant smile. She thanked everyone for stopping in, as if it were a church social, but she rarely provided information. Deputy Amos Moss was an hour away from being the town idiot—a tobacco-chomping bungler in his forties, overflowing in a stained shirt and pants, his badge always lopsided. He spent his days going in the wrong direction.

Chief of Police Caleb Stone, however, was a different cut of cloth, a man as stringy as a long bean, with a prominent jaw, a volatile temper, and a persistent belief in fair play. I considered him an enigma, largely because he was so notoriously close-mouthed. He might be a clever man, this taciturn sheriff, but with his stony reserve he was hard to read. An elder in the First Congregational Church, he was respectability itself.

Appleton was so lazy and peaceful a town that the chief and deputy spent their days wrestling with trespassing, wandering cows and sheep, barroom brawls, neighborhood spats. The horse-drawn patrol wagon hauled drunken souls to the city lockup, baby-faced Horace Grove at the reins. At times, staring into the wagon, I saw grimy, stone-faced Oneida Indians, drunk on corn mash illegally sold to them, deadened men headed for lockup where, according to Byron Beveridge's report in the *Crescent*, they spent the night playing euchre.

No, the truth of the matter was that the police had little to do in town, most days. How many times could a vagrant goat trespass in Mrs. Meeson's flowerbed? Read the *Crescent* or the *Post*. Nothing but baseball statistics and at-home socials.

Which probably explained why both Chief Caleb Stone and Deputy Amos Moss were at the high school now, two hours after Frana Lempke's disappearance.

Amos Moss stopped short and I nearly collided with him. "Going somewheres, ladies?"

"I'm a reporter for the *Crescent*, as you know, Mr. Moss."

"This ain't news."

Esther leaned into Amos, her eyes flashing. "We're good friends of Frana, Mr. Moss. We were with her…"

He nodded. I sighed. Why hadn't I thought of that? Girl reporters seemed to have meager currency in this town. Esther's fluttery eyelids and pretty face had more authority with the simpleton law.

Chief Caleb Stone had been summoned by Principal Jones, who, frustrated by the bizarre disappearance and verbally assailed by Christ Lempke, had asked teachers to remain behind. Some returned to the school from their homes. I'd not known what to expect, but surely not this gathering. Sitting in rows in the auditorium, the fifteen or so teachers and staff looked at one another, stupefied.

The chief had been talking to the principal down in front and glanced up at me. "Newsworthy?" A trace of sardonic smile. Once or twice as I passed by him on College Avenue, he'd greeted me with similar wry amusement. Even this—this situation, whatever it was—seemed to bring his sarcasm.

"So," he began, "we have a young lady who stepped out of class and into thin air."

Esther and I slipped into seats at the back of the auditorium.

I heard grunting. Frana's uncle, Christ Lempke, was sitting apart, not in an auditorium chair but on a bench, his back against the wall, hunched over.

"Is time I went home." He attempted to stand.

"Not yet." Caleb Stone eyed him. From the way he spoke, I sensed he'd been using those words over and over with the impatient man.

"I need get home." A thick German accent, almost impossible.

Chief Stone ignored him.

Scratching the back of his neck, Amos Moss glanced at Lempke, using one of his two practiced stares: accusation and vacuity.

Caleb Stone cleared his throat. "I asked to meet now to review some facts. I know some of you teachers had arrived home and had to travel back here. I'm sorry to inconvenience you. Now we've been hearing around town that Frana was seen getting on the 3:01 with"—he looked down at his notes—"a chubby drummer, but I ain't got no idea where that rumor started."

Kathe Schmidt, that's where, I was certain of it. The spiteful Kathe bustling over town with accounts of Frana eloping to New York and to Broadway footlights. Odds are, Kathe *created* that rumor. But why? Frana and Kathe, two sparring friends, often together but often at war with each other. Kathe was the problem here. She had to be connected to this ugly scene. If Frana did run off, perhaps Kathe was part of the story.

Caleb Stone was going on. "Far as I'm concerned, frankly, the last time Frana was seen was in the hallways of this school." Suddenly, peering over the heads of the faculty, he addressed Esther and me. "I gather you two were friends of the young lady?" He waited.

Well, I never liked her, fatuous beauty that she was, but...
"Yes." I sounded lame. "Somewhat."

"Somewhat?"

"From our high school days, last year," Esther offered in a hurry. "Sometimes she would visit with me and, well, Kathe Schmidt...and...and sometimes Edna here."

Caleb Stone raised his eyebrows. Edna here. Frana, the local beauty; Kathe, the pretty; Esther, the stunning Semite. Edna—here. Girl reporter. Here.

"So what do you two know?"

Once begun, Esther chattered about the rumor she'd heard of Frana seeing an older man—"I heard really older, I mean, twenty-five or even thirty"—to which one of the younger male teachers twittered, then gulped, apologetic. Esther talked of Frana's family's horrid wardenship, her being locked up in her room at night, and she glanced nervously at the scowling Christ Lempke. Dramatically, she ended with an account of Frana's desire to be an actress in New York and marriage and...

Caleb Stone cut her off. "I suspect it's Kathe telling the stories of the train departure. You ain't the first to tell me that." Nearby Amos grunted, and I fully expected and welcomed the sight of Kathe being led away in leg irons.

"You don't believe she left with a drummer?" I asked him, surprising myself.

"Well, anything's possible. Ain't saying yes, ain't saying no." He scratched his chin. "You know the name of this older fellow?"

Esther and I shook our heads. He turned away, through with us.

"What kind school is this?" Christ Lempke struggled to his feet in a spurt of hot anger. "Hands young girl over to lecher. Hopping train ride to hell." He shook his fist in the air.

The room got silent. Caleb Stone deliberated, nodding his head. Esther giggled, nervous. "Hopping train ride to hell," she whispered. Caleb Stone kept his eyes squinted at Christ Lempke, who finally dropped back into his seat.

Amos Moss gurgled with the wad of tobacco in his cheek.

"Way I see it," Caleb Stone began, "Mr. Lempke here arrived his usual time to retrieve his niece, only to learn she'd left the building an hour earlier."

Miss Hepplewhyte, the guardian secretary, was livid. "She had a note. There was a *note*." The last word screeched, hysterical.

Caleb Stone was, in fact, holding the note.

"Is fake," muttered Christ Lempke.

Chief Stone looked as if he had no idea what to do. He watched the redoubtable Miss Hepplewhyte bristle. Skinny as a twig, wrenlike, Miss Holly Hepplewhyte claimed she'd been working in education back to the days of Reconstruction. That was probably true. Nothing got by her, and she prided herself on vigilance. Which, sad to say, she now considered under attack.

Miss Hepplewhyte worked in a small anteroom just off the front entrance, at angles to the first floor main corridor, and thus had a bird's eye view of the universe. The past four days, she insisted shrilly, glaring at Christ Lempke, Frana's uncle walked Frana to the front entrance and stood there "like Cotton Mather," never saying a word except for something muttered to Frana in German, and then he'd be off. Miss Hepplewhyte had been told via the principal that Frana's father, who worked at the Appleton Paper and Pulp Works and was gone early morning to late night, had given orders that Frana be discharged to her uncle each afternoon. She was only seventeen.

Miss Hepplewhyte gathered—here she smacked her lips, judgmental—there was a dire problem with the girl's behavior, some frivolous conduct, some disobedience at home. Frankly, she wasn't surprised, given Frana's brazen flirtations in the hallways, which she herself had admonished more than once. Glancing again to the gaunt, bitter man on the bench, Miss Hepplewhyte insisted her one attempt to greet Christ Lempke civilly was met with an icy, unresponsive stare. Each afternoon he was there like clockwork, dragging home the young girl.

"Is time I leave. Foolish, this," Lempke muttered.

Caleb Stone ignored him. "And today?"

"Nothing different," the secretary said. "I only glimpsed him in the doorway this morning. I was about to say something but I was called away for a few minutes"—she turned to Vice-Principal Timm "as Mr. Timm had a question about one student's tardiness, Markham Tellin, who's always late. But then I prepared my tea and biscuit." She breathed in. "I was next door, an eye on the hallway. When I got back to my desk, the note was there in an envelope, staring right up at me. I assumed Mr. Lempke had planted it on my desk, not wanting to speak to a human being…"

"I no leave note." Furious.

She didn't look at him. "I know that now, sir." She spoke to the wall behind him. "I thought it odd, but…" Another shrug, suggesting she expected odd things from the likes of Christ Lempke. "The outside read, simply, 'School,' one word, and inside a penciled, scribbled note, saying…"

Here Caleb Stone opened the note and read it aloud: "'To school. Her uncle comes for Frana Lempke at two this afternoon. Is family trouble.'" He paused. "Trouble is spelled *truble*." I wondered why he shared that last bit, but no matter. Oddly, it did sound like Christ Lempke talking, but perhaps it was the chief's voice, the addition of a slight thick-voweled accent to his words.

"I no write such thing." The fist in the air.

"So," Miss Hepplewhyte continued, clearing her throat, "I duly informed Mr. Timm, who let Miss Hosley, Frana's teacher, know." A dramatic pause. "We do have policies about early leave-taking, you know. But"—now her voice got strange—"Frana never left the building at two, nor of course did I see her before that. I thought it curious, but then I assumed plans had shifted, and he'd be arriving at the end of day. I paid it no mind."

Christ Lempke grunted. He struggled to his feet. "I go now."

Caleb Stone motioned for him to sit down.

It turned out that Frana had made a point of telling Miss Hosley that she had to meet her uncle at two, and, according to Miss Hosley, Frana used the same words—"family trouble." Family trouble. Frana's concoction, clearly. Some ruse to flee—to meet that mysterious lover.

Miss Hosley swallowed and spoke in an uncertain tone. I could tell she didn't like this public spectacle. Her eyes darted from Caleb Stone to, of all people, Amos Moss, who was off in his own world, dreaming, chewing his tobacco like a cow with its cud. Miss Hosley looked as if she were on a witness stand, deliberating slowly before each calculated response. She'd taught me Latin IV with fierce assaults on Cicero and ablative cases, rapping the front of her desk with a pointer as each student misfired when declining a noun on the chalkboard.

Yes, Miss Hosley said, at two o'clock she excused Frana from class, admonishing her to complete a homework assignment and, truth to tell, Frana seemed giddy—"Yes, that's the word, giddy"—as she left. But, Miss Hosley concluded, drawing in her breath and touching her iron-gray curls and then fingering the cameo brooch stuck on her bosom like a postage stamp, Frana was *always* happy to leave class. "She is not friends with Cicero." Amos, rousing himself briefly from his stupor, sputtered and mouthed a word: *What?* Miss Hosley glared at him, and he turned scarlet.

"And so the mystery begins," Caleb Stone said, more to himself than anyone else. He outlined the layout of the long hallway, which everyone in that room already knew. Frana's classroom, five more classrooms to the end of the corridor, a quick turn and you were facing Miss Hepplewhyte's anteroom, and beyond that, the front door. Frana never made it that far.

"But that's impossible," Miss Hosley exclaimed, and then seemed to regret her outburst. "I mean—she *left* my classroom. She *had* to walk that way." Because there was no other way out of the corridor.

Mr. McCaslin had the classroom next door to Miss Hosley's. He was a youngish man, a dandy; spitfire shiny in a Milwaukee-cut suit with glinting watch fob, his goatee so manicured students whispered it was a fake paste-on, stolen from a passing circus act. Not only was he the drama coach—he directed me in *A Scrap of Paper*—but he taught English grammar and literature, and, while his students gaped in wonder, he would wax eloquent, bellowing out the climactic lines of Shakespeare and Marlowe, then masking his sobbing behind a gigantic floral-patterned handkerchief. The football team called him Cassie Mac, which meant nothing to me, though I'd attempted to analyze it. When I thought of him, the one image that came to mind was his voracious gobbling of apple strudel at the Elm Tree Bakery, crumbs speckling his careful goatee.

Speaking in his best Milwaukee voice, he added one more bit of information. He'd been standing near the doorway when he noticed one of his students waving at someone in the hallway. Through the window of the closed door, he spotted Frana, who was notorious for her flirtations. She waved back, a grin on her face. He turned to admonish the waver, and when he looked back, Frana was gone.

That left four more classrooms. Chief Stone had learned from Principal Jones that two were empty at that hour. The other two teachers had not been gazing into the hallways, so they had no idea if Frana passed by or not. Frana could have skirted by. Yet, Caleb Stone concluded, she never made it to the end of the corridor where, Miss Hepplewhyte petulantly declared, "I was sitting faithfully. Faithfully."

"That leaves two empty classrooms."

"Which should have been locked," Principal Jones added.

"One wasn't," Homer Timm admitted. "By mistake."

"A mistake," Mr. Jones echoed.

Sitting across the aisle from me, Mildred Dunne grunted, then thought better of it. She sat apart from Miss Hepplewhyte, and Miss Hepplewhyte frowned when Miss Dunne grunted. Also glaring at the secretary was Mr. McCaslin, who drew his lips into a censorious line. Quite a cast of characters, this bunch!

So much had changed since I left high school last year. Back then the town—and my prying eyes—yawned over the familiar sight of our principal, Mr. Hippolyte Jones, arm in arm with his chatty and equally rotund wife Muriel, the two sitting at a baked-bean supper at the Masonic Hall, gabbing with the same three close friends: Miss Holly Hepplewhyte, fearsome school secretary and hall sentry; Miss Mildred Dunne, librarian and Sunday-school moralist; and Mr. Philip McCaslin, English teacher and drama coach, a bachelor who bore an uncanny (and unfortunate) resemblance to Ichabod Crane. The fivesome made cookie-cutter appearances at every civic function. My mother said Mr. Jones, a favorite of hers, was a model of Christian charity for putting up with the imperious Miss Dunne, the strident Miss Hepplewhyte, and the squeaky Mr. McCaslin—and even, lamentably, Mrs. Jones, a woman who never paused to take a breath or to forgive a seeming transgression.

But the picture changed, suddenly, woefully. Muriel Jones died from a heart attack at the end of last summer; and Mr. Jones seemed ready to follow her to the graveyard. Worse, Mildred Dunne, discovered shopping at Pettibone's by new-to-town Gustave Timm, became his companion and then his betrothed, the two sitting alone at the Masonic Hall dinners and laughing foolishly over nonsense. Miss Dunne seemed transformed from the dour martinet in the library into a fluttering schoolgirl asked to a picnic for a lemon phosphate. She told some folks that her life was ready to start now. Everything up till then—her shopping sprees, her unhappy time as guardian of schoolbooks—was preamble to what she'd always dreamed of…a husband. The extra dollop of happiness came from Gustave's being so…handsome. My mother, hearing the gossip, remarked, "She'll learn that marriage is one more hallway without an exit."

With Mildred Dunne gone from the group, Miss Hepplewhyte and Mr. McCaslin now discovered they didn't like each other. So by the Christmas dance and supper, Mr. Jones sat with Miss Hepplewhyte and Mr. McCaslin, but no one spoke. My mother said speaking to the principal made her uncomfortable because his loneliness oozed out like sour sap from an aged tree. When the winter carnival supper was held in February, their table was there, but occupied by Mildred Dunne and Gustave Timm, laughing uproariously over a private joke. Gustave's brother

Homer, strolling past with friends, mumbled something to his brother, but Gustave merely laughed louder.

Miss Hepplewhyte, abandoned by her spinster friend Mildred, chose to stay home and, according to some, devote herself to missionary work, though I couldn't imagine how you can save savage souls by sitting in a small drawing room cluttered with embroidered antimacassars and porcelain Chinese dogs. Worse, she stopped talking to her friend, believing that Mildred Dunne's betrothal to Gustave was a betrayal. Rather than be happy for her friend, she chose bitterness, fury, silence. They passed each other in the school hallways like women who'd never been introduced. Mildred reached out to her—invitations to the homestead she shared with her parents, invitations to go to Milwaukee for shopping, a proposal to be in her wedding party, but Miss Hepplewhyte refused to reply.

That much had changed in one year at Ryan High School. It was better, I observed to Esther, than the melodramatic histrionics in a Bertha M. Clay romance.

I also watched the interplay of principal and vice-principal. Mr. Jones, a favorite of mine, had been a genial, spirited man whose overflowing girth matched the expansiveness of his personality. Now he seemed to be lost in melancholy. How different he was from Homer Timm, who stood next to him now, a man severe and dark, the moustache on his upper lip twitching, always a little untrimmed; a man comfortable in his broadloom suit but, oddly, uncomfortable among people. You could be telling a story of great sadness and there'd be that smile stuck to his face.

"But," Mr. Timm went on now, his voice raising, "the door to that classroom was closed. Frana would have had to *try* it to see whether it was unlatched. She wouldn't have *known*."

"Unless she knew," Caleb Stone said.

Mr. Timm snapped. "And how would she have known that?"

"I'm only suggesting."

"But she could have hid in the room until school closed," said Mr. McCaslin.

"Impossible." From Miss Hepplewhyte.

"And why is that?" Caleb asked.

Yes, why was that?

Miss Hepplewhyte harrumphed, a very Dickensian sound. "Until *when*? Classes were over? Sir, Mr. Lempke"—again the furtive glance to the unhappy man against the wall—"showed up before the last bell and was standing on the top step, hat in hand. I thought to myself—well, someone's plans have indeed changed and no one had the courtesy to inform me. So be it. And I watched as students streamed down that corridor toward the door, as I always do—I feel it my duty to remind a few of after-school obligations—and Frana was *not* among that crowd. As Mr. Lempke can testify."

Christ Lempke was nodding furiously.

Miss Hepplewhyte added, "I was surprised, in fact, because Mr. Lempke was actually *early* today."

Christ Lempke stormed, "I am not a clock."

"Perhaps she climbed out the window," Amos Moss said, and everyone looked at him.

Principal Jones was shaking his head. "No, Zeke Puttman was pruning the bushes at the front of the school, was there all afternoon. I already talked to him. I think he'd have mentioned the sight of a young girl climbing out of the window, don't you think? It was the first thing I thought of when I found the unlocked classroom."

Caleb Stone actually yawned. I could read his mind. This was a lot of pettifogging about a wanton, hell-bent youngster who'd obviously schemed her way out of the school to rendezvous with some surreptitious lover. Doubtless she'd be back home by nightfall, punished by her stern father and whipped by the unrelenting Christ Lempke. At this point, the chief was going through the motions of being the marshal in town. It was either this curiously anemic incident or a walk to Lawe Road to warn Farmer Burnett—for the umpteenth time—to keep his sheep from bothering the grazing cattle of the widow Peters, who inhabited the hell-to-ruin cabin by the river.

"Well," he drawled out the word, "she ain't disappeared into thin air."

So we'd come full circle: Frana, the ghost in the sky.

Mr. Timm decided to speak. "I might add that I was in that corridor at half-past the hour, more or less; and I did glance at my pocket watch"—he extracted the elaborate gold timepiece and flashed it to the onlookers—"and all was quiet. The empty classroom door was closed. Of course."

"But not locked," Chief Stone said.

"I didn't check." Suddenly Mr. Timm seemed flustered, as though he'd said too much. "I mean, why would I?"

"Of course." The words escaped from the mouth of Mildred Dunne, who suddenly looked sheepish. "I only mean, well, we all were where we supposed to be. It's a *school.* It must function…"

Mr. Timm showed a sliver of a smile. "Of course, Miss Dunne. Thank you, but I need no defense."

Miss Dunne's cheeks reddened.

Mr. McCaslin made a whistling noise, but a withering glance from Miss Hepplewhyte seemed to elicit an unintentional snicker from him. Mr. Jones looked none too happy with his staff. In fact, for a moment he looked teary-eyed, shaky.

Caleb Stone stuck the phony note into a breast pocket. "Seems to me this Frana girl is pretty clever. Somehow she worked her way out of the building, unseen. Someone batted an eyelid"—a sidelong glance at Miss Hepplewhyte, who was decidedly not happy—"and slipped out. Young children do those things. We can't keep an eye on them all the time, you know. My own children, well…" He trailed off. "There is no other explanation. People don't move through walls like Houdini."

Outside, Esther stopped by the willow tree that brushed the building. "Why did Kathe Schmidt tell everybody about someone seeing Frana hopping a train with some drummer from the Sherman House?"

"I'll tell you. Because she *wanted* that to be the truth. She'd like to see Frana really disappear from town."

"Because of Jake Smuddie?"

"What else? Maybe Kathe told people that story because she *knew* Frana was up to something. Maybe Frana confided in her. Maybe, in fact, Frana did get on that train with a drummer. Maybe it's not a rumor. But Chief Stone doubts she's left town. Maybe Frana actually told her fair-weather friend that she *planned* on being on that train with a certain drummer. So Kathe just assumed it happened."

Esther was wide-eyed. "And plans changed?"

"Maybe not. Frana could be in Milwaukee as we speak."

"I can see Frana lying to her."

"Because Kathe would believe her."

"You know, Frana is up to something bad."

"And Kathe is involved somehow. But I don't understand how Frana mastered leaving the school unseen, not with Miss Hepplewhyte sitting there. Was that the only way she could get away from her uncle's eagle eye?"

"She was a prisoner at home," Esther insisted. "They put bars on her bedroom window. They *watched* her."

"How'd you first hear of that?"

"Kathe was happy to tell me."

"So she obviously saw her chance to flee only during school hours…"

Esther looked puzzled. "Why go to such lengths to get out of school unseen?"

"Meeting up with someone," I concluded. "But she must have known there'd be a price to be paid later on…a beating, more confinement."

"Unless she wasn't planning on going home again."

My mind was racing. "Then maybe she *did* get on that train."

"The chief will find her."

"But where is she? Frankly, I never thought she was that clever to do something like this." I bit my lip. "Unless…"

"Unless what?"

"Unless someone told her to do it."

Esther nodded. "The lover."

"Yes, the lover."

"But where are they now?"

I clicked my tongue. "Not in a honeymoon Pullman suite, I'd hazard a guess." A pause. "She'd—they'd—know everyone would look on that train right away."

"So…"

"So she'd be hiding out in Appleton."

"Until…"

"Until she can escape."

"How?"

"Maybe a boat. Catching the Goodrich Line tonight at eight o'clock. From the dock on Sycamore." In my mind I ran through the possible ways to escape Appleton.

"But the chief will be watching that boat, no?"

"I'd hope so."

"So long as he doesn't assign Amos Moss to keep an eye on it."

"Then Frana can blithely sail up the Fox River, arm and arm with her paramour, waving goodbye to Appleton."

"Paramour—I love that word," Esther laughed.

We strolled casually back home, enjoying the idle speculation, gossiping, fascinated with our pretty little schoolmate who now had made herself the subject of discussion. Frana, the girl who never left home without a mirror, now talked of, sought, condemned, hiding somewhere, perhaps by the river or in the mill district. Somewhere. Perversely, I was wondering how I might make it an item in the *Crescent*, though I realized it was hardly news. Sam Ryan never allowed tidbits of scandal or idle sensation, no matter how scintillating, to pop up in his serious columns. *Frana Lempke disappeared on a riverboat with Chester Smedjen, salesman from Minah Malleable Iron Fittings Company.*

I was itching to jot down notes in my pad, to describe the scene at the high school.

"I feel sorry for her when she's found," Esther whispered.

"If she lets herself be found."

◇◇◇

The next morning I woke to the sound of rain beating down on the roof, and I snuggled under the covers. It would be a drifting Saturday, a chance for me to read the F. Marion Crawford romance I'd picked up at the library. For a moment, lying there, I thought of Frana Lempke, disappeared from town. Or had she? Downstairs Fannie was complaining about the rain. There would be no beating of carpets and Kathe Schmidt would simply not show up, most likely overjoyed at not having to help the Ferbers. I'd forgotten the day's intended chore; I'd have to help, too, working with Kathe, doubtless the two of us ending up in a verbal skirmish.

By midday the rains were worse and my mother returned from My Store for dinner.

"Everyone comes into the store and talks of Frana," my mother told me. "But everyone thinks it's…amusing. Like it's a foolish little-girl adventure."

"Well, Frana can be a foolish girl."

"Strangely, her mother stopped into the store just before noon. A nice woman, but not a talker. I asked her about Frana and she just nodded, looked a little embarrassed. You know what I think? Frana came back home last night, and now the family is a little ashamed of the fuss that's been made."

"But I wonder just what she's up to?" Fannie asked.

I kept my mouth shut.

It rained all day, and Fannie sat by the kitchen window, staring out at the empty clothesline. I avoided her, sensing she was ready to do battle.

Sunday morning was bright and clear, and in the early afternoon I wandered to Esther's house, where we sat on the veranda, sipping coffee and chatting. Later, buoyed by the welcome sun, we took a stroll, drifting in the placid June air, a gorgeous day, the slight breeze rustling the sycamores and sugar maples. We meandered off the Avenue, headed toward the river by way of Lovers

Lane, the quiet promenade of overarching elms and birches, with its hard-packed dirt lanes and the rough-hewn fences. There old men walked ancient hounds, college freshmen from Lawrence University rode their fashionable bicycles, and sixteen-year-old girls sat on the moss-backed hillocks under the aromatic white pines and read Ella Wheeler Wilcox verse aloud…

Most of my most fanciful dreams happened when I sat, alone, on the benches there.

We rambled toward the river, my favorite destination, but our ramble was cut short, when, nearby, Old Man Travers, a man in his nineties who periodically drifted into town from his shack in the mud flats and announced that he was the rightful heir to the throne of Slovakia, started making gasping sounds as he pulled at his border collie who was straining on his leash. The animal would have none of it, yipping in counterpoint to the doddering owner. Esther and I stopped, watched, and saw Old Man Travers crumble to his knees, moaning. Panicked, we rushed to help the old man—*Don't die don't die don't die*—only to discover, as we neared the gasping, choking man, that his faithful border collie Wilhelm was pawing at the body of Frana Lempke.

Chapter Eight

I sat by myself on a bench. Esther's father had taken her home. I'd refused to leave, my reporter's instinct taking over, but, more so, I had to grapple with my own dreadful, numbing discovery. I'd never seen a body before and certainly not a murdered body—nor of a person I knew, maybe not a close friend but a school chum. I preferred to sit quietly, thinking, watching, shaking, removed from the frantic men assembled near the dead body. I'd already told Chief Stone my story, which was no story, really, watching Old Man Travers topple and then…the gruesome sight of sad Frana lying there, her fair hair, as light as moonshine, askew about her head. The eyes wide open, startled, yet glassy. The face ashen and contorted, as though she couldn't believe her life was ending so horribly.

Caleb Stone and Amos Moss strutted around, out of their element, as Dr. Belford, the district coroner, pulled up in the dark-curtained death wagon. A crew of bustling men—ten or more townsmen—circled the body, trampling the scene. Shouldn't they keep their distance? In the damp spongy mud perhaps a few foot indentations, left behind, might be evidence. Or maybe a bit of clothing, a hair, or…or what? I tried to think of how police or detectives in Sherlock Holmes or Anna Katherine Green mysteries acted. I'd just finished reading *The Filigree Ball*, though I disliked mystery romances. All that bother about nothing. Folderol. This murder was the province of those men, with

Chief Caleb Stone, the best of the sorry lot, obviously thrown off by the severity of the crime.

Murder had its own rules…or the breaking of rules. I understood that, but I also sensed, emphatically, that this assembly of Appleton gentlemen was delirious with confusion, from the good sheriff himself to Johnny Mason, the local town drunk and all-around handyman, who was positioned over the body.

Dr. Belford mumbled to Caleb Stone as the body was hoisted into the dark mortuary wagon. "Some fool strangled the poor girl." Said simply, an awful declarative line. Caleb Stone winced.

Head spinning, I stood and walked toward the men. At that moment I heard labored breathing and turned to see Matthias Boon, late on the scene, pipe in his mouth, reporter's pad in his hand. He stopped short and nearly barreled into me. "Miss Ferber, what are you doing here?"

"I found the body." I pointed to the disappearing wagon.

Boon rocked on his heels, ended up on tiptoe, hoping to become as tall as I, but he pivoted and teetered, much like a wind-up children's toy my mother sold in My Store at Christmas.

He sneered through his teeth. "Were you looking for it?"

I frowned and lied. "Frana was a friend of mine, Mr. Boon. My friend Esther is her close friend, too." Boon stopped looking at me, staring instead at Caleb Stone and Amos Moss, their heads huddled close together, looking like confused referees debating a call at a Lawrence University football game. He headed toward them, pompous as a rooster at daybreak, when I said to his back, "I'll write up the murder for the *Crescent*."

Boon faced me, his face purple with rage. "What did you say?"

"I'm a witness."

He stepped up to me, narrowing his eyes. "Look, Miss Ferber, this is news."

"Precisely. I'm a reporter."

"I'm a reporter," he mimicked.

"I know the story from the high school through her disappearance, and I'll put together a piece…"

He interrupted, venomous. "You'll do nothing of the kind, Miss Ferber. You forget that I'm city editor, and murder is my story."

"It's my story. I'm part of it."

He slid his tongue into the corner of his mouth, making his moustache shift like a caterpillar realigning itself on a tree branch. "All the more reason for me to handle it. Reporters are dispassionate, objective, they…"

"I can tell the facts…"

"Like your Houdini piece, I'm afraid. You do love the flight of fancy, the…"

"The fact of murder, sir, calls for a bitter realism."

"You're not Theodore Dreiser, Miss Ferber."

"And you're hardly Joseph Pulitzer."

"No matter. This is a man's province. Consider yourself one more person to be interviewed for the story. By me. You will *not* have a byline here." He turned away to see the mortuary wagon creeping its lugubrious way out of Lovers Lane, and Caleb Stone and Amos Moss and the other officious men already leaving the park. Boon cursed loudly. I'd heard Sam Ryan use every profane word in some sinister devil's dictionary. Nothing surprised me anymore. Now and then Mac exploded in a volley of scatological fury from the pressroom. After a year on the *Crescent*, I'd considered using some of the vocabulary myself. So Boon's blustery "Shit!" simply made me laugh. He went charging after Caleb Stone who tried to avoid him.

That evening's meal, supervised by Fannie, was roast beef, browned and crusted at the edges, pink in the center, juicy and rich; cloud-light mashed potatoes, a well of hot butter pooled in the center of each heap, with thick, steamy gravy; and winter squash blended with a dash of ground pepper and maple syrup. On the counter was Fannie's creation: the three-layer chocolate fudge cake, the one the family deemed Alpine Mountain, towering, with peaks of chocolate and vanilla icing.

Ordinarily I would have ravaged such a meal, famished, but tonight, dispirited, I had no appetite for food or conversation. The Ferbers were a chatty family. Not my father, to be sure, who'd retreated into monosyllables, but the three fiercely strong women shared vignettes of shopping, passersby, public figures, politics, sewing, chicanery, life's obstacles: all of it, none of it. Tonight the family scarcely spoke. Fannie pouted. My terse and shaky summary of the horrendous day had silenced them all. Sitting there with mounds of food on the ample table, with that delectable cake beckoning, we lapsed into mournful silence.

The evening ended when my father spoke for the first time. "She was so young." A pause. "At least she's spared the agony of life to come."

The sentence hung in the air, so wrong. Too bitter, too laced with melancholia. This wasn't my father who lacked my mother's dark European *weltschmerz*, the ominous cloud that hung over all our horizons. I'd never heard my father say anything so cynical, so stark, so plaintive. Or so filled with doom.

Suddenly, helplessly, I started to sob. My mother rose and wrapped her arms around me, soothing, touching. My family thought I was crying for the late Frana Lempke. But I wasn't. I wept for the death of something beautiful in my father.

The next morning the *Crescent* office hummed. Boon had already written the front-page account, garnered piecemeal from Caleb Stone and Amos Moss, from the other men at the Lovers Lane death scene, even from hasty interviews with Principal Hippolyte Jones and Vice-Principal Homer Timm. I sat at my desk.

"What do you think?" Sam Ryan passed me the typed sheets.

I was mentioned in the article, though gratuitously. "The body was discovered in Lovers Lane by Linus Travers, signaled by his faithful dog Wilhelm, and then assisted by *Crescent* reporter Edna Ferber and Esther Leitner, daughter of Rabbi Mendel Leitner of Zion Congregation."

That was it: no more. But Sam Ryan rustled the returned sheets, poring over Boon's typescript, doodling with a pencil, fiddling with it. Surprisingly, he asked me to share my own observation. I refocused the story that Boon had covered, starting with the mystery of Frana's leaving the high school, unnoticed. I rambled on and on, never glancing at Boon who sat there, pipe dangling from his mouth, puffing away, while I told Sam Ryan about the mythic chubby drummer secreting the girl away, taking her to New York. I mentioned Frana's juvenile obsession with becoming an actress. Sam listened, rapt, as did Miss Ivy. Sam scribbled on another piece of paper, rewriting lines here and there, a paragraph. He quoted a line from me, asked me to repeat it, jotted it down. Finally, he handed the sheets back to Boon, wordless. Boon, his lips drawn into a tight, unforgiving line, contemplated the additions to his piece, unhappy, and simply nodded.

"We need a good headline." Sam was looking at me.

Boon slurred his words. "Girl Reporter Edna Ferber Discovers Body in Lovers Lane. And underneath that: Girl Reporter Frequent Habitué of Lovers Lane."

Sam reddened, "That's not very funny, Matt."

Miss Ivy *tsk*ed *tsk*ed.

"I'm not trying to be funny," Boon smirked.

I raised my voice. "You're not trying to be a gentleman either."

Sam walked away, baffled, disappearing into the pressroom. When he returned, he stood there in the doorway, staring from me to Boon.

"Miss Ferber, I'm trying to protect your virtue." Boon's voice was cloying, sweet. "Why do you want to be the subject of gossip in town?"

I fired back. "Let me worry about my own name."

Tension in the city room: voices raised, curt responses, silence heavy and arctic. Should I speak again, I would be shouting. Time stopped around us. Abrupt movement from the back room broke our suspense. I jumped. Mac stood there, a smear of black ink on his cheek, a sheaf of copy in his gigantic hands hanging down to the floor like spilled leaves. He was focused on me, which rattled me. I couldn't make out the impassive expression. Slowly, he turned his head toward Boon, who hadn't noticed, intent as he was on smiling stupidly at me. The corners of Mac's mouth twitched.

The door opened, and Byron Beveridge tripped down the five steps, brimming with news. When I looked toward the printing shop, Mac was gone.

"Got the latest on the murder." Beveridge's movements were a little too jaunty, his voice too spirited. "Not from Chief Stone, of course, that piece of incommunicative granite, but from Jarvis Hull, who barbers his hair. The coroner says Frana was killed on Friday. Sometime that afternoon or night. It rained all day Saturday and no one went into Lovers Lane. Another thing. It seems the chief interviewed Christ Lempke again, and the man mentioned scaring away a young man from under Frana's locked, upstairs bedroom window the other night, a young man identified as Jake Smuddie from Lawrence University."

"I know him." I spoke in a small voice.

"You do?" Miss Ivy asked.

"He's a freshman at the University. He used to be Frana's boyfriend…"

Sam looked perplexed. "What was he doing playing Romeo under her balcony the other night?"

Byron Beveridge kept trying to interrupt. "If you all would let me finish…" We waited. "The uncle said Frana had seen him sometime last year, but had jilted him, forced by her family who insisted she wasn't ready for marriage. He didn't take rejection kindly. He's been a pest at the farmhouse, and Frana's father once scared him with a blast from a shotgun. Kept coming back like a bad penny or a hungry dog."

Boon sneered. "Nice friends you have, Miss Ferber."

I spoke to Byron. "Did Chief Stone talk to Jake?"

"He did. Out at the university. But Herr Professor interrupted and put an end to the interrogation. Said his son had nothing to do with Frana any more, whose death, he said, was the result of a life lived carelessly. Caleb remarked he was not through questioning the boy, not by a long shot."

I fought the sudden image of the strapping footballer Jake, those strong hands twisting Frana's delicate neck. No, no.

No.

When I returned home around three to take my father for a short walk, I discovered Kathe helping Fannie with cleaning the parlor and dining room carpets, the beginning of Fannie's early summer housekeeping. In a hurry to be done, she was dragging carpets to the back clothesline and attacking them with the ferocity of a Saracen warrior. I sought her out in the yard, but Kathe didn't want to talk about Frana's death. She closed her eyes and shook her head vigorously when I expressed sympathy. Frana and Kathe were friends—though rivals. When I asked about Jake Smuddie, Kathe glowered.

"Leave him out of this," she snarled. "He ain't part of this. He got nothing to do with it."

I asked her about the rumor of Frana getting on the train with a drummer. "Who told you that, Kathe?"

She turned away, dropping the carpet beater. I'd learned that Caleb Stone and Amos Moss were interviewing the guests at the Sherman House, especially the traveling salesmen there; and I'd heard through Sam Ryan that, in fact, three men had left on the 3:01 on Friday afternoon, alone. Chief Stone was tracking them down. Could one of those men be the murderer of Frana? One of those bilious, portly, scratching men who tucked themselves with their indigestion and gout and sample cases into the worn seats of the Chicago and Northwestern train. When I mentioned the drummers, Kathe looked ready to say something, but stopped.

"Where is Jake Smuddie?" I asked her.

Infuriated, Kathe swung around, eyes blazing. "You leave him alone."

I suddenly knew where to find the footballer.

Of course, he wouldn't be at his home. Doubtless Herr Professor wouldn't lock up the young man as Frana's parents unsuccessfully tried to do with her. No, watching Kathe assault the carpets in a fury, I realized Kathe would be joining Jake after she left the Ferber household. I knew that Kathe and Jake often lingered, out of both sets of parents' forbidding eyes, in the gazebo in City Park, the sheltered retreat set back in a grove of white pines, a cool summer haven and now, in serene June, a hiding place. He'd be there, waiting for Kathe to finish her work.

Within minutes, walking briskly, I approached the gazebo from the side and startled Jake Smuddie, sitting on a bench, dressed in his football jersey. He was leaning over a thick tome, concentrating, his face inches from the book. He turned, expecting someone. "I'm not Kathe."

He smiled and stood. The book toppled to the ground. I noticed the title: *Elements of Moral Philosophy*, and I thought, cruelly, a little too late, no?

"I can see that." A pause. "Hello, Edna."

My heart fluttered as I looked at the handsome boy.

"What are you doing here?"

"I'm not hiding. We—Kathe and me—we always come here." Then he swallowed. "Yeah, I guess I'm hiding. From my father. He thinks I'm at the college library, studying." He pointed at the book, which now rested on his boot. "But I couldn't stay at home. He's not happy with me these days." He gave me a wispy smile. "He says I've brought shame to the family."

"Well, have you?"

He looked hurt, and I regretted my sharpness. I stared into his wide, milk-fed boy's face on that rough-and-tumble physique. I'd never thought him capable of anything untoward, though I gave him considerable license because he was so handsome. Attractive souls, I'd learned long ago, had a freedom in life that mere mortals—the bland, the dull, and the otherwise—didn't possess. Plain girls learned that lesson early.

Unlike the other boasting boys, Jake Smuddie was always a decent sort, with a quiet manner. Boys like Jake never noticed me, but, peculiarly, Jake *had*. He laughed at my stories and sometimes talked to me. The afternoon following my performance in *A Scrap of Paper*, he stopped me on College Avenue and told me how much fun he'd had. "You make me laugh out loud, Edna." That surprised me, and I blushed. Jake reached into a cloth satchel slung over his shoulder and took out a thin volume, thrusting it out toward me.

"What?" I stared into his handsome face.

"I want you to have this."

A beautiful edition of *A Midsummer Night's Dream*. I held the slender leatherbound volume in my hand, an awful weight, as he mumbled something I didn't catch, turned, and walked away.

That night, showing off the book at the dinner table, perhaps saying the name "Jake" a little too much, Fannie boiled over. I'd been watching her simmer. She, the pretty girl, had a not-so-secret crush on the footballer, and, unlike me, had notoriously (and unsuccessfully) flirted with him at school dances and even in broad daylight on College Avenue. Jake had ignored her. Now, eyeing the Shakespeare in my hand, she sniped, "He probably stole it from his father's library."

"I think it's a touching gift."

Fannie drew in her cheeks, narrowed her eyes. "He probably knows the only companion you'll ever have is a book."

"Fannie!" my father thundered.

"Well, I'm not sorry."

Jake's only fault was his lap-dog devotion to the beautiful young blond girls of town. Which must be some sort of punishable crime in the universe I created in my mind.

"I've been foolish." Jake picked up the dropped book.

"Chief Stone giving you a hard time?"

He blushed. "I should have told him right away about my stupid visit to Frana's home."

"When was that?"

"The night before she, you know, died." His voice cracked.

"Good God."

"I know, I know."

"Why did you go there? You're courting Kathe Schmidt, no?" I waited, but he didn't answer. His eyes were watery and he rubbed them with the back of his hand. "Who you'll be meeting here shortly, right? After she pounds the Ferber carpets into perdition."

A genuine smile, warm. "Kathe's a little slip of a girl, Edna, but she packs a mean wallop with a stick." He considered his words. "No, no, I don't mean anything bad, you know. I'm trying to make a…" He stopped.

"Why did you go there?"

"My father says I shouldn't be with a high school girl now that I'm at Lawrence. But we're just a year apart, really. And what he really means is that I shouldn't be courting *any* girl. He's made that clear."

"You and Kathe?"

He looked away for a second. "I was thinking of Frana. I used to be with her all the time, Edna. Last year at Ryan. You know that. You saw us together. She was a grade behind me, but that didn't matter. She *liked* me. Then out of the blue she left me last fall. Just told me to go away." He hesitated to say what was on his mind. "She had trouble at home," he whispered. "It made her, I think, *afraid* of people."

"I don't understand."

He licked his lip. "It was a secret she let slip out. She was crying one night and…"

"Tell me."

"One of her brothers…bothered her a lot. He, you know, tried to…but …" He stopped. "She was scared, Edna."

My mind swam. Violent, horrible images floated before my eyes. I recalled a mysterious remark from Esther. *Frana doesn't like to go home sometimes.* Why? I'd asked. Esther just shook her head.

Secrets, I thought. The real lives of Appleton, lived behind closed doors. When I started out at the *Crescent*, that plump girl whose visions of life came from Dickens and Thackeray, I'd been woefully innocent, and Sam Ryan purposely kept me from the dark underbelly. It wasn't possible. Now, a year later, I understood that darkness loomed on too many lost souls' horizons. The first time I saw a drunken man slap his wife as I joined a noisy celebratory crowd outside a beer hall, I was stunned and couldn't sleep that night. Yet last week when I was sent by Sam Ryan to interview a doctor who was hawking some new, improved health elixir, the august doctor, a slobbering man in his seventies, was startled that a nineteen-year-old girl was doing the interview. All of a sudden he reached into a drawer and thrust before me some photographs—the kind of risqué French postcards I'd seen high-school boys tittering over. The doctor watched me closely, expecting—what?—screams, horror…fainting. But I'd been on the streets of Appleton for a year now. "Interesting," I stated. And stood up to leave.

Now, beside a sad Jake, I questioned, "Did you ask her about it?"

He shook his head. "I couldn't bring myself to do it."

"So she just left you?"

"Just told me to go away. It drove me crazy. I'd see her around town, and she'd stay away from me. But then we met by chance a month ago or so back, bumped into each other on College, and we talked a while. I guess I…went a little crazy."

"But you are seeing Kathe." A fact, stated bluntly.

He nodded. "I started seeing her right after Frana told me goodbye." The last word hung in the air, awful and loaded. "I guess Kathe had been around me a lot and I didn't notice. When Frana said goodbye, suddenly Kathe was there, and, well…" He waved his hand in the air.

I knew all of this. I'd watched parts of the curious evolution and heard the rest of it through Esther, who'd blathered about all the ups and downs of Jake Smuddie's infatuation with Frana, as well as Kathe's shameless pursuit of the jilted boy. Kathe had been telling friends she and Jake were "close" long before they appeared at a barn dance at the Masonic Hall this past February. "I know, I know," I told him now.

Jake looked away for a second. "I never lost my feelings for Frana, and I was angry that she told me goodbye. When I talked to her last month, she said she had a way out. That surprised me. She was always talking about New York. You know, I said to her—Frana, you've never even been to New York, much less Broadway. She got mad at me. She really wanted a different life…away from her home. But I don't think she knew how to get away clean. I suspected there was somebody wooing her, whispering something in her ear."

"No idea who?"

"Somebody not in high school, that's all I knew."

"Why?"

"When I said we should talk again, she laughed. 'Isn't that pushy Kathe enough for you?' She made fun of me. She wanted to be around a *mature* man who valued her talent. What does that mean—*valued* her? She ain't a…a porcelain vase."

"But after all that you went to her house?"

He gazed over my shoulder, his face reddening. "After we broke up, I used to wander to her yard…until her uncle chased me away with a shotgun. When Kathe told me that her family locked her in at night, guarded her, and even sent that uncle of hers to and from school, I had to see her. She was a prisoner. Kathe told me she was seeing an older man who promised her a new life away from Appleton, a man with bucks in his pocket, and I got, well, bothered." His lips trembled. "Edna, I never lost my feelings for her. I wanted her back in my life, and I thought if I *talked* to her…"

"What were you thinking?"

"I know. It was stupid. I went through the Lempke back fields in the dark, bumping into the chicken coops so that the whole world was alerted, and I threw pebbles against her window. They locked her in at night and the window had bars nailed across it. She could open it a few inches. I thought she'd be happy to see me, the two of us whispering there, the rest of the house asleep. The house dark. But you know what she said to me? 'Go way. Just go away. I'm getting married. I'm going away. Tomorrow.'

That was crazy—she looked like a nun or something, standing there in this dark robe in the shadows. And then I saw a flash of lantern light behind her, all shaky, and her crazy uncle was there, peering down at me. It was awful. He yelled at me, 'I kills you, I kills you, bad bad person.' I panicked and ran away. But as I did, I saw him slap her right across the face. She screamed like a polecat, I tell you. So I ran. You know, I ran and ran. Edna, I just wanted to *save* her."

"Jake, you know…" I stopped. There was a shriek behind me. Kathe Schmidt ran lopsidedly, stumbling, toward the gazebo. I expected to see a carpet beater flying in her hand. She'd obviously abandoned her chores at the Ferber backyard. Fannie would be livid and blame me.

"I knew you'd be here, Edna. You're *not* a friend." Her words ended in a scream.

True. We didn't like each other. An indication of taste on my part, foolishness on hers.

"Jake, she's a *reporter*."

Jake shook his head. "Kathe, she's one of the people we know."

Kathe glowered. "What did you tell her?"

"Nothing I haven't told the chief of police."

"What?"

Jake talked to me. "You know, after my father closed down my interview with Chief Stone, I decided to see him myself. I stopped in at the police station before I came here and told him everything I just told you."

Decent, this young man. A commendable act, a boy better than his esteemed father.

"You did *what*?" Kathe yelled.

"It was the right thing to do."

Kathe was beside herself, swirling around, out of control. "What's gonna happen to us?" she barked, shoving her face close to his. Jake was watching her with wide and, unfortunately, mournful eyes.

"Frana's dead." Tears matched his words. "That just happened."

The line surprised me. *That just happened.* What did that mean? Her death was a chance event? Or her death just occurred yesterday? Or he hadn't *planned* it but it happened? What was he saying?

Kathe was caught up in a mindless rant. "You know, Jake, you didn't think I knew about your…your foolishness about that girl. When her name came up, you got quiet and dopey. How was I supposed to feel? You're with *me* at the Easter dinner at the Methodist Church, and she walks in, and you start to stammer, can't take your eyes off her. Think about it, for God's sake." She caught her breath. "You know, I *wanted* her to run away with someone. I really did."

I interrupted. "Is that why you told folks about her getting on the train with an older man?"

Kathe wanted to stomp me as if I were a bug. "I thought that's what she did when they couldn't find her. She *told* me her plans, Edna. She told me. She said she'd be leaving with a man who said he'd marry her…"

"Why didn't you tell us?" Jake was perplexed.

"I keep secrets."

"Did you know about the note to the school—the whole plan?"

She hesitated, but then shook her head. "I knew she had to get away. She was afraid of her uncle. He was getting crazier and crazier. Her brothers. My God, they nailed bars on her window. They locked her in right after school."

"They knew about the older man?" I asked.

"She'd told them, throwing it in their face, I guess. That was a mistake. You know, her uncle told her he'd kill her if she didn't obey the family. They're old country German Catholics, you know, severe as everything, and she was just too fun loving. They were always beating her. Her brothers…You saw the welts and…"

I was curious. "Are you sure you didn't know about the note she slipped on Miss Hepplewhyte's desk?"

Kathe purposely ignored me. She probably helped Frana in her scheme and had something to do with the letter.

Kathe faced Jake. "I just thought, you know, she'd run away."

Jake narrowed his eyes. "You wanted her out of Appleton, Kathe." Flat out, weary.

Silence. "Well, she wanted to go to New York, Jake. She *left* you, told you to go away. Here you are, traipsing after her, mooning under her window. How does that make me look? We're together now. Really. Think about it." Her tone was more strident, clipped. "Maybe I should tell *you* goodbye and you'd come crawling around my yard, begging and pleading and bellowing like I don't know what." Sharp as glass, that voice of hers. His face flushed, Jake rose, nestled his textbook against his chest and moved away.

"Where are you going?"

"You're happy she's dead."

"Jake…"

"You…you wanted her on that train…away from me."

"I ain't to blame. Just because she's dead."

"You know, Kathe, I can almost understand your jealousy and all. But not this. You wanted her dead." Spoken out loud, it became an unwelcome epiphany, hitting home. "Well, she's not on that train, Kathe. She's dead. Does that make you happy?" He stormed away.

"Wait," Kathe cried. "Wait. Come back. I'm sorry, Jake. I'm sorry. It wasn't supposed to happen like this. I didn't plan on it like this. I didn't. I'm sorry."

Dubious, troubling lines again. Plan what? What was I missing here?

Jake was gone, hidden by a copse of thick holly bushes.

Kathe, teeth clenched, flew at me. "This is all your fault, Edna. Your fault."

Chapter Nine

Appleton had one big story: the awful murder of the young German girl Frana Lempke. It was everywhere, friends dropping in at the Ferber household and lingering over coffee and cherry-studded *Schaumtorte*, neighbors talking over back fences, customers at My Store shaking their heads. My wonderful Houdini interview, for a moment the talk of the town, was immediately eclipsed by the gripping account of Frana's murder. Even the back-to-Jesus street-corner evangelist Mad Otto the Prophet (his name was Hosea Thigpen but long ago someone called him the odd nickname, and it stuck) talked of nothing else. That morning I spotted him standing in a vacant lot on Washington. By noontime, he'd be on College by the Masonic Hall. Most days, and some evenings, he stood on the corner of Lawrence and Cherry, back by the breweries and the railroad tracks, standing on a cabbage crate and screaming Biblical passages at the workers headed to and from their jobs. "Predestination and damnation," he boomed…"fire and brimstone…the yawning maw of hell…a young innocent taken at the flood…the Doomsday book…the hand of the devil palpable and gripping…God in his awful wrath…"

People always rushed by him, a little nervous. But I filled my reporter's pad with descriptions of the crazed man. I once suggested I interview him for the *Crescent*. Sam had grimaced. "Really now, Miss Ferber. The *Crescent* a soapbox for a madman?"

On Tuesday morning I fielded calls from out-of-town papers, talking with the *Milwaukee Journal*, even the *Chicago Tribune*. I told the same practiced story, rote now, succinct; but the calls kept coming. Sharp-eyed journalists, spotting my name in the telegraphed stories, asked for in-person interviews with me and Esther, but Esther's father, bothered by the attention, had made it clear his daughter was to be left alone.

Yet once her initial squeamishness passed, Esther was eager to talk to anyone. At one point, late in the morning, she unexpectedly appeared at the *Crescent* office where she had never visited before. She stood at the bottom of those five cement steps, looking around the room as though she'd discovered some new and even lower rung out of Dante's inferno. "*This* is where you work?"

"What did you expect?"

"It's so small. So cluttered." She squinted. "So dim."

Sam Ryan grinned. "My theory is that an unpleasant office makes my reporters want to go outside and get the news."

His sister Ivy laughed. "Except for the bookkeeper, condemned to darkness visible and infernal chicken wire."

I was happy with their remarks, taken as they were with Esther. Boon was not there, thank God, and Esther conveniently perched herself on the edge of his desk. Earlier, Boon had left on the 7:52 for Milwaukee, one hundred miles away. Through Caleb Stone he'd learned that the Milwaukee police had detained the three drummers who'd left Appleton the afternoon Frana was murdered. Boon, Sam said, was convinced one of these itinerant gentlemen was the killer. All three were seasoned travelers, men in their forties or fifties, each one unmarried and, at least in one case, notorious for idle flirtations with the harried waitresses at the Sherman House dining room. Matthias Boon was convinced one of the three would confess that afternoon, and he wanted to be there. Sam told me it was a wild goose chase.

"What do you think?" I asked Sam when he finished telling Esther about Boon's hasty trip to Milwaukee.

Sam's instincts were solid. A reporter's heart to the core, though a publisher who couldn't scribe a decent paragraph himself, Sam sighed. "The murderer is still among us." A twinkle in his eye. "Matthias Boon has a favorite restaurant in Milwaukee, and perhaps a lady friend."

I mumbled to the rapt Esther, sitting nearby. "Obviously a woman in need of being institutionalized."

Byron Beveridge walked in and circled around Esther as if she were Eve in the garden, grinning foolishly and bowing. He mentioned that Caleb Stone and Amos Moss were meeting at the high school at noon to "review" the evidence.

"What evidence?" I sat up.

"Well, now that it's officially a murder, Stone has to go back to the beginning. This isn't just a runaway girl now." He waved a copy of yesterday's *Crescent*. "The *Post* is sending a reporter, I hear."

"Be there." Sam gestured to me. "You're already deep into the story. Maybe you'll see things others won't."

Just before noon, I headed to Ryan High School, trailed by an excited Esther. "Do you think they'll mind if I tag along?"

"I'm assuming the men would demand your presence."

Once there I learned Caleb Stone had already interviewed the frightened young students who had classes in that hallway and learned nothing he didn't already know. No student, gazing dreamily through the small glass of the classroom door, bored perhaps with math or Christopher Marlow or a parsed sentence, had spotted Frana Lempke walking past. Then Chief Stone, with the imprimatur of the principal, sent the students home for the afternoon. While Esther and I stood in the hallway, hordes of excited, gabby students rushed out over the lawns, headed away from the school. They buzzed about Frana, the police, the murder. I nodded to Titus Sharpe, the craggy reporter from Appleton's other paper, the morning *Post*, slouching in a chair in Miss Hepplewhyte's office, gazing into the hallway. He'd never said a complete sentence to me. He had a skinny reedy upper torso, with a giraffe neck under a freckled, blotchy face, all resting on an enormous bottom that shook like a bowl of unpleasant aspic when he walked. Like Sam, he was a Civil War veteran, and claimed to have been in Washington D.C. when Lincoln was shot.

"Yes?" he said to me as I walked into Miss Hepplewhyte's office. It was a dismissive word.

I focused my eyes on his Adam's apple, the most delicately inoffensive of his many questionable features. "No," I answered flatly. His eyes grew wide. I shuttled by him, Esther close behind me.

Chief Stone walked into the small room, nodded at me and Titus, but looked askance at the presence of Esther, who, nervous, stood so close to me we kept bumping into each other. Still, he said nothing. When Deputy Amos Moss, clearing his throat and deciding to become officious, pointed at her accusingly, Caleb Stone gave him a look, and the deputy shut up. Chief Stone led everyone into the deserted corridor, a small group of teachers and staff huddling around him, and announced that he wanted to reenact the time sequence, if only, he said brusquely, "to give me a sense of what in tarnation happened that afternoon."

"I've told you…" Miss Hepplewhyte began, but the principal's stare made her keep still.

Principal Jones looked drained and I felt sorry for the man. When he lifted his chubby hand, it was trembling. Homer Timm stood there with a pad and pencil, his eyes following Caleb's every turn, and I wondered whether he'd been appointed recording secretary.

Miss Hepplewhyte, severe in a slate-gray smock, her hair drawn into an awesome bun at the back, seemed ready to do battle. Doubtless she felt accused. She was a collector of slights, I realized; of accusations, real or imagined. That important note *had* been placed on her desk, and she'd informed Miss Hosley of Frana's intended premature departure. She was a featured player in this tragedy.

Standing as far from her as possible, Mr. McCaslin, an English primer gripped between his fingers, looked miserable, and kept glancing at Miss Hepplewhyte as if she were to blame for everything. Mildred Dunne was absent.

The diplomatic Caleb Stone announced that no one—staff, teachers, even (his quick glance suggested) Esther and me—was to *blame*. He wanted information. "Frana had to leave the building somehow." He even mustered a chilly smile. "This is a reconstruction"—he stretched out the word, deliciously—"like, say, Sherlock Holmes would do."

Homer Timm grumbled and tapped his foot, then regretted the move when heads turned toward him. His sheepish look suggested an apology.

Everyone stood in front of Miss Hosley's classroom.

Amos Moss, directed by Caleb Stone, played Frana, leaving class at two o'clock and waving to a friend in Mr. McCaslin's classroom. He started to mimic girlish gestures, but a cutting look from Chief Stone stopped that indelicacy. Everyone trooped into the notoriously unlocked classroom. Caleb pointed out a cloakroom where, he said, Frana could have hidden. Everyone breathed a sigh, as though the answer was in front of us.

"Impossible!" Miss Hepplewhyte preened herself like a peacock. "As I told you before." When Christ Lempke appeared and did not find Frana waiting, and she knew Frana had not left with other students, she thought Frana might still be in the building. She noticed the unlocked classroom. "And, of course, having dealt with students for many, many years, I immediately opened the cloakroom door. After all, I knew Frana was not happy with her uncle's guardianship. Frana wasn't hiding there."

Everyone looked at everyone else.

Caleb Stone wanted to know about the empty locked classroom. It was still locked, Principal Jones announced. Then the chief wanted to know about another door at the other end of the corridor. "It's an unused storage room," the principal said. "It's never been used, so far as I know. Not in all the time I've been here." Everyone gathered by the sealed door. The principal turned the knob, which didn't move. "It's locked, of course. I doubt if there's a key." The windowless door suddenly seemed ominous to me.

"Of course there's a key," Caleb Stone grumbled.

Homer Timm shrugged his shoulders. "This is an old building. There are a few closets and storage rooms not in use. With no keys."

"That makes no sense," Caleb Stone insisted. "Frana could have hidden inside the storeroom."

"Impossible!" Homer Timm used the same word Miss Hepplewhyte just used. "How? The door is locked." He snorted. "Or maybe you haven't noticed."

Caleb Stone ignored him. He tried the door again. Not only was it locked, it seemed frozen to the frame. "Where are the keys kept?"

Everyone looked at Miss Hepplewhyte, who raised her eyebrows and shook her head. A little grumpily, "I'm not in charge of keys." A pause. "I'm sure Frana Lempke never paid it any attention either."

True, in my four years at Ryan High School, I'd barely been aware of storerooms, locked or otherwise.

Mr. McCaslin babbled something about this being a waste of his time—he had work to do on the Senior Play—but stopped, suppressed a belch. Miss Hepplewhyte rolled her eyes. Even Mr. Jones frowned, ready to say something.

"Find Mr. Schmidt," Principal Jones ordered Homer Timm, who seemed loath to move, his expression suggesting that he was not an errand boy. He shuffled off while we waited.

Homer Timm returned with August Schmidt, the school janitor and Kathe's father. He looked nervous and frightened, his head flicking left and right. I knew him, of course—everyone did. He'd been the janitor at Ryan for years, ever since he'd emigrated from Germany years back. Now a beefy man in his forties, with balding head and large droopy ears, with saucer eyes and a bushy white moustache on a round face, August Schmidt spent his days cleaning the hallways, taking out the trash, and nodding repeatedly to passing students, who baffled him. I knew he spoke very little English—unable to master the new language, according to Kathe—and tried to be as unobtrusive as possible in the noisy school hallways. When students filled the hallways between classes, he stood with his back to the cement wall, eyes half-closed. Sometimes, passing by, I heard him singing in German, some soft *lieder* that sounded sad.

No, he said, in a garbled blur of German and fragmented English, he'd never opened the door. No need to because all his supplies were around the corner. In *that* storeroom. Yes, there was a key, he assumed. Maybe. He didn't know. Yes. No. In the other storeroom, next to where he hung his coat, he said, there was a bracket loaded with old keys. He rushed off, bowing first to everyone, very Prussian, I thought, and returned with a dozen wrought-iron keys, several looking rusted and ancient. Methodically he inserted one after the other, so jittery that at one point he dropped the keys to the floor. He inserted the same key more than once and lost track of which was which. Impatient, Amos Moss shoved him aside, grabbed the key ring, and started over. At last everyone heard the hesitant click. The deputy tugged at the door, gripping the knob with both hands. The door sprang open as though freshly oiled, and everyone stared into a large storeroom filled with pieces of furniture.

Light from the hallway barely illuminated the shadowy space.

The principal located a kerosene lantern and Caleb Stone took it and stepped inside. Sidling near, I saw shafts of dust particles in the air. A stale smell, old wood and moldy books. An oak desk was pushed against a back wall. A glass-front bookcase occupied the left wall. Old desks were stacked alongside it. Some chairs were pushed against a wall. Caleb Stone motioned to his deputy, who joined him. When Homer Timm went to enter, the chief waved him back. I spotted what Caleb Stone was studying. There was a thick layer of decades-old dust covering the desk. But in the flickering glare of the lantern I saw a clear area, a stretch of exposed wood where something—a leg? an arm? —had either rested on the desk or slid across it. As Caleb Stone lowered the lantern, I saw a confusion of smudged footprints everywhere. Stubs of burnt candles were bunched on the desk.

Someone had been inside recently. Amos Moss, in a burst of discovery, exclaimed, "Someone was in here, I ain't kidding." Caleb Stone, angry, yanked him back.

The chief directed everyone to stand away as he walked out, eyeing all of us. He held something up to the light. It was an embroidered ribbon, a young girl's bit of frippery from a dress or bonnet. I gasped, recognizing Frana's embroidery. Frana, adroit with a needle, often decorated her bonnets and dresses with ribbons. Sometimes she wore them in her hair. She favored blue and gold. I once cruelly remarked to Esther that Frana was readying herself to be the Hester Prynne of Appleton.

He turned to me. "Could this be Frana's?"

"It is hers." I was emphatic.

"How do you know?"

"I know." Behind me, Esther nodded.

"So now we know where Frana was hiding," Caleb Stone concluded.

Rumbling in the hallway, everyone talking at once.

The principal spoke in a tinny, hesitant voice. "But how could she get inside? She had no key. Why would she even think to do so?" He looked flustered. "The door was locked. You'd have to have a key."

Everyone turned to look at the quiet German. August Schmidt had been trying to follow the events, his head swiveling back and forth. baffled by most of it; but his gaze had become more and more agitated as time passed.

In German, Caleb Stone asked August Schmidt who else had access to a key. Schmidt mumbled something incoherent but suggested the only key he knew of was in his storeroom and never left the wall.

Amos Moss bellowed, "No way Frana Lempke couldn't have had no key." He turned to the janitor. "August Schmidt, did you grab Frana Lempke and drag her here?"

The man squirmed. "Frana Lempke?"

Caleb Stone asked him, "Did you know her?"

The man nodded. "*Ja, ja*. Yes. She come to house with Kathe. Yes. Frana."

Amos Moss was beside himself. "Somebody let that girl in this here room."

Schmidt clearly did not understand what was happening, except that every eye was on him, accusing. He started to blubber, and for some reason reached for the jangling key, still in the lock, and the deputy put out his hand, stopping him. Schmidt started to cry inconsolably, twisting his body as though looking for escape; and he whispered a torrent of rambling German. What I gleaned, in bits and pieces: *Mein Gott…Ich…in himmel…bitte… nicht…mein Gott…zufiel ist…bitte…*Sorry… I…So sorry… " Sorry sorry sorry. On and on, pleading, apologetic; confessional. He crumpled, wrapped his arms around his chest and shook.

"But," I remarked, "Frana had that fake note. She planned to sneak out at two. She *planned* it. I don't think anyone *grabbed* her. She…"

"Please, Miss Ferber," Caleb interrupted. "Not now."

Staring at the whimpering man, lost in the tense hallway, I knew in my heart of hearts that August Schmidt had nothing to do with Frana's murder.

Not so with Amos Moss, who boomed out, "Clear to me this here man lay in wait and he abducted her, the pretty young girl he probably watched every day, seen his chance, she alone in the hallway, maybe she *was* planning to sneak out of school, yes, maybe he saw her alone in the hallway, maybe tied her up, strangled her, left her there till darkness when he was the only one here, and then dragged her body back of the school to Lovers Lane." As he spoke, he punctuated his fast declaration with angry glances at Schmidt. "Nobody around, late at night. Seems simple to me…"

Caleb Stone was not happy with his deputy's declaration. He turned to August Schmidt and said in a surprisingly kind voice, "Mr. Schmidt, I'm afraid you have to come with me to the station. Just a little more conversation, where it's quiet…" His voice trailed off.

Good Lord. That was the gentlest, most unthreatening arrest I could imagine. But to August Schmidt, shaking back and forth, the words spelled doom. He bellowed like a wounded animal, "Is wrong, is wrong. I begs you."

Amos Moss kept yelling, "Admit it, admit it," approaching the shaking man who kept muttering in German. When the deputy touched his sleeve, August Schmidt caught my eye and held it, a desperate stare that rattled me. The look said: Help me.

I couldn't turn away. Help me.

The craziness of the hallway was shattered by the slamming of the front door. Christ Lempke lumbered in, dragging the dead leg against the hard marble floor. It made an echoey sound, eerie as nightmare, and I got chilled staring at the gnarled, bitter man moving toward us. No one said a word. When he drew closer, he stopped, tried to balance himself by leaning on a wall.

"Mr. Lempke," Caleb Stone greeted him.

But the man exploded. "You no waits for me."

"I just assumed you couldn't make it…"

Lempke tried to straighten himself up, full-size, but he wobbled. "You see this leg that dies in that stupid war? You sees that?"

"I'm sorry, I…" The chief stopped, glancing at the blubbering August Schmidt.

Amos Moss jumped in. "Mr. Lempke, we got here a suspect in Frana's murder." He pointed at Schmidt.

Lempke looked at August. "This is your murderer? This man?" His laugh—a thin broken cackle, really—filled the hallway.

Amos Moss yelled, "He had a key…"

Caleb Stone held up his hand. "Mr. Lempke, we have more investigating to do…" A pause. "Maybe Mr. Schmidt can give us some answers about locked doors."

"Is no matter now."

"But justice…"

Lempke actually spoke out the side of his mouth, and his face twisted into a hideous mask, contorted and crimson. "Justice is myth in this America."

I spoke out. "Frana deserves justice, no?"

Lempke looked at me, a creepy smile on his face. "You is reporter, no? Live on peoples' disgrace and anger and pain. Shame shame shame on you. Shame. Foolish girl. What you know of justice?"

"Sir!"

"Frana her mother planned send her back to Germany, put her in convent, maybe. Now she is dead girl. Is probably die in time. Maybe. She disgrace family with this boy, this man. Who knows? She talk crazy to family. She run to New York to be on stage and paint herself maybe and bring great disgrace, more so, to us. The way she die to me disgrace." No one spoke. "Last night we find deck of cards in her room. Cards for playing games." For some reason he pointed at me. "Forbidden, this pleasure. Like dancing. Like…"

"Well," I said cavalierly. "No one should die because of a card game."

Lempke's eyes got hard, dull. "You think games is for little Catholic girl? She wants to pedal a bicycle. Like circus girl. The Virgin Mary she frowns in heaven. Our people cross themselves in this sinful America. She…" He waved his hands in the air. "Enough. Now a tombstone will keep her good."

Chapter Ten

I returned home from work exhausted. The events at the high school—and the subsequent, manic conversations in the city room—made me tense, almost ill. Matthias Boon, back from Milwaukee and in a surly mood, had minimalized his failed mission. All three drummers had been released because all three, evidently, had no connection with the murder of Frana. Boon disagreed. The Milwaukee police force, he insisted, was staffed by an assembly of "bumbling magpies, speaking in tongues," taking the word of one particularly smooth-talking, shifty-eyed drummer. Boon also wasn't happy he'd missed the scene at the high school…and the questioning of Schmidt. "So you're saying the German strangled her and hid her body in the storeroom?"

"I never said that, sir."

"Lust, Miss Ferber. Think about it."

"I'd rather not."

Boon snickered as I turned away.

I straggled home and was surprised to see Kathe Schmidt. When Fannie walked out of the back room where she and Kathe were cutting and sewing patterns, I whispered, "Why is she here?"

"Her mother sent her over."

"Did you hear about her father?"

"Of course." Fannie was testy. "It's all over town. Kathe told me about it, in fact. She says it's ridiculous."

"Of course, it is. But shouldn't she be home with her family?"

"Caleb Stone sent her father home, so he's sleeping now, she said."

"But doesn't she want…"

Fannie shrugged. "Imagine detaining Mr. Schmidt for murder! Have people in this town lost their minds?"

"Yes, they have."

Fannie eyed me suspiciously and left to tend to supper. Over her shoulder, she told me, "We're having goose with cranberry sauce."

When my mother returned from My Store, she questioned me. "Why is Kathe here?"

"She had nowhere else to go, I guess."

"What does that mean? Don't be sarcastic, Ed. Poor Kathe. The poor dear. When a family is suffering, daughters need to stay close to home. Everyone knows that."

Curious, I walked to the back sitting room, a small alcove where I liked to read my novels during the icy winter months, a drafty space that looked out on white-crusted stone walls. Now, Fannie's dress patterns covered a pinewood table, and Kathe, her back to me, was bent over the narrow table, snipping away with scissors. I cleared my throat, but Kathe was slow to look up.

"Kathe, I'm sorry about your father."

I lost any sympathy for her because the look on her shiny face was hardly what I expected, some softening, some weepiness, some helplessness. Some—vulnerability. No, Kathe looked mean and fierce, eyes hard as polished agates, lips pressed into a thin angry line. Scissors suspended in the air, she wagged their points at me and glowered.

"What?"

"Nothing." Kathe dropped her eyes.

"Kathe, are you mad at me?"

"My father ain't guilty of nothing." I corrected the grammar in my head.

"Well, I know that."

"Then why were you and the others there today…crucifying him? You and those people…"

"I had nothing to do with it."

"Yeah, like you didn't chase down Jake in the park and make him talk about Frana."

Well, true. "I'm a reporter. Frana Lempke—your friend—was murdered. I would think you'd want…"

"You want my father to be guilty…"

Outside, I noticed, it had started to rain, the heavy drops pinging and plopping against the window. For a second Kathe stared out into the rain; when she looked back at me, she appeared dazed.

"You're making no sense, Kathe."

She stabbed at the fabric with the scissors. Her shoulders hunched, tight. "Leave me alone."

"So your father is back home?"

Kathe seethed, silent.

Intuitively I sensed that only one subject would get Kathe talking. "What *does* Jake Smuddie have to do with this?"

"What?"

"Have you spoken to Jake since…since the park?"

"No. He won't *talk* to me. Guess whose fault *that* is."

"Well, he's hurting."

"Maybe if you left him alone…"

"Did you know that he was still pursuing Frana?" It was a cruel line, said deliberately.

"I ain't a fool. I had evidence."

"Evidence?"

For a second the rain distracted her. Then she raised her chin and locked her eyes on me. "I knew he went there that night because Frana told me the next morning. The day she died, in fact. She tossed it in my face like a…a insult. She didn't want him around because she was leaving Appleton with that man or something. But she knew how to *hurt* me. 'Jake came to my window last night,' she said. Just like that. Laughing. 'He begged me!' She laughed and said, 'My uncle was gonna kill him.' She thought the whole thing was real funny. You know, I couldn't *wait* for her to get on that train with some old fool who'd use her and then abandon her on some New York street like a dirty rag or something. It ain't right what she did to me."

"No, it wasn't."

Kathe snorted. "Like you care, Edna."

"Of course, I do."

"You took Jake's side."

"That's nonsense." A second passed. "Tell me, how did Jake react when he learned Frana was sneaking out to see some older man, if she actually did that."

The rain picked up, streaking the windows, turning the room chilly. I glanced outside, and Kathe followed my gaze. "He ain't sitting in the park now, you know." Then she added, "Of course, he knew about the man. I made sure to tell him. Me. God, even Frana told him. I could see he didn't like that."

"But Jake was seeing you, Kathe."

She bit her lip. "He used me. I was the other pretty girl, but not the favorite. Second best. I was the dress"—she pointed to a pattern of fabric spread on the table—"that you wear, maybe not to the ball, but to a hayride. That's what I was. You don't care if it's wrinkled a little and…and…" She faltered.

"You still have feelings for Jake?" A blunt question.

"No. Yes. I don't know. I don't think he's nice to me and I don't think…"

"Kathe, certainly you don't think he'd hurt Frana, do you?"

A long silence. "He's a football player."

"What does that mean?"

She spoke in tinny, nervous voice. "He's strong, ain't he?"

"Kathe, really."

Kathe, hands on hips, spat the words out, deliberately. "And he went to Ryan High School, ain't he? He ain't no stranger to those hallways." She thought about what she'd said, arching back her head, and suddenly seemed happy with her words.

"You're accusing him of murder?"

"No, no, I ain't saying that." She dropped her shoulders, ducking her head.

A liar, I thought, a dissembler, a sloppy girl without moral boundaries. "Just what are you saying?"

"You're attacking me, Edna. Like you always do. You get me all rattled." She looked outside. "Now I have to walk home in the rain."

"I'm merely…"

"You just won't leave me alone."

"I need to know…"

"No, you don't. Maybe you *think* you do, but nobody ain't made you God here."

"Kathe…"

She slipped into German. "I should have stayed to home." *Zu hause.* She tossed the scissors down, swiveled around, and snatched her jacket, cradling it against her chest. "Just tell Fannie I left." I didn't move so she had to walk around me, nearly dropping her jacket as she edged out of the room. She collided with Fannie, who was rushing in.

"You're leaving?" Fannie took in her furious face.

"Your sister won't stop asking me questions." She swallowed a sob. "She's treating me like a criminal."

I kept my mouth shut.

Her wailing intensified. "I shouldn't be treated this way in your home, Fannie. She makes me feel like I'm the one who *murdered* Frana. Frana was my good friend." She choked out big sloppy tears, brushing by Fannie, and flew out the front door, slamming it.

Fannie whirled. "Edna, how can you *interrogate* her?"

"I merely…"

Fannie cut me off. "Don't play reporter in your own home." She surveyed the unfinished dress pattern on the table and squinted at the wet windows; she was ready to cry.

"Play?" I took a step back.

"Whatever you *do*."

"I have a job."

"Not in these four walls you don't."

We two sisters squared off.

"Fannie, there's been a murder in this town, and Kathe is somehow a part of it…"

Fannie threw up her hand inches from my nose. "For heaven's sake, Edna, you're talking just like a character in a novel by The Duchess."

I didn't step back. "Kathe is making accusations against Jake Smuddie."

"What?"

"Accusing him of murder." I was steaming. "She virtually called him a killer."

Fannie gave an elaborate sigh. "Edna, for Lord's sake, are you writing a story in your head? Some melodrama…"

A fight was brewing, one of our bloody battles born out of the nagging, grating resentments that scraped at our workaday life till it tore open; Fannie, the serene homebody who flounced around the house like a butterfly and me, the literalist, uncomfortable with idle time or pretty fripperies.

Fannie hurled the first deliberate salvo. "Edna, the fact is that I overheard a few of your comments to Kathe. I was listening, purposely."

"So?"

"And you seem to have forgotten how a person behaves politely in her own home. You do not *harangue* the guests. My God, you went at her like a dentist's drill."

"She's not a guest, she's an employee," I insisted. "And minimally competent."

"Even more reason to be kind…"

"I need to get some answers…"

"Perhaps you should not even be asking questions. Perhaps this is none of your business. Edna, this…job has turned you into a shrew." Fannie drew her lips into a thin line. "You'll do anything to disrupt this household."

"For God's sake, Fannie."

"I mean it. You gallivant out there"—She pointed toward the center of Appleton, unseen—"and have allowed yourself to be…coarsened by life there. You're not a man, Ed."

"And you're not a lady, despite the finery."

"You're jealous because I'm pretty…"

"And I'm not?"

She made a great show of chuckling. "Oh, please, Edna. In Cinderella, we know which sister you'd be."

"Yes, the intelligent one."

"Men don't want intelligence."

My turn to smile indulgently, as if she were stupid. "Of course, they do. They just don't know it. That's why women have to be smart. They have huge jobs to do, starting with the men in their lives."

"No man seeks out a sassy reporter."

"You say it like it's a perversion."

"No one's going to marry a girl reporter," Fannie finished. "Especially one that looks like you."

"Marriage is a trap women fall into, like children toppling into an unprotected well." I regretted the words because I knew my father, sitting in the parlor, was hearing his daughters in battle again. I added, "For some girls," but hesitated. I never liked to qualify my statements.

My mother stood in the doorway, for a moment hypnotized by the rain battering the windows. Her voice was high pitched. "Enough of this. I deal with crazy housewives and smelly farmers all day long, and come home to warfare. Enough. The food will burn…the…" She closed her eyes and rubbed her temples. "Will you two come into supper? Stop this nonsense."

My father banged into the edge of the table, a purposeful gesture because he maneuvered his sightless way easily through the rooms. He was telling us something.

"Supper?" he called.

We three Ferber women nodded.

After a stony meal I lingered in my upstairs bedroom, trying to read that F. Marion Crawford romance that made no sense. Bejeweled countesses in elegant Roman society; whispered intrigues on the Via Venetto; drawing room infidelities and alliances. I looked around the room that I purposely kept Spartan, save for the rich velvet counterpane I'd sewn for the four-poster red oak bed. A hand-carved black walnut chair with plush leather seat occupied one corner, positioned so that I could look out on the backyard, directly onto the blooming cherry tree. On the dresser a lace antimacassar, given to me by Fannie last year.

On the walls two pictures: one—a sepia-toned scene from a maudlin stage production of *Uncle Tom's Cabin*, the scene in which Uncle Tom is pontificating to frail little Eva. I'd won the gilt-edged print as a prize for second place in the oratory contest in Madison three years ago. First place had been a gold chalice, engraved. This lackluster print reminded me that there was only one place I allowed myself in any contest: first.

The second picture, also in heavy gilt-gold frame, was one I had purchased in an emporium in Chicago. I gazed on the glitzy chromolithograph each night before turning down the gaslight: a slender young girl with auburn hair stands alone on a cliff overlooking a vast periwinkle blue ocean, puffy white clouds in the sky. A breeze rustles her white dress. Her alabaster hand is reaching to the distant horizon, wanting to be somewhere else, out *there*, beyond the white-tinged horizon. The sentimental caption was a quote: *Beyond the horizon is the world you dream of.* Each night, glancing at the print, I asked myself: *But is that true?*

Contemplating the print, I wondered what Houdini had seen in my eyes. What hunger? Imagination and concentration—cornerstones of a lifetime. The whole world could not confine him, yet I was locked inside these four walls. Bound by the geography of Appleton. On my bureau was the clipped interview. I read it over and over, not out of vanity, but because I believed it held the clue to something I needed to know. Even as I became obsessed with Frana's murder, I pictured Houdini on that street corner. Echoes of his voice stayed with me. And, I admitted to myself, thrilled me.

A gentle knock on the door. "Edna?" My father opened the door. "Edna, let's take a walk."

Quietly, I gathered my jacket and held my father's elbow as we went downstairs and out the front door. I was pleased. So many nights, especially after the cutthroat skirmishes I had with Fannie, he chose me to walk with, the two of us strolling downtown. Tonight I'd expected him, actually, because supper had been stilted, heavy with frost. Fannie talked about the dress she was making, but my mother seemed distracted. No one mentioned Frana or the questioning of Kathe's father. We avoided the story that so riveted Appleton. That angered me, though I chose not to bring it up. When I said Sam Ryan praised my Houdini interview again—he'd heard from subscribers—my mother said, *sotto voce*, "The praise of lesser men."

I had no idea what that meant but felt, again, that it was part of my mother's dislike of my being a reporter, as well as her familiar championing of Fannie's side when we argued. I kept my mouth shut.

Slowly strolling with my father, holding his elbow, rarely speaking, we moved off North Street, down Morrison, onto College. I sensed my father had something to say because the gentle man, his body so loose-limbed and free, the Hungarian wanderer, tensed up, a tightness in the elbow. I waited.

We strolled past the Lyceum. A poster in the glass-fronted display window advertised tomorrow night's show. Houdini's benefit. "The Master Escape Artist. See the Handcuff King in a Show to Benefit the Children's Home. The Greatest Mystery Novelty Act in the World. Known in Every Country on the Globe." I thought of the genial, humorous man I'd interviewed, and chuckled.

"What?" my father asked.

I recited the braggadocio of the poster and described the fuzzy picture of Houdini bound in chains, hunched forward, showing the camera a hard glassy stare. My interview, published, had been the talk of the visitors to the Ferber household. All the Ferbers, including my father, planned to attend the show. That had surprised me, this change of heart. He would see nothing of Houdini's antics, but he said he wanted to *experience* Houdini. "This is an event." Houdini's show, of course, was a visual extravaganza, a magician's sleight of hand punctuated by a rattling of chains and the whoop and holler of a frenzied audience. I dreaded it because I feared I'd be constantly leaning in, explaining, describing.

The Lyceum was dark now, but on the second floor, off to the left, was a hazy light.

"Maybe Houdini is rehearsing."

"Maybe he was rehearsing and they turned off the lights downstairs. Now he can't find his way out." He was grinning.

I felt hollowness in my chest. Was my father talking about himself? This man condemned to grasping at fleeting shadows, condemned to awful blackness and pain. I thought of Milton: "When I consider how my light is spent." Or was it: "When I consider how my life is spent." Suddenly I couldn't remember the line. It didn't matter because they both said the same thing.

He touched my shoulder. "I don't like it when you and Fannie do battle."

"I know."

"But it won't change." He gripped my shoulder. "You are two different people. Fannie wants life to be a calm lake, a boat ride with parasols and moonlight. And that's good. You want life to be a storm-tossed clipper on the high seas, perilous and thrilling. You two will never agree."

I liked the image he created of my life. "I'm the girl reporter."

"You know, your mother hates that phrase. Your mother also knows that she's *like* you, or you're like her, rather—look how she runs My Store, better than I ever did. She likes being out of the home. She won't admit it—she can't—but she loves that store." He could be talking to himself. "She's not happy when she's home. She gets quieter and quieter as the days go on. I sometimes don't know she's in the house." He swallowed. "Edna, you are like your mother. You like to be out of the house."

No, I wanted to cry, I'm like you. But I knew I wasn't. I didn't know how to dream, I told myself. I only knew how to act...to move...to question...to probe...

"I like my job..."

"I know you do." An awful pause as he stopped walking. "You are determined to be a part of this murder investigation."

"What?"

"I heard you talking with Kathe…all of it."

"I'm sorry."

He touched my hand. "No, no. Edna, I'm not unsympathetic. You're a bright girl. There's a fierceness in you"—that smile again—"and a sassiness, a penchant for hurling barbs at hypocrites." He laughed. "You'll spend your life scaring people, Edna."

"Father!"

"No, no. There's nothing wrong with that." He turned toward me. "Edna, you'll have to do what you have to do."

"I always do."

He smiled in the darkness and started walking. "The girl who got the interview with Houdini! Nineteen years old and so determined."

"I have to be."

His hand brushed my shoulder, affectionately. "I'll never understand you, Edna." He must have sensed me tense up. "I don't really have to."

Chapter Eleven

The next evening the Ferber family trooped to the Lyceum for Houdini's benefit demonstration. No one was happy. I'd been late to supper, staying too long at the city room and neglecting to telephone home. Fannie, still roiling and fussing from the altercation the previous evening, served an undercooked spring chicken, lumpy mashed potatoes, and a sauerkraut cauliflower so vinegary my father gagged. I apologized, but Fannie would have none of it. Convinced my dawdling had been purposeful and malicious, she blamed the failed supper on her nerves. Kathe, scheduled to help that evening with supper, hadn't shown up, and Fannie insisted that "Edna as Appleton's Spanish Inquisition" had badgered the girl to a point where she probably would never set foot again in the Ferber household.

"And just how am I supposed to manage all these rooms?" She flung her arms out melodramatically and let her hand hang in the air like an emphatic punctuation mark.

"Perhaps if you weren't so imperious with the help..." A rumbling from my father stopped me.

"Edna," my mother wondered, "why *were* you late?"

"A witness has come forward."

"To the murder?"

"No, but a farmer from Neenah, visiting his daughter on Friday, was taking a stroll in Lovers Lane, headed to the river sometime after two o'clock in the afternoon, and swears he saw a girl who looked a lot like Frana Lempke—he saw her picture in the paper—running off into a cove of bushes, running ahead of the man she was with."

"Older?" From my father.

"He couldn't tell except that the man seemed to be stumbling, losing his balance as he ran."

"And he's sure it was Frana?"

"He claims, yes. He said he noticed her because she was so pretty—and he said she drew his attention because she was laughing loudly." I pushed away the sauerkraut. "He insists others can back him up. Because, minutes later, headed back to town, he saw a man and a woman nearby, the man leaning against a tree, the woman pulling at his sleeve. Lovers, teasing each other, playing games. Then the woman laughed out loud, and the two scampered out of sight. He said they would have crossed paths with the girl and her friend."

"Good Lord," my mother said.

I took a deep breath. "Chief Stone is trying to locate this couple, but the witness simply described them as 'fancy dressed.' Whatever that means. If true, then Frana somehow got out of the building by her own free will and met some man, happily so, and she was running—that was his word—running in the woods. It means she did not hide in that storeroom for hours— she left at two. More importantly it means that Mr. Schmidt didn't grab her, pull her into that room, strangle her, then carry out her body after dark, as Amos Moss suggests."

"Now what?" my father asked.

"Chief Stone doesn't know if he believes the man."

"Why?"

"I gather he…well, rambled, got confused. And I guess the chief would rather believe Frana was in that storeroom. She *was* in there that afternoon. So how could she have been outside at two?"

"So maybe the farmer is wrong." My father rested his fork beside his plate.

"But if he's not, something is really strange here. She hid in that room and then, well, I don't know…"

"I bet that dullard Amos Moss has some ideas." My mother, I knew, had little respect for the deputy.

"He's probably arresting the farmer now for lying to the police."

My mother frowned at the sauerkraut. "Well, it does seem to suggest that August Schmidt is innocent. I can't imagine that poor man romping in the woods with Frana."

"Of course, he's innocent," I said.

Fannie eyed the chicken that had been scarcely touched. "Do we have to talk about murder at suppertime?"

"You prefer your unpleasantness served with dessert? Lemon pie?"

"Edna!" From my father.

So the Ferber family, walking to the theater, moved with frozen spaces between us, save for my father who leaned on my mother. At the Lyceum, I nodded to old friends and felt a little proprietary about Harry Houdini. The evening was sold out, and I felt responsible, though that made no sense. In the packed lobby under the blazing chandeliers, I spotted the brothers Timm standing by the ticket window. Homer Timm, dressed in his high-school face, smiled at me as I neared. He half-bowed to my mother. His brother Gustave was as frantic and harried as he always was on the nights of performance. Standing next to Homer, though not speaking to him, stood Mildred Dunne, her eyes on Gustave. Dressed in a purple velvet dress that must have cost a week's wages, she wore an enigmatic yet oddly triumphant smile on her face, much as, I mused, Balboa had when he stood on that peak in Darien contemplating the vast Pacific. In that resplendent dress, Miss Dunne hardly looked the severe high-school librarian. Such elegant plumage and ostrich feathered hat would, I feared, alarm the quiet shelves of Dickens and Thackeray and Bulwer-Lytton.

Gustave moved through the lobby, nodded at Miss Dunne, disappeared behind his office door, circled back, bowed to folks. At one point he shook my father's hand and spent a few minutes chatting about Houdini, who, he confided, was an old friend.

I refused to believe him because Houdini was *my* friend. But I was happy to see him single out my father. So often Jacob Ferber, standing in a crowd, seemed lost and abandoned, a deserted island in a storm-tossed sea. Backslapper though he was, Gustave seemed genuinely interested in my father's well being. Showmanship, I thought, but I appreciated the effect.

As we stood among friends, none of us in a hurry to find our seats, I confirmed that the brothers Timm did not like each other. Lately, given my plodding journalism up and down College Avenue, I prided myself on my powers of character observation, my delight in observing the foibles of the souls I encountered. The Timm brothers filled up pages of my reporter's notebook. I didn't care for Homer, put off by his rigid physiognomy; Gustave I tolerated because of his jovial demeanor. But they disliked each *other*, even though they were often seen together. Every time Gustave sauntered near Homer, I detected a slight frown on Homer's face, a momentary flicker of disgust. Gustave either didn't notice or he didn't care. He'd smile foolishly at Mildred and move off, called away by a theater patron who wanted to shake his hand or to ask something. The minute Gustave's back was turned, Homer's eyes followed him, and, had I been a nineteenth-century writer of melodrama, I'd have described Homer's glare as baleful. Hmm, the brothers Timm as Dickensian characters. Well, well.

Put that on your library shelf, Miss Dunne.

The observation thrilled me. In my reporter's notebook I'd jotted down imaginary scenes with the two brothers, and now, to my satisfaction, they acted as I had drawn them.

Mr. McCaslin arrived, dressed in a theater cloak which he wore on nights when his high-school drama club performed for parents, and announced to someone behind me that the Lyceum stage should be reserved for classic drama. "Not vaudeville antics."

A bell rang, and we all rushed to our seats.

Houdini strutted his stuff on the stage to the maddened delight of the audience. Expecting sensation and glorious exhibition, I found myself bored. Not that I didn't marvel at the transformation of the short, unassuming man into a stage Goliath. Houdini appeared in a black frock coat, stiff collar and black tie. He cried, "Are youse ready to witness the marvelest escape of our time?" I cringed, though the rest of the audience waxed ecstatic. His voice managed to echo off the far balconies—thickly accented but peculiarly melodic and entrancing.

Accompanied by his brother Theo and his admittedly sheepish friend David Baum—who kept stumbling into the footlights and almost fell off the stage, to the delight of Houdini himself and the Appleton folks who knew Baum as the genial owner of Baum Hardware—Houdini moved slowly across the stage but created the illusion of rapid movement. Each calculated step was a masterpiece of planning. Every eye locked onto his every movement. He filled up the room, ruled the space. He was marvelous to watch because the stage show was a deliberate manipulation of the audience's expectations.

For his first act, Houdini encouraged two strapping farm boys to tie him up with a cord and then handcuff his wrists behind him. He drew it out with much twisting and jumping and struggle, groaning, the footlights capturing the beads of sweat cascading off his brow. He cried to the crowd, "The path of a handcuff king is not all roses." While the audience sat pensive and restless, he twisted, and suddenly he stood there, ropes collected about his feet, handcuffs snapped open and held out to view. The audience erupted. I knew he could have extracted himself within the first few minutes, but the man understood the psychology of anticipation. Ode, I thought, on a Grecian urn, as it were—vaudeville style. He understood the power of presentation, the need to interact with an audience, the swell and thrust of human drama. This was what Sam Ryan had also told me: You need to understand what your audience is hearing you say. Now, watching Houdini, I understood.

Some of his trickery I found tedious, yet I was more interested—though not *that* much more—by his climactic exhibition, his being bound again in ropes, then lowered into a coffin with the town's master carpenter Hermann Grower noisily banging nails into the lid and, prompted by the audience, examining the box closely. Grower mumbled to the audience, "It's real, let me tell you," spoken with so much wonder and awe that he garnered a round of spontaneous applause. The coffin was lifted into the air and suspended above the stage as a curtain was drawn over it, leaving an open space below it. Silence…minutes passing… shuffling of feet and elbows in the audience…whispers…nervousness. Waiting…waiting.

I fought a vagrant mental image of laughing, happy Frana Lempke escaping into the woods on the arm of her murderous lover. Trapped, unable to free herself. What happened to them? What turned that joyous moment into such disaster? Again and again and again: How did Frana get out of the school? Where was the evil lover waiting? The lawn behind the high school led, a few hundred yards away, into the dense park of Lovers Lane. So many places to hide. The back door of the school opened onto that wooded expanse. I drifted off, an unwelcome reverie, imaging myself in Lovers Lane the moment Esther and I happened upon that body.

The curtain lifted. I jumped, emitted a little yelp, and my mother scowled at me. The box rested on the stage, and from the wings a triumphant Houdini appeared. He invited the carpenter to examine the box and beamed as Hermann Grover announced that not a nail had been removed, everything was just as he had hammered it minutes before. Removing the lid, a disheveled brother Theo popped out. He bowed. Hermann, excited, reached over to shake Houdini's hand, and Houdini, winking at the audience, put something in Hermann's hand. Baffled, Hermann opened his palm and grinned. He was holding, he announced, the watch fob that had been clipped to his vest.

"Genius," he shouted, and the crowd roared.

Masterful. The pint-sized dynamo, all sinew and muscle, a Jewish boy from Appleton, the performer who once called himself the Prince of the Air, stealer of crabapples and peaches. The wonder of it all.

Afterwards in the lobby, that hum of wonder covered the room like a spray of warm river mist. I was standing near the front door, ready to leave, watching as Gustave Timm, preening like a barnyard cock at dawn, leaned into my father, but I had no idea what he was saying. Yet my father was pleased, even smiling a bit. So it was all right, then, this chat.

When I approached, I heard Gustave inviting him to join him and David Baum and some other men for a luncheon two days hence, the day before Houdini was scheduled to leave. That thrilled me, but my father said, "No, thank you."

Gustave implored him, saying that Baum had requested my father be there. "Houdini wants to meet the father of the feisty girl who ambushed him on College Avenue."

Baum, like Jacob Ferber, of course, and Houdini himself, had been born in small impoverished villages in Hungary. They had all fled to the golden land.

"No," my father said, a little more empathically, "I would be uncomfortable."

Gustave walked away. Listening to these few plaintive words, I wanted to go home.

Suddenly Houdini was there, a small, clean-shaven man now writ larger than life, his black curly hair messed up. He maneuvered his way through the packed crowd. Someone tapped me on the shoulder. I turned, expecting to see Sam Ryan or Miss Ivy. It was Homer Timm. He looked none too happy away from the corner of the room where he'd been rooted. Mildred, nearby, watched him, a frown on her face. Another observation for my notebook: The future brother-in-law and sister-in-law disliked each other. A trio of unhappy players.

I knew Homer had moved into Mrs. Zeller's rooming house years back after his wife took sick and the children went back East to the grandparents. Gustave, the newcomer, rented the small cheap bungalow on South Street, just up from the boat dock near the mill district. The brothers didn't share lodging. Well, I thought, grimly, I understood that perfectly because I anticipated the day when Fannie and I would be miles apart, independent of each other's lives, my older sister married and probably stopping by on the High Holy Days or, more likely, Christmas. It would be nice if she lived in California, where I had no intention of ever going.

"Houdini wants to say hello to you," Homer said. "He sent me to ask you because he can't escape the sycophants." A strange run of words, mechanical and flat, said while looking over my shoulder and seemingly addressed to the wall behind me. I caught Houdini's eye. He was being monopolized by the overbearing Helena Poindexter, Appleton's quintessential club-woman, all bosom and bamboozle. He couldn't escape. Her dress had a sweetheart décolleté neckline, and under the overhead lights her wrinkled neck sported an ostentatious rope of pearls, a look that didn't serve her well. Homer Timm slipped back to his necessary wall next to the frowning Mildred, while I made my way to Houdini, who looked relieved.

"You like my show?"

"Of course."

"I knew you would. I'm the Handcuff King. The world flocks to my shows." He actually puffed his chest out, a bantam on home ground.

And I'm the Queen of Sheba. Immediately I feared he could also read minds. "Very impressive."

"I read your interview in the *Crescent*."

"You did?" I was pleased.

"Wonderful. I love what you said about my devotion to my mother. And the money I make. I am a success story for Appleton."

"You are, indeed."

"I cut it out, two copies, pasted one in my scrapbook I carry."

I thanked him, pleased. "I'm just…"

He cut me off. "You are going to say you're just a small-town reporter." I shuddered. My God, he did read minds. "You remember my advice to you?"

He waited for me to answer. "Concentration and imagination."

He chuckled. "A good student."

I caught my mother's eye. Let's go home, her glance indicated. But when I looked back at Houdini, suddenly I didn't want to abandon the conversation because I had an idea. I leaned into him. "Mr. Houdini, perhaps you've read of the murder of Frana Lempke?"

He seemed startled by the quick shift in subject. "Yes, David Baum and I discussed it. It's a sad story, no?"

"It's baffling." I tried not to raise my voice.

"Baffling?"

"The way it happened. We…I mean the police can't make any sense out of the way it happened. It's a mystery."

"What are you telling me?" His head was bobbing, his face close to mine.

"Well, watching you tonight on stage…"

"You liked it?"

"Of course, but watching your show, I thought…" I stopped. What did I want from him?

Houdini watched me closely, his face now soft and his eyes unblinking. "And you think all mysteries can be answered? Like in my show?"

I was surprised. "I hope so. I've always believed there's an answer to everything."

"That may not be true."

"But there is a murderer…"

"You know, my dear Miss Ferber, murders are like escape from handcuffs—there's always gotta be an answer, even though it looks impossible. Concentration and imagination. Logic and romance, the two together, you know. Any crime has to have an answer. It's just a question of how to locate the answer."

"But that's what's baffling."

He whispered. "Before I let anyone tie me up or handcuff me, I already know beforehand—always—how I will be free. Otherwise I'd panic. It would be chaos, disaster." He paused. "Even death. You gotta know how to escape." While he was talking, a young man was dragging at his sleeve, thrusting a paper and pen for an autograph. Houdini tried to ignore him but hurriedly scratched his name on the sheet. He turned to me, "A minute of conversation in my dressing room, perhaps. Is all right?"

I agreed. Hurriedly, I told my family to leave without me, though my mother didn't look happy. I wove my way through the still-milling crowd to a side door where Houdini waited. Gustave Timm was standing outside his office, his hands holding a stack of papers, and he looked surprised.

Houdini winked at Gustave. "I have a reporter guest for a second."

Gustave nodded.

As we walked by the open door to Gustave's office, I spotted the imperious Cyrus P. Powell seated at Gustave's desk. Oddly, Homer Timm was standing behind him, unmoving, his eyes focused on the money. Powell was counting the money with undue concentration, but he glanced up at Houdini and me, and his look was sour, disapproving. He looked ready to say something, but the stack of dollar bills he gripped seemed more appealing.

Gustave was stranded outside his own office, one he dared not enter.

I followed Houdini into a narrow hallway and trailed him up a small flight of stairs into a shabby square dressing room. I had expected something more glamorous than the threadbare chairs, the dirty chintz draperies, and the faded Currier and Ives prints hanging lopsidedly on the wall. It looked like a room nobody came to…or at least stayed in very long. A musty smell, years of unwashed bodies, too much stage makeup, forgotten clothes left piled in corners. Houdini sat opposite me, poured himself a glass of tonic water, and sipped it. He offered me some, but I refused.

"I don't drink spirits. It harms my body, saps my energy. I don't smoke either. Cigars, never." He made a face. "The body must be kept pure. Remember that." He smiled as he sat up straight, his eyes fixed on me. "Now tell me the facts. The story of the murder."

For the next few minutes, a little in awe of the man who drew close to me, blue-gray eyes shiny in the flickering gas light, I

narrated the saga of Frana sneaking out of the high school, the
phony note, the rumors of assignation with an older man—he
frowned at that—the finding of the body in Lovers Lane.

"But why do you think of me?"

I breathed in. "When I saw you get out of that box…" I told
him of the locked storeroom, the dusty space with the smudged
footprints…and Frana's bit of ribbon.

"So?"

"So she got into that storeroom and we thought she hid
there—or was held there against her wishes, perhaps strangled
there—but a witness now claims he saw her running in Lovers
Lane a few minutes later. It's impossible."

"It doesn't sound too complicated."

"Well, it's baffled us all." I waited a second. "It doesn't seem
possible."

"She could have walked out. People miss what's in front of
their eyes, you know. Illusion."

"You haven't met Miss Hepplewhyte."

He tilted his head to the side. "So it's a box of illusion, that
room."

"Perhaps you can help."

"Maybe yes, maybe no."

This was not what I wanted to hear. "I'm bothered, Mr.
Houdini, I must tell you, because the school janitor is considered the murderer, so far at least. He's a gentle man, harmless, a
German immigrant who doesn't understand what's happening to
him. A witness claims he saw Frana and her friend frolicking"—I
paused, hesitant with the word—"in Lovers Lane. Well, sir, Mr.
Schmidt is not one to frolic. Believe me." I was going on and on,
becoming impassioned, and I realized that Houdini was smiling
at me. No, he was grinning widely.

"What?" A little peeved.

"I enjoy your spirit."

"Well…"

"It's good, really. You write with flavor, and you speak with
a passion. And you are how old?"

"Nineteen."

"A child."

"Hardly."

"Are you married?"

"Of course not." What was wrong with this man?

"I married my Bess young, knew her a matter of days. A slip of a girl, though the love of my life, this wonderful woman. She is better than my career, of course. In a few years I'll stop this nonsense and have children. Lots of them."

"I have no intention of getting married," I announced, surprising myself.

"Then you better get famous fast."

"Why?"

"We all got to have someone to applaud for us."

That made no sense. I wanted to get back to the story of Frana. "Mr. Houdini, people can't walk through walls…"

"Of course they can."

"No, no, realistically." I was getting frustrated. "I know you do an *act* on stage, but you can't just walk through a wall." I pointed to an outside wall, bright under blazing gaslight.

"You just have to know how to do it."

He was toying with me, as he'd done before, and, again, I realized I took myself too seriously. All right. But this pleasant banter was getting us nowhere. Frankly, it was time for bed. Eight hours of blissful sleep each night, my practical regimen, my requirement, no less.

"All along," I emphasized, "I was thinking Frana was hiding in that locked, unused storeroom, but maybe she was running through the woods, happy as can be." I made eye contact. "That means she got out."

"Happy, until someone snapped her neck." Houdini dramatically twisted his wrists.

I trembled. "It seems impossible."

"Mysteries are like handcuffs…"

I interrupted. "I know, I know. They always have an answer."

"Let me think on this. I'm here for three more days." He stood. "Now I'll walk you home."

"Oh, no. That's not necessary. Appleton is a safe town. It's not that far."

His face set, firm. "I am a gentleman. I can do no less."

I acquiesced reluctantly, though flattered. As we walked out, Gustave Timm was turning off the gaslights and locking the doors behind us. Mildred Dunne had left. Cinderella back at the hearth, dreaming of September and her honeymoon at Niagara Falls. Outside, waiting for his brother, Homer Timm stood with his arms folded over his chest. He seemed startled to see Houdini and me together, Houdini cradling my elbow. We turned down the sidewalk, crossing the street. When I glanced back both brothers were still outside the Lyceum, two shadows against the dark façade, unmoving.

Under a moonlit sky, we walked to my home in comfortable silence. The only thing Houdini said was that the night reminded him of a recent stroll on the Nevsky Prospekt in Moscow.

"The sky was the same pale blue with a hint of sulfur in the air. Like here in Appleton from the paper mills out at the Flats. I never forget the odor of sulfur in the air. In Moscow I feel like I'm in prison. The Czar's police follow you everywhere. It ain't America, Miss Ferber." He grew quiet, neither of us talking until I pointed out my house, dark now, on North Street. He bowed and I thanked him.

"I have an answer for you," he said, suddenly. "There is only one possible answer."

I turned back. "What is it?"

"Not yet."

"When?"

He chuckled in the darkness. "The impatience of young people. I will sleep on it."

He disappeared into the dark night.

Chapter Twelve

The next day I met Esther for a lunch at Volker's Drug Store, famous for its curious cardboard sign in the front window: *Hier wird Englisch gesprochen*. On Thursdays Mrs. Beckerstrader baked her German delights, an array of succulent confections, plum tortes, *Pfeffernusse*, the cottage cheese *kuchen*, and the cinnamon rolls topped with slivers of almonds—the best in Appleton—and both of us knew the delicacies would be gone by Friday. Each week I treated Esther from the allowance my mother gave me from my salary. It made me feel…independent. Afterwards, sated, I staggered back toward the city room with Esther, who'd be shopping for her mother's kitchen at W. L. Rhodes, Grocer, just around the corner from the *Crescent* office. As we approached Morrison and College, we nearly collided with Ivy Ryan, her arms around a basket of poppy-seed rolls.

Miss Ivy gushed, "You'd best get back to the office. You have a visitor waiting on you."

"Who?"

"The man who warrants these rolls." Miss Ivy's eyes grew wide. "Sam first mentioned a pail of beer from Glassner's Grog Shop, but Houdini said no. Never."

In an awed voice she told us that Houdini had stopped in at the office asking for me, and Sam Ryan sent her to purchase some breads. The office was in a titter. "Even Matthias Boon seems at a loss for venom."

Esther said goodbye, but I insisted she meet the great Houdini. Flustered, Esther started to hiccough, debating what to do. Her rabbi father had forbidden her coming with us to see the show at the Lyceum, but she'd peppered me with questions about it. "The opportunity of a lifetime, Esther."

As we descended the five cement steps, Houdini stood, smiled, and bowed, first at me and then at Esther. Of course, he was immediately taken with Esther, which irritated me. After all, Houdini was my friend. Sort of. Somewhat. Esther slipped into a convenient chair and produced a smile that seemed frozen onto her captivating features.

Byron Beveridge was sitting back, his fingers idly tinkling the keys of his typewriter as he watched Houdini. Matthias Boon had maneuvered his swivel chair to the edge of his cluttered desk, as close to Houdini as he could be and still seemingly remain positioned at his own desk. He gave me a mock friendly look that reminded me of Homer Timm's transparent attempt at friendliness at the high school. Sam Ryan slumped in his rickety chair behind that chicken wire fence (I wondered what Houdini thought of such a makeshift construction in a newspaper office), conducting a lively talk with Houdini.

Sitting back in a chair pulled close to Sam's desk, Houdini seemed a nondescript man, as unassuming as the town cooper or gunsmith, someone stopping in to place an ad in the *Crescent* and chatting about local politics. Sam was puffing on his cigar, and a cloud of dense, stagnant smoke floated above the desk like a low-hanging storm cloud. Sam's wrinkled face looked more creased and pitted than usual because cracking a smile seemed to set in motion layers of chafed, dry skin.

"Miss Ferber, join us." Sam Ryan motioned to me. "There's a man here to see you."

As I walked by, Boon mumbled, "The novelty may be too much for her."

I shot him a withering look. I introduced Esther to Houdini, though she remained frozen in a chair by the door. Houdini responded, "Lola Montez has nothing on you, my dear." For

God's sake. What was I? Dishwater with an intellect? Yes, a part of me was pleased that a friend of mine garnered such attention. After all, I invited her here. Still and all…I surveyed the room. All the men were gaping at Esther, rapt as schoolboys at their games. I caught Miss Ivy's eye when she looked up from placing the rolls onto a plate. Her puzzled glance suggested that men were such abysmal fools. They always missed the point. Beauty was…well…

"You came to see me?" I asked, loudly.

"I have an answer to your question." Houdini looked into my eager face.

Sam Ryan was smiling.

"And?"

"And Mr. Ryan agrees with me." A moment passed, Houdini's face assuming a faraway look. "You know, Miss Ferber, Mr. Ryan actually remembers my family from years back. He remembers the early Jewish families moving in. The frightened immigrants in the strange town."

Sam tapped his cigar in his ashtray. "His father, Rabbi Mayer Weiss, used to stop in with news items. A fine man, a scholar. Let me tell you—he created quite a sensation as he walked up College Avenue, looking like an old-world prophet in his Talmudic shawl, a white neckband, and that hat…"

"A barrett," Houdini finished for him. "The four-cornered miter of German Reform Judaism. I used to be embarrassed…" He stopped. "A man who found nothing in America but sadness and death." Then he shook his head. "Listen to me. Family stories." He saluted Sam, pleased. "It's good he is remembered."

"And well," Sam added. "A dignified man."

Houdini nodded. "But now it is time for our business, Miss Ferber. I've suggested to Mr. Ryan a little of what I think needs to be done, but you and I have work to do. We have a performance to stage."

"I'm not following this, sir."

"Mr. Ryan has already contacted the chief of police, and we're meeting at the high school at three, very shortly, when the students leave. I have an *idea*…"

"Tell me," I demanded, hungry.

Houdini laughed. "I'm a showman, my dear. Seeing is believing. You asked me to perform magic. You have to learn that magic has its own rules. Would you rob me of my moment?" His tone became serious. "I'm not gonna name the murderer for you—I don't have any idea on that, I tell you—but I think I can show you how to walk through a wall and not be seen. You have to find the murderer yourself."

I held up my hand. "You misunderstand me, Mr. Houdini. I'm not trying to find a murderer…"

He interrupted. "Of course, you are. I know you, young lady." He ran his hands through his hair, and a clump of hair jutted out. He left it there. "It's a story that needs an ending."

"We have a chief of police and a deputy…"

"They may need a little help from you."

Sam Ryan was enjoying Houdini's baiting of me. "Mr. Houdini," he admitted, "is quite a persuasive man."

"I can persuade men to chain me, tie me up, handcuff me, throw me into jail cells. People like doing that. It's the *freeing* people from shackles that people resist. Wherever you look, people are in the chains they wrap around themselves." His eyes got bright. "Freeing people is the job of the newspaper." He stood. "We need to leave for my *real* Appleton show. Miss Ferber?"

A little dazed, I stood. Sam turned to Matthias Boon. "Matt, get your hat and notebook."

I would have none of it. "This is my story."

Sam shook his head. "Mr. Boon is the city editor, Edna. You know that. This is his story."

"But I'm at the heart of the story."

Houdini was watching me.

"No."

And that was that. I glowered at anyone who looked my way. Matthias Boon preened, swelling up like a spoiled child indulged one too many times with sticks of sweet peppermint. So be it. Let the episode of Houdini be reported by a man who didn't have a sensible notion in his fat head.

Houdini bowed to Esther. "And this pretty lass can be my stage assistant, seeing as my bride Bess is in New York and my brother is off with friends." Esther blushed and stammered a thank you. I frowned. Was sight the only operative sense for the male of the species?

So Houdini, Esther, Boon, and I headed a few blocks away to Ryan High School. As we walked, I kept my distance from the strutting editor who led the way, as though we'd never gone that route before. At the corner, turning from the police station, Caleb Stone spotted us, and waited. Rushing up, out of breath, was Amos Moss. In his agitation he had mismatched the buttons on his vest under the shabby old suit. That proved my theory—men function with only the sense of sight, always impaired.

A few students straggled out of the building, but the hallways were empty. Miss Hepplewhyte stood, flummoxed. "Has something happened?"

Yes, a murder.

No one had told Principal Jones and Vice-Principal Homer Timm about the visit, and both men were not happy, though the principal shrugged his shoulders. "What do you want me to do?" The usually genial man seemed a little startled, and rightly so. This was his domain, invaded.

Homer Timm had been speaking to Mr. McCaslin, who looked relieved when Timm, spotting the regiment of souls marching in—with Houdini as leader, no less—simply abandoned him. He stood there, a frown on his face. The drama teacher looked puzzled, eyes dark, and quickly stepped into a classroom, shutting the door behind him.

Caleb Stone apologized for the intrusion, an apology clearly not genuine. For some reason, he was relying on the element of surprise. But why? After the explanation—"Mr. Houdini has an idea"—a line that seemed weighty and somber, a kind of leaden exclamation—the two men nodded to each other, and Principal Jones waved his arm to the notorious corridor. "Down here, Mr. Houdini." He stammered, "It's a honor, sir."

Houdini bowed slightly. "Of course it is. But first I would like to walk around the school, if I might."

He strolled the hallways, peering into classrooms, offices, standing on stairwell landings, though I noticed he did not go upstairs. He did walk into the auditorium and into the dressing rooms, and at one point he stood on the stage, down front, and seemed ready to do his magic act. He'd probably never met a stage he didn't immediately dominate. I wondered if he'd be followed by a troupe of sword swallowers? Of fire-eaters? Where were the Siamese twins?

He wandered through the small school library, empty of students, and Miss Dunne, surprised as she shelved a book, actually gasped and dropped it to the floor.

"Houdini," she exclaimed, and he laughed, bowing.

"All right, enough of this." He turned to me and asked to be directed to the locked storeroom He stood there, contemplating, his eyes focused. Then he took Esther's hand and leaned in to whisper something to her. Blushing a deep scarlet, Esther nodded and walked out of the building. "My lovely assistant has an assignment."

What? To amass boughs of lilacs to be strewn at your feet? To hire a brass band?

Houdini faced the offending door, now locked. "You have a key?" he asked the principal. "Can you open it?"

Homer Timm sneered, "You can't be of help?"

Houdini regarded him with narrow eyes. "I get out of situations, not into them."

So the door was opened and Houdini peered at the knob, as well as the inside of the door. "Shut me in." He paused, then seemed to speak to himself. "Ah, it locks when it closes." He stepped into the dusty, dim space, and Caleb Stone slammed the heavy oak door shut. He jiggled the knob, but the door was locked.

"No key needed to lock it," the chief said.

Yes, I believe that's what Houdini just announced.

Everyone waited and my heart pounded. I noticed a sheepish Mr. McCaslin had slipped into the hallway, though he stood away from the rest of us. Obviously he didn't want to miss this new scene in our play. We waited as three four five six minutes passed. No one said a word, expectant. Every so often there was pounding or scraping from within, and one time Houdini let out a low-throated groan. Good God, was he stumbling around in the dark?

Then, abruptly, the door flew open, and Houdini stepped into the hallway with a flourish.

"So?" Caleb Stone's voice wavered.

"I'm playing with you," Houdini said, cavalierly. "Opening this door is no trick." He pointed to a knob on the inside of the door. "To get out all I had to do is to turn the knob." He bowed. "This is no challenge."

I realized that, as with his stage show, he delayed freeing himself for dramatic effect. Yes, I told myself—you build a scene craftily; you need to understand crescendo and climax.

Amos Moss grunted. "Ain't a question of getting out anyway. It's a question of how she got in."

Houdini looked at him, "No, you're wrong, sir. It is a question of how she got out. But we know she ain't got out back into *this* hallway. Again, I'll lock myself in."

"Why?" Amos Moss asked.

Matthias Boon was scribbling furiously on his pad, and I wondered how he was going to write up this episode, though I knew my presence would be minimal, if mentioned at all.

Houdini stepped back in, and Caleb Stone closed the door. He looked irritated. This was all tomfoolery.

Again we waited. This time the minutes passed, perhaps ten, maybe fifteen. Everyone in the hallway was getting restless, and I noticed Principal Jones was leaning against the wall, looking drowsy, though Homer Timm stood like a sentry, spine erect, arms folded. One sleeve of his suit jacket was smeared with chalk. Now and then his eyes caught mine, though I couldn't interpret the look: stony, quizzical, even a little sardonic. Miss Dunne had quietly joined us, abandoning her books for this impromptu theatrical. She kept away from Miss Hepplewhyte, who, of course, avoided Mr. McCaslin. Enemies, all.

We waited and waited.

And waited.

A scraping noise from within, the sound of a board snapped, splintered. Still toying with us?

"Maybe we should check on him," Homer mumbled, but Caleb Stone's look said, of course not.

I cleared my throat. "I think we should trust him."

Silence in the hallway.

I heard the front door open, and I feared Christ Lempke would come lumbering in, filled with accusation and bile; but, surprisingly, Esther came rushing around the corner. "Come with me." She practically sang the words.

Everyone trailed her outside, down the steps, alongside the building where I expected to see Houdini. But Esther kept moving, away from the building, beyond a copse of shrubbery, off a pathway into a bank of blue hemlock scrub. There, standing with arms folded, his hair all out of place, his clothing dusty and crumpled, was a beaming Houdini.

"Well, well, well," Caleb Stone said. "I'll be darned."

I breathed a sigh of relief.

"It's very simple," Houdini announced as Esther moved beside him, taking her role as stage assistant a little too seriously.

Back inside the high school, standing outside the storeroom, Houdini described what he said was obvious to him. "I told myself there had to be another way out. If she ain't come out one way, she comes out another." In walking around the building, he'd noticed the proximity of the storeroom to the auditorium wing. In the back wall of the locked room was a panel, perhaps five feet high and two feet wide, hinged but latched on the other side. It opened to another storeroom on the other side.

"A little pressure on the panel," he informed us, "undoes a latch that, once sprung, lets the panel door swing open."

Everyone stared at the small opening. Why was it there?

Houdini explained how it worked. The panel opened to the other room, which opened onto a small landing leading down into the auditorium. From there, he said, it was easy to walk along the side of the stage to the back of the building, a route that led to a back door. Then he was outside.

"Is easy," he explained. "Once I saw how close the auditorium was to this wing of the school, I knew there was a way." He sighed. "That young girl simply walked out of the school through a door. Simple. No mystery."

"Yes, but how did she know it was there?" I asked. "I mean, how did she even get *into* the storeroom?"

"That's the question," Caleb Stone agreed. "Someone helped her."

"Impossible." From Miss Hepplewhyte.

The chief went on, "Someone had to tell her—or somehow entice her into this room."

My mind was racing. "Interestingly, Frana seems to have walked the other way first, past Mr. McCaslin's classroom, waving to a friend. Then she scurried back to the end of the hallway to this storeroom. She *planned* it."

Mr. McCaslin spoke up. "I did see her walk by." He looked rattled.

Caleb Stone noted, "If you stand in the storeroom, you can't tell the panel's there. The latch is on the other side."

Houdini nodded. "It was easy for me to undo it. But someone else…"

"Someone would have to have opened it from the other side." A pause. "Someone was waiting for her." My voice was rising.

"Who knew about this passageway?" Caleb Stone asked.

Both principal and vice-principal shook their heads because there was no reason for anyone to know of it. Homer Timm grumbled, "We have enough to do policing wandering students.

We hardly have time to explore the catacombs that wend their way through this building."

"But someone did," Caleb Stone insisted. "And it warn't Frana who discovered it. That's for certain." He wanted to see what was on the other side, and the group moved around the corner and into the auditorium. The chief walked up three steps to the landing and into what was clearly the janitor's storeroom—shelves filled with mops and brooms and pails, as well as hammers and saws and planes. The cluttered paraphernalia of school housekeeping.

"This is where August Schmidt keeps his tools," Homer Timm told us. "This is his space."

"Is he back at work?" Caleb asked.

The principal shook his head. "No, he's too frightened to return. And we can't allow it. The students would be alarmed."

That was news to me. I imagined the timid German at home, awaiting arrest for murder. Worse, this storeroom yawned before us, one man's domain, and its contents seemed to suggest guilt.

Caleb Stone peered into the room. "Who goes in here beside Mr. Schmidt?"

"No one." From Homer Timm.

But I interrupted. "Well, students rehearsing our plays would sometimes run up for hammers…"

Mr. McCaslin added, "And, you know, nails and…" He shrugged his shoulders.

"Show me how the panel works," Caleb Stone demanded.

All of us pushed closer, peering. Houdini walked up the stairs and into the janitor's storeroom, and I moved next to him. "There really is nothing hidden here," he pointed out. "Look." He showed us a panel built into a wall. "It looks like one of the series of panels that make up the back wall. Very basic. With a simple latch to close it. Another storeroom. Whoever built it probably figured there might be a need for moving from one space to the other. A place to put unused furniture." I noticed that a small table was set against the panel, covering part of it. Closed and latched, the panel became part of the wall.

Examining it, I realized it was easy to not see the latch. Would August Schmidt have known this? Houdini undid the latch, and suddenly there was the other secret room. I stepped closer to examine it, then I backed out as others moved up the steps to look. I stood on the small landing that led out of the janitor's room and down to the auditorium. If I craned my neck, I could glimpse the back of the stage. From the landing I spotted the work smocks and caps hanging on hooks, aprons lying on a table, even boots placed along the wall—all the possessions of August Schmidt.

Caleb Stone and Amos Moss nodded at each other. I sensed what they were thinking—Here it is. It has to be August Schmidt. That unassuming man, that sad soul who played his role well, masking his true murderous intent, a man who hatched some nefarious plot, discovering the unused storeroom, opening that latched panel. Somehow, he seduced the innocent Frana, confusing her, enticing her, promising wonders.

That struck me as nonsense. Wouldn't someone have seen him? Who knew there'd be no one watching? But these men wanted to believe Frana planned an escape, slipping into that room at two o'clock to meet an anxious Schmidt, the two running out the back into the woods, laughing as they escaped.

The scenario was impossible. Someone waited for Frana. But not the meek Schmidt. What life in New York could he offer her? Absurd! No Sherman House drummer was familiar with the school building. But it could be anyone in town, some old-timer who knew the school, maybe even a former student or teacher who long ago discovered the locked storeroom when visiting the janitor's room for a pail or a broom, and, years later, now an "older" man, suddenly found a use for such information.

I turned to Houdini, who was now standing apart from the others. He looked tired, drawn; these exercises carried a heavy toll for the man. Concentration and imagination, indeed.

"Thank you," I said. He was waiting for someone to acknowledge him.

Caleb Stone gave his thanks, and Houdini bowed. He turned to go. "My work here is done." He smiled at me. "This was not really an escape, Miss Ferber. This was just a discovery I made. You could have done this. This is just a door in a wall. A panel. That's all. No one bothered to look."

Chief Stone interrupted, sheepish. "It was common sense, really. But it never occurred to me. We never came back to look." He scratched his head. "I'm feeling a little foolish."

Houdini interrupted him. "Why should you think that way?"

"Well, it was right in front of our eyes." The chief's head twisted around. "For Heaven's sake, a storeroom door. I never thought…"

"No, it wasn't." Houdini was kind. "There was no latch visible from the inside, sir. You see, I'm always looking for means to escape. That's the way my mind works."

"But, my God, a doorway…"

Quietly Houdini assured him, "Once you'd reexamined the room, you'd have found it. Surely."

The chief started to say something, but Houdini held up his hand. "It's just that I got here first. And, you know, I do like to put on a show."

"But…"

"No trickery, really. You didn't need the great Houdini for this. You needed to open your eyes."

I shook my head. "What was obvious was obviously not obvious."

Boon frowned at me.

Houdini's look took us all in. "Isn't it strange, then? With all my elaborate escapes and tricks and illusions, I find a door in a wall…and, well…you may remember this one day as my finest performance."

Chapter Thirteen

I headed home from the *Crescent* office late in the afternoon to take my father for his walk. I passed in front of the fountain near City Park, where Hosea Thigpen or Mad Otto was declaring perdition and wrongdoing and the wages of unrepented sin. No one was around to hear him and I doubted whether he knew I was there. Usually I paid him little mind, but today I paused and watched him gesturing and posturing, eyes wide and teary. I wondered what drove a man to become so monomaniacal, so maddened, so removed from reason and common sense?

A man like Houdini practiced deliberation, logic, order, discipline...and a spirit of freewheeling fancy. His geography was always the world out there. Somehow Houdini had realized that life was magic—not just the pyrotechnics he enacted on stage but the wonder of his days. He saw everything as adventure, as thrill. Though he dressed like an out-of-town drummer, when he moved through the streets he became an explorer searching for uncharted continents.

Appleton was filled with vagrant souls whom no one bothered—Mad Otto the Prophet, Minnie the Hatrack, Isaac Solid who drove hay wagons up College Avenue and hurled lumps of horse manure at fleeing matrons. Mary McGregor wandered the lanes with a bundle of toys wrapped in a blanket hugged to her chest as she told passersby of her new-born infant; Barry Knott, one hundred years old, fell asleep in the outhouse every day. They wandered and no one thought ill of them. People here assumed goodness in others, even among the lunatics. No one locked their doors at night because they believed no one would ever think to rob them.

Until now, that is.

Until now.

Frana Lempke's murder had altered the comfortable landscape. The Ferber household was never locked, nor were our neighbors' homes. As I walked along busy College Avenue, I noticed something new in town. A well-dressed businessman checked his gold watch, a woman shopping in Voight's filled baskets with tonic and hairpins, an East End society matron picked over notions for whist prizes at My Store, children pumped hoops across the wooden sidewalks or played leap frog in the park—they had all become worriers now. They started when you approached quickly from behind. They *watched* you. Or was I just imagining it? Who do you trust when that golden bowl has just been shattered?

In my talks with folks, I sensed panic. Would this murder plague the town, unsolved, throughout the summer? Merchants worried, and I'd overheard one fussy shopkeeper berating Caleb Stone, demanding the murder be solved by the Fourth of July. Appleton's huge patriotic celebration, barges and fireworks on the Fox River, was in jeopardy. Hordes of out-of-towners crowded the avenues, spending their money, and the specter of heinous murder might prove a damper on the festivities.

Chief Stone had muttered, "Don't you worry, sir. Appleton will be the same old town by then."

But at that moment I knew in my heart that Appleton would never be the same town again. The awful blemish of such a crime had stolen some of our soul.

I suspected Houdini's revelations might have fueled Matthias Boon's intoxication because, back in the city room, he wrote his copy in a white heat—and hummed as he did it. Somehow he'd convert that prosaic discovery into sensational headline. At my own desk, I had trouble focusing on the nonsense I was typing.

Despite the discovery, Frana Lempke's murder still remained a mystery.

Suddenly I thought of Jake Smuddie. High school footballers lingered after school in the auditorium, running in the hallways, up and down the stairs. We all did. I sat on those very steps leading up to August Schmidt's storeroom when I worked on my part in *A Scrap of Paper*. Students often drifted up there for paintbrushes, for brooms, for…I stopped. Anyone could have spotted that panel, that latched door. But most would pay it no mind. There was no reason to. No one would think it a convenient hiding place. Again, my mind flashed to Jake Smuddie, an image of the brawny, tough boy with his amazing hands around Frana's neck. God no! I recoiled. Who else? What former student, now grown into a man, inheritor of that secret knowledge of that panel, came back to use it to lure the hapless Frana? Or…a present student. Or…who?

Even before I turned onto North Street, I heard my father's rich laughter. He was sitting with Gustave Timm who was telling him some anecdote, his hands flapping like wild birds. My father leaned in, enjoying it. I was happy. So many afternoons I dropped back home to check on my father, only to find Gustave Timm and Jacob Ferber sitting next to each other in the parlor or on the porch, the two men huddled together, Gustave puffing on a Golden Night cigarette. He'd met my father last spring when I brought my family to the theater, my desperate attempt to connect him to something. How deeply he'd once loved the theater! But he sat stiffly throughout the evening. Unable to view the actors onstage, baffled by the laughter from the audience, he got rattled. We left at intermission, and Gustave Timm, standing in front of his theater, had offered to escort my father home. The afternoon visits began, the two men yammering on and on about politics and Appleton and even, as I once overheard, the outlandish price of coffee. Gustave confided his dislike—his nagging *fear*—of Cyrus P. Powell, who owned the Lyceum and was thus his boss. Once I'd heard him say, "I was brought up to respect authority, especially one's employer, but the man always seems to find fault with me. He's always checking on me. I turn around and he's there." He sounded like a whiny child, freshly reprimanded. "I fear Homer speaks against me."

Gustave Tim spotted me. "Your reportorial daughter has returned home." He waved a welcome.

"Hey, Bill."

"Hey, Pete."

I drew up a chair and told them about Houdini at the high school, filling the account with enough drama to impress Gustave as well as entertain my father.

Listening, my father shook his head. "The sad tale continues."

Gustave joined in. "Tragic. She was just a child, such a misguided young girl."

"You knew her?" I asked.

Gustave shook his head. "No. But she wandered into the theater some afternoons with one of her friends, another girl. I thought that they were sisters but…"

"Kathe Schmidt?"

"I don't remember her name, the other one. She fidgeted, but kept her mouth shut. Frana did all the talking. She'd show up during rehearsals after school was dismissed and announce that she wanted to be an actress. She plagued the visiting artists till they ran from her or complained to me. She'd ask for an autograph, then beg to be in the show." He shrugged. "Over and over, the same pleading, yet grandly, like she was already on the stage." His smile was wistful. "It was sad."

"Why?"

"She thought prettiness made you an actress."

Sharply, from me, "It certainly helps."

Gustave disagreed. "Only in vaudeville revues. One time I asked her what she knew about being an actress, and she had nothing to say. It was the *idea* of fame and money, the allure of Broadway, that propelled her. She wanted to hear stories about Broadway. I told her I'd never been there. She found that strange. Like, how can you manage a theater and not have been to New

York? Lord, when she went on and on, her friend rolled her eyes and grimaced. She thought it was funny."

"What did you tell her?" my father asked.

Gustave considered. "She wanted to act at the Lyceum. I told her that we mount shows with traveling companies of professional players who bring their shows to *us*. We don't put on local shows. I'm not a director—I'm a theater manager. I know the business, not the plays. We get Joseph Jefferson and Lillian Russell and the Weber Brothers, popular acts that people want to see."

"How did she take that?"

"Not well. The last time she was there, just before a dress rehearsal—the two of them, that is—I told her to stop pestering us. Quit loitering outside, approaching the actors, bothering them. She followed William McCreary, and he was not happy. He told me she trailed him to the Sherman House, went on about joining his company when they went to New York. He wanted to call the police on her, and he expressed his concern to Cyrus P. Powell, who spoke to me about it. Harshly, I might add, warning me to shoo such pests away. I gather Powell wrote a letter to Frana's father, but I heard that from Homer. What good did it do? She drove Mary Allibone crazy, and I was ready to call the police. But in the lobby I put my foot down. She got angry. What did I know about theater, she yelled. I was a mediocre backwater manager. She'd leave and come back to Appleton a star, she said. It was a little tiresome, but she was young, naïve and, well…"

"Pretty?" I suggested.

He looked at me, squinted his eyes. "I was going to say…sad."

"That, too." My father turned toward me. Disapproving.

"But then I said the wrong thing. I said she could be hired, summers, as an usherette. We use three or four young people each summer. Ryan High school girls. Most like it, but…"

"The wrong thing?"

"She burst into tears. It was a little scary, frankly, and her friend had to take her by the arm. 'I'm not an usherette,' she yelled. 'I'm an actress. Look at me. I'm beautiful.'"

In the quiet, my father said, "Was she beautiful?"

Both Gustave and I looked at the blind man. A rasp thickened Gustave's voice. "Yes, she was pretty. There are thousands like her. But she didn't have that…well, spark. A Lillian Russell steps on stage, beautiful, but there's something else. A Mary Allibone. A Sophie Toomer. An electric charge that shoots over the orchestra and audience."

My father spoke. "She was a little girl. Maybe she'd acquire it."

Gustave weighed his words carefully. "I think no. You need to be born with it. The sad little girl was pretty. That's all. That's not enough." His eyes darkened. "Her friend kept saying 'Let's leave' in a snippy voice. Frana babbled about a friend who had a place in New York, across the street from a theater—but that made no sense. Luckily, Mildred stopped in with her mother, and the two women calmed her down, even drove the girls home in their carriage. Mildred has little patience with such nonsense. An iron will, Mildred has. Comes from being in charge of so many books, I guess." He beamed.

"Miss Dunne knew Frana from the high school."

"She never liked her, she told me. I guess she *talked* in the library." He flashed that winning smile. "A crime against nature. Mildred complained that Frana would step into the library, her laughter already covering the room. Frana needed to be…seen. Admired. Mildred thought her desperately lonely but, well, Mildred has little patience with lost souls." He smiled. "She believes you set your sights on a future and that's where you'll end up."

I interrupted. "Well, so did Frana. She had a dream of a future."

Gustave clicked his tongue. "The difference is that Mildred is a disciplined woman—strong—and Frana seemed to me an idle dreamer. Let me just say that I was happy that Mildred and her mother were at the theater that day. Mary Allibone looked at me as if to say—what kind of place do you have here?"

I rolled my tongue into my cheek. "Did you tell this to Chief Stone?"

"Of course. For what it's worth."

"A place in New York, across from the theater," I echoed.

Gustave Timm shrugged and made ready to leave, saying he had to meet his brother Homer for supper at the Sherman House. "It's an obligation I have a couple times a week." He made it sound onerous. "Mildred thinks Homer demands too much of my time. She thinks he controls me—that I'm too passive."

I was curious. "You know, Mr. Timm, when you arrived a couple years back, no one thought you were brothers. You don't look alike…"

"Of course we do. He's older by a decade, yes. And a tad heavier, and darker complexioned, but we both take after our mother—prominent chin, big eyes, and"—he laughed—"the floppy ears we cover up with wild hair."

My father said what I was thinking. "Perhaps it's the personality. Your brother is very serious, while you…"

"It's the nature of the profession. He deals with schoolchildren, day in, day out, and over the years he's developed a severe exterior. Sometimes I think he's forgotten how to laugh at things. When you run a theater where half of your shows are rollicking, roustabout comedy revues, and when actors miss performances, or when snowy nights keep Appleton home in front of the fireplace, well, you learn to laugh a lot."

I remembered my conclusion that the brothers disliked each other. "You don't live together?"

I sensed my father's disapproval again. Edna, the inquisitor.

Gustave kept his smile but it thinned considerably. "It's the same old story. Proximity breeds contempt. As boys, with a ten-year age difference, we fought tooth and nail. You know, we do love each other—he's the one who recommended the job at the theater two years back—but we know better than to spend too much time together."

Like Fannie and me, I thought: blood-curdling battles royal. Over the hem of a dress. Over the dropping of a saucepan. Over an innocent sarcastic barb from one sister to another.

"I keep expecting your brother to leave for the East to join his wife or for her and the children to return here." I stopped, sensing a violation. My father was frowning.

A long silence. "Sophie may not be returning to Appleton. Homer begs her to, as she's no longer in a sanitarium, of course, and he misses his boys. But she delays. She seems to enjoy a marriage of...distance. Each year Homer plans to tender his resignation, head East, and reunite. But each year Sophie...suggests he'd best stay here..." He stood. "I'm airing family laundry on the Ferber porch. Mildred says I talk too much." His ready smile. "She says silence is a virtue. Spoken like a true librarian." And he was off, tipping his hat and walking away.

After a while my father said, "They don't like each other."

"I know that."

"But you have a way of intruding into people's lives, Pete."

"I'm curious, Bill."

"You can't stop asking questions."

"I know."

"Family business is private. There are secrets in every home." A sloppy grin. "Remember that, Edna, when you write your books someday."

A smile of my own. "I have to get back to the office." I leaned over and kissed him on the cheek.

When I returned home that evening, Kathe Schmidt was in the backyard walloping the stairwell runner with a beater. From the kitchen I could hear her creaky, off-key voice:

Casey would dance with the strawberry blonde
And the band played on
He'd dance 'cross the floor...

She didn't know how the stanza ended because she repeated those same three lines and paused, mid-line, and then began again, as though she were a wind-up toy that malfunctioned. I thought I'd go mad. I wanted to scream: *with the girl he adored.* It was not singing but some labored keening, mindless and mechanical. Her thoughts were elsewhere, perhaps in a dark place.

Fannie, kneading dough for strudel, her hands and elbows coated with flour, simply raised her eyebrows when I pointed to the backyard. "Fannie," I began, but my sister held up a powdery arm.

"No, stop. Leave her be."

I wandered into the parlor where my father slumped in a chair, his head nodding as though to a song in his head. He roused as I walked in, said hello, though he did not to want to talk. I didn't linger.

Heading up the stairs to rest before supper, I saw my mother enter the parlor and speak sharply to him, a low, cutting remark. "How can you sit in the same chair all day?"

I froze. I hated it when my mother carped at the helpless man. Herself a driven woman whose energy demanded movement, she had little patience with a husband whose blindness was only the last in a series of failures—from business and money to, well, marriage. Lamentably, she had seen him as ineffectual long before the blindness struck. She had little tolerance with his placid movement through life, his desire that the world be painted in soft rainbow pastels, with muted chamber music underscoring his inactive days. She balked at that. Cut from a different cloth, steel-ribbed, taut, indomitable, she wanted her daughters to be molded similarly. Jacob Ferber was willow, she was oak.

She'd had a bad day at My Store. I could always tell because she assailed her sitting, immobile husband. She couldn't help herself.

"The bank manager stopped in today." A cold voice. "Again. Money due." A bitter laugh. "And I can't even discuss it with you." I saw her punch a pillow on the settee and shift an end table so it was just out of his reach. She mumbled as she disappeared into the kitchen, "Chicago." I cringed. It was, I knew, a prayer. It seemed to be the word that let her survive these bleak moments. Salvation in Chicago, sheltered among her family. A number of times I'd heard my mother and Fannie whispering about the ultimate move to Chicago. I always filled in the missing words: *when father dies*. The store would be sold, the house and furniture sold…and Fannie would marry the shopkeeper there she'd flirted with for years, an earnest fellow everyone loved, though I thought him lackluster.

Where would I be? I often wondered as I eavesdropped. Would I be the unmarried sister tending to sniveling brats through windy Chicago winters?

Something had shifted in the Ferber household these past few months. My mother's outbursts—her attacks—had long been volcanic. Her anger went on and on, thunderous, until the rafters shook. Fannie had inherited that anger and largely directed it at me. But lately my mother had become…quiet. Coldness replaced fury when she talked to my father. She had stepped backward and realized she didn't have to care anymore.

Upstairs I lay on my bed, burying my face in a pillow. Outside Kathe Schmidt was singing those same three lines. There was no escape, I thought. None whatsoever. Madness creeps into this home from the very corners.

Later, I found myself alone in the kitchen with Kathe. Last time we'd fought, and I regretted that. This time I vowed to be silent and decent, two qualities I had trouble executing.

"How are you, Kathe?" I asked, quietly.

Kathe looked up from the potted chicken she was spicing. She looked ready to cry.

"What's the matter?"

Kathe made a smacking noise with her lips, sighed. "Nothing."

"Something's the matter."

"It's *mein vater*." In a sloppy blend of German and English, she described her suffering father. She sobbed like a sickly child. It was like watching a dumb farm animal caught in a trapper's cruel leg iron, squirming and flailing—helpless before the randomness of life. Kathe cried that life at home was horrible; her father sat all the day long on a chair in the kitchen and faced an empty table, while her mother, a maddened hen, clucked around him. August Schmidt, I learned piecemeal, had lost the will to live: a desire never to return to his lowly job as janitor, surely; but more so, a nagging belief that there would be a sudden rapping on the front door and he'd be led away in irons—to be hanged by the state. August Schmidt would start to whimper and slip from his chair to the floor, slumped like an old dog, afraid of noise and sudden movement. Her mother moved like a ghost through the halls, whispering that the family would flee back to Germany.

Kathe gasped. "I can't live in that place no more. It's a house of…of dead people."

"Kathe, your father did not kill Frana. You know that."

"Do I?" That answer made me furious. I wanted to slap the stupid girl. "Yeah, I know that. But *everyone* thinks he's guilty."

"Not so, Kathe." I kept the fury out of my voice. "Reasonable people don't believe it…"

Kathe cut me off. "People *look* at me on the street. Like… like…" She trailed off. "People don't talk to me."

I understood something. "Like Jake Smuddie?"

Kathe pouted. "Yeah."

"Well, Kathe, you accused Jake Smuddie of murder."

"I did *not,*" Kathe was no longer sobbing.

"Sort of. You were angry with him."

Hands on hips, she swung around. "Well, he left me, you know. Frana always came first. And ever since that day in the park he won't *see* me."

"But he didn't kill Frana either."

"Then who did?"

"I wish I knew."

"Help me, Edna," Kathe pleaded.

"Me? What can I do?"

Kathe's tough façade disappeared as quickly as it had surfaced. "You know people. In town. Talk to them." Her lips trembled. "I just want things to go back to where they were before. You know. Back then."

"Kathe, for God's sake, things can't go back to where they were. Frana is dead." I thought of Jake Smuddie, hidden in that park gazebo, searching for an escape from his father's regimented world. "And you have to accept that Jake is gone from your world."

Kathe flared up, drawing her cheeks in, a sudden gesture that reminded me of a squirrel gnawing on an acorn out back. "We'll see."

My Lord. For a simple girl she could run the gamut of emotions from weepiness to sullenness to anger to pouting... to desperation. And then optimism. Each level, I considered, having the depth of oilcloth.

"I don't mean to offend you, Kathe. I'm just trying to make you see..."

"Oh, yes, you did," she snarled. She threw back her head so that her fair hair caught the light "Of course you did."

"Kathe, I've been wondering about something. That afternoon Frana disappeared, you seemed to know so much about it—I mean, the story of the older man, the rumor of Frana on that train. You said she told you what she intended to do, her plan to sneak out of school. You knew about that note. You must have asked her who the older man was, no? She told you everything..." I stopped. Kathe's face tightened. "What?"

"I *did* ask her."

"And?"

"She'd just smile. A secret. She'd write me from New York."

"So you helped her?"

"Well, you *know* that. She was afraid Miss Hepplewhyte might spot her near the office and she'd have to explain. So she had me drop the note off when Miss Hepplewhyte stepped out. Frana slipped it to me. I put it on her desk. So what? I ain't committed a crime, you know." A hard look, challenging.

"Did you know what it said?"

A pause. "No, it was sealed."

"But you did it."

"Of course. It was part of Frana's plan to leave Appleton with that...that man. She said she'd be on that train."

"But it didn't work, Kathe. Frana got murdered, and Jake is gone."

Kathe trembled. "It ain't my fault, Edna. You can't blame me. I was just trying to help a friend. That's what friends do, you know."

I deliberated. "Kathe, you were always with her. Did you help her sneak out that afternoon?"

"No." One word, hard.

"Did you *see* anything?"

"How could I? I was in the library that period. Last period. I mean, I knew something was gonna happen, but I didn't know what." She swallowed a laugh. "The funny thing is, you know…One of the boys—Johnny Marcus, that clown—yelled something to me about Frana the prisoner locked up in the tower like Juliet. Everyone jumped in, buzzing, about her creepy uncle. They looked at me like I knew what was going on. In a loud voice I yelled, 'Frana ain't gonna be happy everybody is laughing at her.' And then everyone laughed and hooted and carried on. Some of the serious students slammed their books shut, mad as hell."

"And what did you do?"

A pause. "I laughed as loud as the rest."

"Frana was your friend." I glared at her. "Aren't you ashamed of yourself?"

"I got *lots* of friends, Edna." She narrowed her eyes. "Unlike some people I know."

I ignored that. "Yet you helped her with that note."

She closed up. "Leave me alone, Edna. I mean, could you just leave me alone?"

After supper my mother decided that the Ferber family should pay a condolence call to Frana Lempke's family. Frana's mother Gertrud often did her shopping at My Store. At Christmas she bought religious figurines—the Virgin Mary, Joseph, the Christ Child, camels, sheep, little Bohemian figurines in gaudy blue and red and green. "A small, quiet woman, but a good woman. Not the brash army of women who move like stampeded cattle through my aisles, their ample hips sending goods willy-nilly."

Fannie had baked one of her succulent apple pies, dipping into the barrel of winter apples in the cellar. Entering the house, I'd smelled the aromatic confection—the pungent sweep of cinnamon and nutmeg, the savory butter crust, the fleshy winter apples diced and soaked in cider. I was happy to see a second pie on the pie rack, cooling—this one for the family.

Dressed in funereal black broadloom and corduroy tie and black silk and black taffeta bonnets, the Ferbers left home, Fannie swinging a wicker basket with white linen cloths covering the pie. We walked to the edge of the farm district beyond the fairgrounds in the Sixth Ward. The Lempke farm sat on a little promontory that edged a bank of black hemlocks, a tiny farmhouse with pine-slatted roof and whitewashed clapboards, a house that seemed haphazard, a room tacked on as needed, so that the whole effect was one of chance, mishap, even chaos. Dilapidated, with a sagging lean-to on one side. Broken stone paths wound through untrimmed bramble bushes, thickets of wild rose, and I could see, beyond the sagging honeysuckle-covered picket fence, the meager fields beyond.

I knew Frana's father and brothers worked at the Appleton Paper and Pulp Works on the river. The men did the filthiest, smelliest jobs in the acid vat rooms. At home they worked their piddling truck farm of tomatoes, cucumbers, beans, potatoes. A few autumn melons. The mother tended the hencoops and the pigsty out back, while the brothers labored in the barn where the horses, cows, and goats clamored in the dark, tight recesses. An orange-brown mongrel dog barely lifted its head as we stepped onto a creaky porch; nearby a cat squeaked, leapt over the railing, and then climbed into a Rose of Sharon bush.

Gertrud Lempke seemed surprised that anyone would visit but looked grateful, thanking us too much, apologizing for the disheveled parlor with its hand-hewn chairs and rag rugs. She rushed off to brew coffee. There was one photograph on the wall, a sepia-toned portrait of a mustachioed German military officer with much braid and ribbon; and I thought of the Old Testament God, judgmental and contentious. Mrs. Lempke served us a strawberry strudel, but not the apple pie. From my chair in the parlor, I could see that confection sitting on a rough-board kitchen table among the unwashed supper dishes.

Gertrud was dressed in a faded Mother Hubbard smock. She had a tiny, pinched face, a small crinkly nose, a little mouth. One more sad *hausfrau*, I thought, the hidden-away drudge with wrinkled skin and the ill-fitting blue-white false teeth that glistened like piano keys in the flickering gaslight. She had none of her dead daughter's beauty. She sat, stood, sat down again: nervous. I wondered what folks ever visited this isolated farmhouse. Who talked to this scattered, lonely woman?

As we sipped coffee in silence, the back door opened and Oskar Lempke and his three husky sons lurched in, stopped dead in their tracks, and looked ready to retreat back to the fields and the barn. One of the boys carried a pail of beer, and it swung back and forth in his grip. Nervous, he sloshed some suds on the pine floor, and the old man mumbled, "*Du unverschämter Hund.*" The lad narrowed his eyes, fierce. Oskar Lempke, looking at his wife and then at my father, said he appreciated the condolence call, though he didn't seem to. He and his sons sat down in a rigid line, stiff as tree trunks. I looked at all three boys, Frana's older brothers, all in their early twenties, perhaps, blunt-muscled and thick and blond-cowlicky, farm boys and mill workers, all with wide cherry-red faces and hands as broad as ham hocks. Plodding oxen, brutal farm animals themselves, dull. No one said a word; each stared straight ahead. I'd met one of them in a harness shop months back, with Frana at his side; and my memory of him was clear. He kept spitting on the floor.

The brothers seemed inordinately fascinated with Fannie who, conscious of their unblinking stares, fidgeted in her seat. There was rawness in their stares. A barnyard hunger. My mind flashed to Jake's whispered gossip…Frana's fear of her brothers, her dread of going home…the brother who bothered her…

In the awful silence, my mother repeated her sympathies. Frana's mother swallowed and looked away, but I found Oskar's reaction alarming. The tough-looking man, all bulk and weathered line, seemed teary-eyed, putting the backs of his palms against his eyes, and trembling.

Silence.

Then he spoke, his German accent thick, "Maybe we did wrong thing, locking her up like that." He pointed upstairs. "She was rebel, that girl, she was, *meine Kleine*. Fought like wild rabbit. So we nail the bars on the window and we learn you cannot nail in someone who is already living outside the house."

His wife whispered, "We was going to send her to family in Germany. To a nunnery. Is stricter there. I make her dresses but she has to have the *Amerikanische* gown. America is too—too much freedom. The…" She waved her hand in the air. "The… the…open space…"

One of the brothers grunted, or had he belched? He looked pleased with himself.

Everyone turned at the sound of heavy clomping. Christ Lempke was dragging himself down the stairs. He nodded to us and fell into a chair, out of breath. I knew he'd once worked at the Eagle Manufacturing Company, building silo feed cutters, making good money, a hard-working man, well-liked; but his war injury kept him home. Staring at us with hooded, distrustful eyes, he sneered, "I hears you talk. Enough. Frana was girl who chose to dishonor…"

Gertrud made a *tsk*ing sound, but Christ went on, "She should have been in nunnery since little girl, no? Too much looking in the mirrors, too much the *Amerikanish* sass in the mouth, too much with the boys throwing stones at the window at night." His voice rose louder and louder. I thought it peculiar that in this house of grief, this man could only speak ill of the dead beautiful girl. Oskar Lempke stood, tottered a bit, stared down at his hectoring brother, and then left the room, not saying a word. Christ Lempke stopped talking.

We hurriedly stood. No one had touched the strudel.

At the front door Gertrud Lempke touched my sleeve. "She mentioned you. I remember. From school, maybe."

"Yes."

My mother started to say something, but Gertrud Lempke whispered, "Would you like to see her room?"

No. No. God no. But I nodded, and Fannie and I followed Mrs. Lempke up the narrow stairs, leaving our parents waiting downstairs. She opened the door to Frana's bedroom at the back of the house, and in the first flush of gaslight I saw one small window crisscrossed with bars, with nailed wooden panels. Shivering, I felt we were violating the dead girl's bedroom; but I was surprised by the small space, a crawlspace, really, with sloping ceiling just under the roof, a space that was probably a closet converted into a bedroom. A small wrought-iron bed was covered with an old, faded down-feather quilt embroidered with folk patterns, ripples and cascades of red and green floral patterns. It was torn at the edges, with bursting fabric at the center. A simple homemade bureau with a missing drawer was painted a dull green, a stolid paint intended for a floor; and the wide-planked flooring was covered with an oval rag-weave rug, the threads loose. A shadowy mirror in a dull brown frame was nailed by the back window, most likely to catch the sunlight in the morning. On the dresser stood a water pitcher, some brushes, pins, and inside an unclosed wardrobe, I spotted Frana's dresses, her bonnets, her finery.

A Wisconsin nun's cell, cloistered and forgotten among the leftovers of a family. But on the wall just inside the door Frana had pinned pages torn from magazines and newspapers, stories of New York and Broadway and theater, of well-known actresses. A grainy print from a magazine like the *Century* or *Scribner's*—with a black-and-white likeness of Lillian Russell. There were also some glossy chromolithographs from magazines like *Demorest's*, with bright, blotchy colors, actresses like Mary Allibone in her celebrated role as Juliet, the wide-eyed, winsome tragedienne staring into space, hands extended, hair askew. It was a popular print, the one used on the poster when Allibone performed at the Lyceum. Unframed, ripped, tacked on, the print stared back at me, haunting; a talisman of color in an otherwise drab lifeless room. It blazed like a noontime sun in its shadows. I could scarcely turn away from it. It was compelling…awful.

Suddenly I felt faint and wobbled. I'd disliked the vain and fickle Frana with her ribbons and her lace and her fluttery coy manners, her cheap flirtations, her prettiness. We talked now and then, we socialized, we moved in similar circles of young people. In this monastic chamber, illuminated by that midnight sun of an actress in her glossy colors, I saw Frana as a lonely, desperate girl, a lost child in the home of pain, overwhelmed by a new world. I wished, all of a sudden, that I'd paid attention to her. There were things we could have told each other. Maybe.

But maybe not.

Chapter Fourteen

Caleb Stone stopped to say hello as I walked up College Avenue, heading to My Store, and he was uncharacteristically eager to gossip. I was hoping his organ-grinder monkey Amos Moss was elsewhere, but Caleb I liked. I didn't think him too bright, yet I considered him honorable and fair. We chatted about some ruckus he'd broken up at a beer hall, and he joked, "Not really headline news, I'm afraid, Miss Ferber." Then the usually laconic chief told me that Jake Smuddie was no longer attending classes at Lawrence University, which surprised me.

"You probably know that he sits in that gazebo in City Park." He leaned into me. "I sat with him. He was a little testy with me. Seems to think his father sent me over to bring him back to the college."

"And had you spoken to his father?" A little testy myself.

Caleb Stone nodded. "The father—Herr Professor—did speak to me. He's worried about his lad, of course, but I said that the boy ain't doing anything illegal, so far's I can tell. Not going to your classes at the university ain't a crime, though it's a questionable choice of behavior for someone whose father is a high muck-a-muck on the faculty there."

"And what was Jake's attitude when you spoke to him?"

"Angry." He reflected a bit. "But more, I think, bewildered. Hurt. This whole thing with Frana Lempke—the way she died—seems to have snapped something in him. That's all he would talk about."

"Just what did he say?"

"No confession of spontaneous murder from him, if that's what you're suggesting."

"I don't believe that he would kill anyone..."

He scratched his chin absentmindedly. "That's where you and I differ, Miss Ferber. I believe everyone could kill someone. It's just the circumstances that trigger a episode."

"I would *never*..."

"Of course, you would." He had a deep rumbling laugh. "I've walked by North and Morrison on more than one occasion and heard you and Fannie whooping it up like deranged warriors. One of these days I fully expect to lead one or the other of you off in leg irons."

I waved him off with a grin. "It'll be me doing the killing, frankly. If ever there was a girl born to be strangled, it's my sister Fannie..." But I stopped, realized the gravity of my words. Strangle her? Images of Frana Lempke swept over me. "I'm sorry."

This time Caleb Stone waved his hand in the air. "We're just talking, the two of us." He started to walk away. "If you hear anything about young Smuddie, you let me know."

"Like what?"

"I get the feeling he knows something he hasn't told us. Something his father senses as well. Maybe I'm wrong. Hard to say."

"I'll talk to him." The chief expected that to happen; I suspected he'd orchestrated our little talk...

"But don't let me read about it in the *Crescent* first. Come see me."

"I'm a law-abiding young woman."

He tipped his hat and walked away.

By afternoon in the city room I got increasingly angry, feeling that everyone was in league against me. Miss Ivy was out with a spring cold, so it was a male enclave of pipe- and cigar-smoke, belching, and ribaldry, coupled with the excessive use of bodily functions as metaphor for most of what they talked about. I scooted in and out of the office, interviewing a Ladies Auxiliary woman about a spring flower show. Then I interviewed a local milliner and haberdasher about summer fashions—my notes were filled with cotton cheriot, peau de soie, Bishop's sleeves, Valenciennes lace, and gros de Londres—all of which made little sense to me though I dutifully jotted everything down. Fannie, I knew, would relish such European vocabulary for the fabric that she cut, basted, sewed, and ultimately wore.

But something was *not* being told to me, a story that the men knew I'd want to know. It had to do with Frana, though it would be indecorous to ask the male club what with its privacies and strict definitions of what could and could not be told to any woman. Lord, if these men could read my random jottings in my reporter's pad—the suspect behavior I observed around Appleton.

Men shouldn't have a monopoly on discussing base or foul human behavior, even though they were *responsible* for so much of it.

I pricked up my ears, busied myself at my typewriter, silently moved alongside them, left the building and yet lingered in the stairwell, eavesdropped. It wasn't hard to do once I put my mind to it. These men were frantic gossipers who couldn't wait to blather their news to one another, Matthias Boon sputtering, Sam Ryan lamenting, Byron Beveridge becoming salacious in his comedy. I even spotted Mac standing in the doorway, nodding at Sam, when I returned from walking my father at mid-afternoon. So he was part of the mystery. Noisy, chattering men; boys with their marbles.

What I learned, though, stunned me—I pieced it together, fragment by fragment, a scrap of anecdote, a throwaway line, even a licentious or downright lewd remark. Frana was no longer a virgin—or at least that was the scuttlebutt hinted at by the attending physician who served as medical examiner—word of mouth that seeped through the male world, like sewage into already murky waters. Hardly shocking, though such things were rarely discussed, certainly not among the young folks of Ryan

High School. Occasionally, a wayward girl or boy was subjected to public censure and quick removal to a distant relative's home in Tacoma, Washington, or Ecorse, Michigan. Or to a Home for Unwed Mothers on the East Coast, where such homes, I gathered, were commonly needed, and thus plentiful. No, the revelation about Frana stunned but didn't surprise. As the day went on, the overheard comments were even more alarming, for the indiscreet doctor—Horace Belford, notorious, I knew, for examining you with half-closed eyes and beer-nasty breath—had also suggested that the misguided girl was carrying a bastard child in that young body.

That news would never appear in any daily paper.

Chief of Police Stone, according to Sam Ryan who mentioned it to Matthias Boon, had told Herr Professor Smuddie about the—in Sam's word—"problem."

It added a new and fascinating wrinkle to the mystery of her death, and I thought of Jake Smuddie, dazed and disoriented these days, a wanderer in the small city.

Poor Frana, scared, running, desperate to leave Appleton, still clinging to her dream of Broadway though she carried a child in her body. Who could she turn to for solace? Kathe? Hardly. The lover who betrayed her, touched her…The jilted Jake? Somebody else? Worse, her hideous brothers slouching around that decrepit farmhouse? Little Frana, beautiful and…running scared. My heart ached for her. She didn't know how to get away.

By the end of the day the story had more spice. Byron Beveridge, lolling at his desk with his feet up, said in his drawling, Southern sleepy voice to Matthias Boon—just as I was walking back into the room—something salacious about Jake Smuddie and Lovers Lane.

"So what's new with the Frana investigation?" I asked the men.

Silence.

"I gather…"

Matthias Boon interrupted me. "Miss Ferber, isn't your workday over?"

For a second anger rose in me, the taste of ashes in my mouth. But then a curious thing happened. I didn't care. It didn't matter anymore. None of this. Ever since Boon began his campaign against me, I'd bristled and fumed, ready to do battle. Now, sensing another mean-spirited confrontation, I knew to my marrow that the landscape had shifted. Perhaps Frana's murder had something to do with it. Perhaps Houdini's rousing praise was part of it. This city room was too small to contain me now. Yes, there was no escaping the resentment I felt at my unfair treatment at the *Crescent,* but to battle with a pipsqueak like Matthias Boon was a waste of time. I felt calm.

I made a dismissive sound, which bothered the men not at all, gathered my belongings, glanced around at one more pitiful rung of hell…one of the unimportant ones.

That evening, skipping supper and dressed in my take-me-very-seriously outfit of brown chiffon taffeta shirtwaist with a tan linen flounce skirt, I walked to the Lawrence University campus. To gather my resolve, I first strolled among the tree-shrouded buildings of the Methodist university, a place I'd always liked because of its somber appearance and its earnest students. I headed to Eldorado Street, an expanse of elegant white-fenced professorial homes with electric lights and vanilla-soda lives. There stood the imposing home of Herr Professor Solomon Smuddie, his wife Odette, and son Jacob, called Jake, erstwhile Ryan High football hero, now disaffected Lawrence University freshman.

A housemaid dressed in gingham and a French Chantilly cap answered the door and said in German, "*Folgen Sie mir, bitte.*" She had me wait in an anteroom on a plush burgundy side chair that matched the fabric of the draperies and the window-box seats. An oil painting of a European gentleman hung on the wall, framed in an oversized dark-stained black-walnut frame. The shellacked Kaiser Wilhelm moustache made me nervous.

Odette Smuddie walked in, smiling, but nervous; her hands kept grazing her face as though she wanted to stop herself from saying something. She extended her hand.

I apologized for the intrusion and identified myself. "I'm a close friend of Jake—Jacob—and I had to be on campus, and he'd said to say hello if I'm in the neighborhood and…"

Odette Smuddie actually made a yelping sound. "I'm afraid Jacob is not here right now, Miss Ferber…"

"Oh, I'm so sorry." I stood.

Mrs. Smuddie went on, "No, please stay a bit. For tea. Please. He never has guests, and I'm worried about him…" She stopped. "Please, have tea."

In the parlor, settled into an overstuffed armchair, I gazed at the shelves of cut-glass vases, the table with the cushy vellum photograph album, the fireplace with the veined marble mantel, the wrought-brass and copper chandelier, the dark mahogany paneling, and the ceiling with the elaborate plaster rosettes. The housemaid served me a cup of tepid tea and a piece of apricot torte. Not bad, I thought. It needed a little more cinnamon and orange rind, but…

"I'm worried about Jake, too." I swallowed.

I got no further. Herr Professor rumbled in, a bull of a man, thick-chested and bursting out of a Prince Albert coat as crisp and pristine as Switzerland. On his expanding vest I spotted the obligatory watch fob and a pin that identified him as part of some German Unity lodge. The man had more gold plate on him than a self-aggrandizing Prussian general.

"And you might be?" he demanded, not warmly.

Odette jumped up, flustered, banged her elbow against the back of the chair, and fell back down, slumping like a rag doll.

"I'm Edna Ferber." I rose and half-bowed. I made my excuses for intruding, but Herr Professor regarded me with forbidding gray-black eyes, the color of an approaching storm. I looked away because the man frightened me. Around Appleton the epithet most commonly used with him was: *gebildeter*. A cultured man. To me, he was a harsh schoolmaster with a hickory switch.

I almost faltered. "I'm a friend of your son, and I wanted to say hello. I know it's unseemly but…"

"But young women do not pay visits to young men," he grunted.

"I came…"

"You are a reporter. I know you. You're the one who thinks we Methodists are prone to vice." I blushed. In my account of President Plantz's afternoon tea, I'd mentioned that cards were played, a throwaway line added to my innocuous account. Card playing was forbidden on campus. Apologies were proffered (Sam Ryan wasn't happy with me), but obviously Herr Professor remembered my indiscretion. I needed to stop imaginative jottings in my notebook.

"I am his friend. That's why I'm here."

"He has no friends." He scratched his bushy moustache. "He's always been a soft, yielding boy. I thought football and whippings would turn him into a man, but Jacob would rather gaze at the moon than tackle the world out there." He actually pointed through the window at the twilight sky. As though ordered—Herr Professor, Odette and I——turned to see the complex, unmanageable world outside, ignored by the absent Jake Smuddie who was probably sitting out there now, most likely in that gazebo.

"Jake is a smart young man."

Herr Professor was ready to end the conversation. "He's lost."

"Lost?"

"To us." He pointed to his wife.

Dressed in a too-elegant dress to be an at-home gown—a red serge evening dress with strands of black piping (I made a mental note to discuss it with Fannie)—Odette was obviously one of the ornate possessions on show in the cluttered drawing room, a figurine among the porcelain bric-a-brac, the morning glory phonograph, the heavy tiger oak table, the brocade chairs, the feathered pillows. Was she a household pet that would jump at the slightest noise and bolt meowing from the room to hide behind the woodpile at the hearth? I thought of Frana's sad mother, Gertrud Lempke, herself the invisible member of the family. Two women from different worlds, but so alike.

"I know Jake's been through a great deal of…" I paused. "The murder of Frana." There, out there: blunt, purposeful, smack up against his hermetically sealed academic tower.

Herr Professor thundered. "Jacob is not here."

"Miss Ferber." His wife stopped as her husband glowered at her.

I was not through. "It's important that he not be connected with her death…"

Herr Professor, cold, cold. "I do not blame my son, though perhaps you assume I do. A weak boy, coddled by a silly woman. An only child, hiding in the corners of this house. There are such women in the world as this Frana, a wayward…"

He searched for a word, and I interrupted. "She was a young girl."

A raised voice, thick and coarse. "She was a seducer—a sinner, Jezebel, temptress. I constantly pulled him away from her hold. He told me that she'd found a man to make her happy, an older man, hardly a surprise. But when she hurled him away, he… he lost his focus."

"This older man…"

"A myth, let me tell you. Because even after that…that abandonment I saw them together. She was toying with him. We are Methodists and we're not into such shenanigans, young woman."

"Her family was going to send her to Germany. To a nunnery."

"Catholics!" he erupted, venom in his tone. "Germany has no place for her. She was what America does to young people. Germany is a distant memory."

I remembered an interview Herr Professor had given Byron Beveridge for the *Crescent*: He was a noted orator and writer on the topic of "Honor the German Language," part of a Wisconsin-based group of Social Democrats whose essays in the *Deutsch-Amerikanische Buchrucker-Zeitung* protested the loss of the German language as detrimental to their culture in America. The war cry was "German at home!" *Deutsch in Amerika.* Herr

Professor had made it his cause and often dropped his leaflets at the *Crescent* office. One leaflet oddly blamed a recent diphtheria epidemic on the moral decline of America. He'd also protested the Oneida Indians casting votes during municipal elections, claiming they were all drunkards and fools. Jake had never mentioned his father's zealotry, and once, when someone brought it up as we sat with sarsaparillas in the drug store, he walked away.

Herr Professor went on. "I thought her death would solve our family problem."

That was a horrendous sentence, cruel. "Frana Lempke didn't deserve to die…"

Herr Professor was walking toward the door and I followed. "Sometimes one death can redeem other lives. Sacrifice."

"You think she had to die?"

"Her behavior made it her destiny."

"I think…"

He held up his hand, signaling an end. "But she seems to have taken our son with her." He actually stomped his foot on the floor. "As you can see, he's not here. Thank you for your visit, Miss Ferber. I trust we will *not* find ourselves quoted on the front page of the *Crescent*."

The housemaid was holding the front door open, and I walked out.

◇◇◇

Wrapped in a woolen jacket, Jake Smuddie sat in the gazebo in the gathering twilight. "What?" he said as I approached.

"I stopped in to see you at your home."

"That must have thrown the house into a panic." He barely managed a wan smile.

"Sort of."

"We only entertain Methodists."

"They told me you weren't there."

"I only go home late at night…to sleep."

"Your father allows this?"

"He doesn't know. My mother sneaks me in." He shrugged those football shoulders. "Where else can I go?"

"This isn't an answer."

"It is for now."

"You left your classes at Lawrence?" I slipped onto the bench, inches from him. In the fuzzy fading light I saw a tired face, the sharp, handsome features washed out, pale.

"What do you want, Edna?"

"I'm concerned."

"Why?"

"You running away?"

"My father's presence covers that house like a layer of…of, I don't know, stone. I can't breathe there."

"What happened, Jake?"

"What happened, Miss Reporter"—it was actually said gently—"is that my father has condemned me and said some awful remarks about Frana. She's dead and doesn't deserve it."

"Well, he's afraid for you."

"No. He fooled you. He fools everyone. He's afraid for himself. His name in Appleton, at the university. His place in the center of the universe. His image as part of that group of fanatical lunatics. You know, Edna, I have to speak German at home. English is for visitors. If I lapse into English, which I do rarely since I never have friends visit there, I'm banished to my room. Me, a college freshman. A right tackle on the football team. I'm still a child."

"But is this the answer?" I waved my hand around the dim park.

He looked at me, coldness in his voice that reminded me of Herr Professor. "You don't understand the…the fierceness of my father. Unyielding, a rock."

"He's afraid what Frana's murder will do to your future."

"Maybe, but I've had my eyes opened. I'm looking at myself…"

"And?"

"I don't like what I see. I'm a son who kowtows to a cruel man, a boy trapped in a man's body. I'm a man who refuses to build his own character, drifting in his family's shadow, and, you know, a man who left undefended a girl who died."

"Frana's death…" I had to know.

He looked at me. "Do you think I killed her?" His voice was brusque.

The question stunned me. "Of course not."

"My father does."

"No, he doesn't."

"He insinuated as much. In one conversation. My own father."

"But the heat of the moment…passion…"

He let out a fake laugh. "My father has never indulged *any* passion." A baffled look spread across his face. "Maybe I did hurt her. There were times when she infuriated me, her flirtations, her lies about running off with other men, her…"

"She left you, Jake."

"But lately she'd see me and we'd talk."

"You didn't kill her."

A long silence. "I don't think so. I don't remember much, I've been in a fog…"

"You'd remember that!" I felt chilled now.

Another long silence. "I suppose so. Who knows? There are times, this past week, I can't remember what I've said or done."

What was there about him that so captivated me? The handsome face, so much the matinee idol, so striking, like one of the young actors in the stage melodramas. A young fair-complexioned Edwin Booth with those mesmerizing eyes, the square jaw, the authority of movement. But with Jake there was an unexpected softness, almost a feminine pliancy, gentleness… and gentility.

We sat there as darkness fell. I found my heart beating wildly; Jake had charms that alarmed me. Not good, this.

He was intelligent and aware, not the common boy I'd sometimes thought. A smart boy. A contemplator. I liked smart boys.

Crazily, I thought of my father as a young man, the dreamy poet who fled one land and lost his way in another.

"There's something you're going to hear whispered in town," I began.

Jake's lips trembled. "Now what?"

I hesitated, trying to find words I'd never used before. "Frana...was carrying...a child."

Jake seemed not to have heard me. "What?" Then, the recognition sinking in. "My God. I..."

My heart stopped. "You knew it, Jake?" I watched his face but I didn't know what I expected to see.

He shook his head rapidly. "No, God no. But something about the way Frana spoke the last time I saw her on the street. She acted like...like she wanted to tell me something scary. Just the way she talked I felt..." His voice trailed off.

"I'm sorry, Jake."

Jake surprised me. All of a sudden he lowered his eyes and a choked rasp escaped his throat. He sobbed out of control.

"I'm sorry," I repeated.

"Frana." He said the name so softly it came out a whisper, reverential.

"I didn't want you to hear it from the men of town, the gossips..."

Jake reached out and touched my wrist. "Thank you, Edna."

For a long time we sat in silence.

"What will you do now?" My voice shook.

He stood and walked around, aimless, arms wrapped around his chest; and for a moment he disappeared into the darkness, a shadowy figure that moved in and out of the overgrown bushes. He returned and sat down, his voice clear and resolute. "I'm going away."

"Where, Jake?" I did not like this.

"Edna, I've been thinking about this. I'm leaving Appleton. I'm either going East to join the navy—I've always wanted to see the ocean ever since I read Richard Dana's *Two Years Before the Mast*—or I'm headed West to California." He smiled sweetly. "I've also read a lot of Bret Harte."

I whispered. "Jake, I…I've read a lot of O. Henry. I'd like a better ending than this."

"No, I *have* to do this. Leave Appleton. If I stay here, I'll be the whipping boy of my father and the good Methodists. I'll stay at the university and be pitied. I'll be touched by the Frana murder. People will wonder if I was the…one…the baby. Or even killed her. I'll never be able to escape *that*, and the town will look at me and think of it. When the house is on fire, you gotta escape by whatever way you can."

"But you didn't kill her!"

He lifted the collar of his jacket, pulled it tight around his neck, and stood. "I have to walk now. I visit football friends. They feed me like I'm a beggar." He smiled. "Alms for the orphan boy."

He walked away. I stayed in the gazebo, tired, a wave of melancholia suffocating me. How wrong this was, how sad. A leave-taking, an escape, abandoning what you know and cherish and hope for…

The loneliness of such departures.

Suddenly, out of the blue, I had the image of the strapping young man standing on sunlit California beaches, his eyes staring out over the shimmering blue Pacific. There was rightness about it, salvation for him, a beginning. Yes, Jake Smuddie had to go West—or East, though I thought romantic souls naturally inclined to the West and prosaic types headed East…to find the path of his life, though he'd carry the ghost of Frana with him. It exhilarated me, this reflection. As I walked home, I felt happy for him.

But as I stepped into the dark yard fronting the Ferber household on North Street, I panicked. Suddenly I was scared.

Chapter Fifteen

On Monday morning Sam Ryan was in a tizzy. Matthias Boon was out with *la grippe*, so he asked me to stop at Mrs. Zeller's rooming house to pick up some copy Boon had written and taken home with him on Friday.

"Now," he stressed. "The man is sick in bed, and I gotta newspaper to get out."

Mrs. Zeller's rooming house on Fisk Street in the Second Ward was a respectable home. I knew that because Mrs. Zeller announced the fact over and over. A weekly shopper at My Store, she'd linger over a simple cast-iron pot, according to my mother, as though she were "contemplating the brush strokes on the Mona Lisa." Worse, she chattered incessantly in a high, needle-thin voice, words rushing over one another as though trying to escape that annoying mouth. You saw an old woman, in her eighties perhaps, dumpy as a sack of winter apples, always dressed in misshapen kitchen dresses with one or more stays loose or threatening to give way. When her husband of a half-century died—one of the Appleton pioneers, she'd tell you, read about it in the papers, if you didn't believe her, her family was real history—and the last of her eight children either died or left town and didn't look back, she converted her twelve-room monstrosity of a home into a boarding house.

A "respectable place," for as a "Christian lady of the German Lutheran persuasion," she'd abide no dalliance or misbehavior in her blessed walls. A fussy, opinionated woman, she mothered the men she harbored, those bachelors and widowers who came to Appleton to work. Hers was a household of men and three women—herself, a housemaid, and a cook. "Ladies do too much laundry and want to go into my kitchen," she said. So the men came and went and most were harmless souls. You had news types like Matthias Boon, transplanted from Milwaukee; Homer Timm, seeking shelter after his wife took ill; railroad men, laborers from the paper mills; wandering disaffected war veterans, always on the move. But despite her loud announcement that she screened and interviewed, there'd been late night knocks on the door by the chief of police. Deadbeat wanderers shuffled out of the back window, one step ahead of the law.

Mrs. Zeller, of course, romanticized all the gentlemen as models of civil conduct and charitable spirit—her "boys." The likes of Matthias Boon and Homer Timm…more like troglodytes than feckless lads, surely.

I introduced myself to Mrs. Zeller's housekeeper, a sullen looking Bohemian girl with braided hair and a boil on her neck the size of a harvest apple, a girl flustered at seeing a woman at the door. She rushed off to find Mrs. Zeller, who was haranguing the cook in the back of the house. The old woman came rushing into the front parlor, wiping her hands on an apron, and eyed me suspiciously.

"I've come for Mr. Boon's—ah, copy." I spoke slowly. Mrs. Zeller, I'd been told, was also hard of hearing.

"A *fraulein*? The telephone said they would send a reporter."

"I am a reporter."

"You're not." Flat out.

"Indeed, I am." I wasn't going to argue with this old crone. "Mr. Ryan sent me. If I might speak to Mr. Boon, please."

Hands to the cheeks, eyes suspicious. "No."

"Is Mr. Boon able to come to the parlor?" I knew that no women were allowed onto the upper floors or into the back rooms, male provinces unsullied by cloying perfume and tatters of lace.

"Is very sick, is throw up much. Such fine figures of mens, he is, *ja*. Crushed like a boy with *la grippe*."

Good God. I entertained an image of Matthias Boon heaving into a chamber pot. The stumpy Boon, blustery as March wind, confined to a sick bed, fed nourishing, though lardy, soups and biscuits by a smothering Mrs. Zeller.

In the hallway the telephone rang and Mrs. Zeller actually jumped. She shook her head. "Is work of devil, but the mens they need it, is businessmens and professions, they are." She pronounced the words—*beezynezmenz* and *profezzunz*, and at first I didn't have a clue. Mrs. Zeller hurried out of the room, answered the phone, hung up, and looked back in. "I go to knock on his door." I then heard her heavy footfall on the stairs. I relaxed. Boon was probably listening to her approach with dread.

I waited. The upright piano in a far corner was covered with old-country daguerreotypes in gold-gilt frames, perhaps twenty of them in various sizes. I saw resemblances to the withered Mrs. Zeller in some of the old photographs, ancient relatives in starched Sunday-best dress, severe German women with rigid, fierce faces, staring as though at war with the newfangled camera.

Voices drifted from a back room, raised voices, an argument. Bits and pieces of conversation filtered through the wall, and I recognized the pitched voice of Homer Timm, his words sharp and furious. He was countered by another voice, lower in pitch, but oddly familiar. Gustave Timm's voice, the younger brother sounding defensive and apologetic. I could make out only random snatches of talk, though there was mostly silence, eerie patches of space between the spat-out words. I glanced toward the open archway that led to the hallway and expected Mrs. Zeller to come trudging down, reams of uninspired copy flowing from her hands. I pushed my ear against the wall and closed my eyes. Frankly, I liked eavesdropping on a good sibling spat.

What I heard: *I'm a little tired of...you think that Mother would condone...you've never believed...is this good idea...you're a bastard...you think...I don't care...no, you're the fool...I'm trying to advise you...*On and on, and sometimes I couldn't tell which brother—Homer, the Cotton Mather of the high school, or Gustave, the bon vivant—was speaking, so overlapped were their words. They seemed to be saying the same things back and forth at each other.

But at one point the voices emerged clear and identifiable.

Gustave: "You think this is a good idea? Well, I don't."

Homer: "My business. I have no choice."

Gustave: "True to form, a man who…"

Homer: "I can't keep on…"

Gustave: "She's…the children…"

Homer: "…none of…business."

I learned—or had confirmed—a couple of things about the brothers Timm. Yes, there was a keen dislike for each other, but, perversely, some filial bond kept them together. The exchange of hot words also told me something else: Homer Timm, the severe educator, displayed more passion than I'd thought possible, emotion lacing his fiery words, even a note of hysteria seeping in. Gustave, the smiling, genial brother, so cocksure, came off as pliant and servile; the younger brother as docile pleader. The little boy in the shadow of a decade-older brother.

Homer Timm had decided to leave his position at the high school and head back East to woo his freshly recuperated but persistently distant wife—to be a father to his children. Gustave, new to town, thought it a bad move. He'd taken the job at the theater to be *near* his brother. Gustave kept saying how much he adored Appleton, a town he felt at home in. "What home had I before Appleton?" Homer would not be there for Gustave's September wedding, and that rankled.

Homer spoke matter-of-factly. "Why? Mildred has made a point of telling me how little I matter to her."

Gustave responded, "If you weren't so cold to her."

Homer, simply, "I don't like her."

I heard footsteps, so I backed away and found myself staring into the face of Mr. McCaslin, who'd obviously entered from the kitchen. He stood there, his index finger marking a place in an English primer; and the look on his face was slack-jawed, stunned. I yelped, startled, but the teacher simply wagged his finger at me. "Miss Ferber, really now. A snoop, no less."

I stammered something about the photographs on the upright piano, and he glanced at them. I could still hear a hum of voices from the backroom, the Timm brothers at war; but Mr. McCaslin shook his head.

"You live here, too?" I blurted out.

For a second he didn't answer. Finally, cradling the book to his bony chest, he snarled, "I didn't realize I had to provide you with my home address." He coughed, mumbled something about returning to his bed since he was under the weather, turned on his heels and headed to the staircase. But he twisted his head back and sneered, "You know, my dear Miss Ferber, when I directed you in *A Scrap of Paper* at the high school, I observed your tendency to self-importance. A booming voice does not make a Bernhardt." He smiled at his own observation, doubled over with a hacking cough, and began climbing the stairs.

He crossed paths with Mrs. Zeller, descending with heavy thud and waving an envelope in the air.

"Is at death's door, the poor boy."

Frankly, I wasn't that lucky.

I stumbled out, still reeling from my overheard conversation, but more from the verbal attack by the foppish Mr. McCaslin, unfortunately home sick from his classes.

I stepped out onto the porch and screamed.

For I nearly collided with Mac, that odd creature who inhabited the pressroom. In that instant I remembered that he, too, rented a room at Mrs. Zeller's, proving that Mrs. Zeller rented to anyone with a dirty sawbuck and a cardboard suitcase. Cassie Mac, Homer Timm, Matthias Boon, even Mac. The men's asylum, surely. But I also realized it was midday, and Mac should not be standing on that porch. He should be setting type, hovering over the hot trays, wrestling with the linotype machines, his fingertips splattered and stained with printer's ink. He should not be loitering on this noontime porch, and he certainly shouldn't be colliding with me.

"Miss Ferber." A gruff, unfriendly voice.

Standing inches from him, I sputtered, "Mr...." I paused. Everyone called him Mac. I didn't know his surname, and I couldn't address an older man by his nickname.

He grunted. "Mac."

"I had to pick up copy from..." I stopped.

"Nice June day." When he smiled, he showed missing teeth, broken teeth, black teeth. What I didn't see was white enamel. And that sickly grin, coupled with his fetid tobacco breath and the stink of unwashed linen, made me recoil.

"It is." My head was swimming.

"A real nice day." He was uncomfortable.

"It is." I agreed again.

He leaned forward, and I moved back against the peeling balustrade. My Lord, the man behaved as though he'd rarely spoken to a young woman before. Well, perhaps he hadn't. Awkward and gangly as a fifteen-year-old boy caught up in a forbidden apple tree, Mac shifted from one foot to another, unable to move. Cornered, I looked back at the house, but there was no escaping. He loomed before me, more giant-like, more—I hated the word but it had to do—primitive. Removed from the city room, Mac was a panicked animal.

The front door opened and the brothers Timm emerged, both startled by the sight of Mac and me facing each other on the front porch. The men were red faced from their brotherly spat, though Homer found his schoolmaster intonation. "Miss Ferber, my, my, you're a visitor to Mrs. Zeller's establishment? Are we newsworthy?"

"That remains to be seen."

Gustave laughed at that.

But the appearance of the two snapped me from my inertia, and I took a few steps away from Mac, though he turned to follow my movements. "I was just leaving, have to get back to the office." Wildly, I waved Boon's copy as though displaying proof.

"Well, good day." Gustave tipped his hat and walked by me down the steps. Homer stayed on the porch frowning at his retreating back. Mac followed the movements of both brothers, but then his eyes landed on me with that same penetrating stare. I fled the porch. As I rushed to the sidewalk, Homer Timm walked briskly by me. He said nothing as he turned onto the street. I was trembling, bothered by the collision with Mac. Nothing had happened, an accidental meeting with the mysterious man—towering, grim, so very close—but it seemed premeditated. Foolish, I told myself; nonsense. But I couldn't get Mac's horrible face out of my mind.

Crossing onto College Avenue, a little out of breath, I nodded to Gurdon Tanner, a lawyer whose business seemed to be drowsing all day in a swivel chair in front of his office and chatting with passersby; and then I paused to gaze at some framed lithographs in Mayes' Emporium—sentimental scenes of the Italian countryside. I reminded myself to buy my father some cuff links I'd seen in town, the ones with the ivory cameos. He'd be able to feel the intricate carving...

Turning suddenly, I caught a fleeing shot of a hulking figure in the shadow of the Voight building, a few doorways away. I froze. I knew in that moment, even though the specter did not reappear, that I'd glimpsed Mac. He was following me.

Chapter Sixteen

I met Esther later that afternoon at the Temple Zion, where her father handed me a hand-written chronicle of social activities for the summer. Idly, I wondered how I'd enliven it for the *Crescent*. Lately, I'd been taking undue license with my matter-of-fact reportage. My account of the Annual Fireman's Ball became an exercise in hyperbole: "Festoons of red, white, and blue crepe paper dipped and swirled above the candle-lighted dance floor; and the theme of Springtime on the Fox River brought to mind dances of Cleopatra on her barge on the Nile, with garlands of lilac and forsythia strewn on papier-mâché columns." Sam Ryan, peeved, had edited it down to a serviceable line: "The theme of this year's Annual Fireman's Ball was Springtime on the Fox River. Winner of the dance contest was…" He warned me: I was not Frances Hodgson Burnett gushing out *Little Lord Fauntleroy*; perhaps I should read Rebecca Harding Davis' grim reportage on life in the coal mines. As I blithely told Sam, facts bored me. They were, paraphrasing Cervantes, the enemy of truth.

"Maybe you should write fiction," he countered.

I was telling Esther about Sam Ryan's comment as we strolled down College. We dawdled in front of shop windows. I didn't want to return to the city room, so I'd implored Esther to walk with me. In front of the Lyceum, I pointed at the old building. "I don't want to write one more piece on the Elks Club fund-raiser," I whined. "I want to be Juliet on that stage."

Esther smiled. She'd heard it all before, of course. "Edna, Edna."

"Theater is in my blood, Esther."

She yawned. We'd played this scene many times in front of the Lyceum. Edna the tragedienne? Edna the comedienne? Camille? Portia? Lady Macbeth? Edna ingloriously tied to the tracks as a locomotive lumbered toward her. But this time Esther seemed to have forgotten her lines, which annoyed me. This was a play we knew by heart.

Suddenly I was overcome with the image of the hapless Frana proclaiming *herself* the belle of Broadway.

Theo, Houdini's brother, walked out the front door, sat down on a bench in front of the theater, and lit a cigar. I knew he'd been visiting friends in Kenosha, Wisconsin, and was just back in town.

"Is Mr. Houdini at the theater?" I called.

Theo nodded. "Yes, but…"

"Could I say hello? I'm Edna Ferber, a reporter."

Theo smiled. "Oh, I read your interview. Quite…romantic."

That cheered me. "Well, I did my best." But noting the sardonic tone of his voice, I wondered if he was really complimenting me.

"My brother is rehearsing. I don't know if…"

Harry Houdini was suddenly standing in the doorway, waving to me.

"Come in," he called to us. "Come visit. I'm rehearsing."

Meekly, we followed the brothers into the quiet theater. Onstage behind a dropped curtain, Houdini had set up some new paraphernalia. "I'm experimenting with both a straightjacket and this farm harness Theo located. It seems designed to limit the movement of frisky animals." He tapped his foot nervously. "The straightjacket I got from a madhouse in New York. Bedlam and me. I'm going to escape from the dangerous combination of a straightjacket reinforced with this iron harness. I'm escaping from the inescapable." He glanced from me to Esther. "Do you want to watch?"

Theo helped his brother into the elaborate contraptions, tightening the cords, binding the clasps, buckling the straps. The iron brace looked sinister and deadly. I imagined some roving heifer locked into panicked immobility. While Houdini maneuvered his body into the gear, he kept up a stream of chatter, enjoying himself, showing off. He danced around, the class clown in front of giggly girls. As we watched, wide-eyed and a little nervous, Houdini shrugged and strained and fretted and sweated—and seemed unable to extricate himself. He was having trouble.

Finally he mumbled, "This is new for me. I gotta devise a way out." Unmoving, he mulled it over, his broad shoulders shifting under the restraint, his torso heaving, the tendons in his neck swelling. No progress. Theo waited nearby, tapping his foot. Houdini toppled onto the stage, rolled over on his side, huffing and puffing. Sweat poured off his face.

I couldn't resist. "You seem to be concentrating, sir, but you don't seem to be using your imagination."

Theo glowered. Esther threw me a look that said—Have you gone mad? Gustave Timm had walked onto the stage, observing Houdini's machinations, and my comment made him shake his head. But Houdini burst out laughing, a high infectious cackle, his body rolling back and forth in the ungainly jacket and irons. Tears streamed down his cheeks.

"You're too much, Miss Ferber," he stammered. Then, to Theo, "Get me out of this." Quickly, his brother released him and Houdini shook out his arms, exercised his stiff fingers, and rotated his beet-red neck. He pushed the contraption aside, and he smiled sheepishly. "I won't get into a bind unless I know my way out. This one's a puzzle. A few wrinkles." He sized up the contraption. "This will be a sensation on stage. The straitjacket is no problem. I already do that." He winked at me. "Assuming I use my imagination."

"I'm sorry." Though I wasn't.

"You said what you were supposed to say." He saluted me. "Like my wife Bess, you hurl the most cutting barbs when I'm trussed and chained."

I started to say something, but Esther, who'd been quiet all along, suddenly spoke. "You know, sir, Edna's dream is to become a famous actress. Like Bernhardt. She wants to perform on a stage like this."

Said, the line seemed inappropriate, especially in the old, creaky theater and on that storied stage. Outside of my family, she alone knew my precious desire. Why would she say that now? Houdini raised his eyebrows as though Esther were joking; and Gustave Timm looked perplexed. Embarrassed, I didn't know where to turn.

"Really?" Gustave Timm said. "I'm surprised. I picture you as a writer."

Feebly, I sputtered, "It's been my dream." I breathed in. "Well, I love the theater. The Ferber family has survived dismal towns because there was always a theater nearby."

"I know what you mean." Gustave understood that. "Your father and I have had wonderful talks about it. He remembers seeing Edwin Booth in *Hamlet*, in fact. Even Nat Goodwin in *A Gilded Fool*. I find that thrilling."

"So why is it surprising that I want to be an actress?" I avoided eye contact with Houdini.

Gustave Timm acted flustered. "I meant no harm, Miss Ferber. Of course, it's just that given my profession"—he waved his hands around the room—"I hear a lot of such sentiment from many young men and women. People think of the glamour and the…the…" He looked away.

I kept still.

"Miss Ferber has dramatic flair," Houdini jumped in.

"I find it strange myself," Esther added out of the blue, and everyone looked at her.

"How so?" Houdini asked.

Esther's face got red. "To be *anything*. Edna is a reporter. I just want to be a good wife. A mother to lots of children. I…I don't know…" Her voice trailed off. It seemed a bizarre statement, and everyone waited for her to continue. She looked to me for help, but I was silent.

The men were staring at Esther, and I knew what they saw: the absolutely beautiful young girl with those dark ebony eyes and that alabaster skin set against that dark upswept black curls. Here was the stunning Rebecca of Sir Walter Scott's imagination. And me: here, too.

Not happy, I was.

Theo flattered Esther. "You, my dear, should be an actress. Your beauty…Why your face is positively luminous."

"You certainly are…" Gustave agreed, but he stopped, flushed, staring into my stony face. "Oh, I don't mean, Miss Ferber, that you shouldn't be…"

I drew in my cheeks. "I gather only beauty can tread the boards?"

I glanced at Theo, then at Gustave.

"I didn't mean that." Gustave nervously looked over my shoulder.

"And yet that's what you just said."

"I'm sorry," Theo added. "I was just trying to be complimentary to your friend. I…"

"But not to everyone." I was furious.

Houdini interrupted, laughing. "Now, now, Miss Ferber. Frankly I can see you as a hellfire Kate in *The Taming of the Shrew*. And I mean that as a good thing."

Well, I'd made everyone uncomfortable. So be it. It wouldn't be the last time I'd disturb the peace.

Theo hurriedly glanced at his watch, mumbled something to his brother, and told us all goodbye. "I'm off to meet a friend." He walked off the stage.

Gustave Timm was sputtering some gibberish about my talent as a writer.

Hmm. The homely girl as wordsmith; the drudge as hawker for his melodramas. Cinderella's stepsister turning pieces of coal into words of diamonds.

Houdini obviously enjoyed the flash fire exchange, which bothered me. Was I overreacting? I was hurt, not only by Theo's insensitive dismissal of me as a future actress but by Gustave

Timm's ready agreement with him, though perhaps he was just making idle chatter. A word came to mind, one to be added to my list of deadly sins: *shallow*. A cousin to *boring* and *annoying*. Pride and greed and lust and the other deadly sins were the stuff of literature—and classical theater. The niggling little petty vices were the ones that rankled and were thus especially unpardonable.

Gustave hurriedly changed the subject. "Miss Ferber, I saw you talking to that strange man who lives in my brother's rooming house."

"Mac?"

"I hadn't realized you knew him—worked with him. He's quite the oddity. He talks to no one in the house, even stares down the formidable Mrs. Zeller." He mock shivered. "Everyone is quite scared of him."

Well, so was I, but I declared, "He's a highly accomplished printer."

Gustave squinted. "Really?"

"We all have our idiosyncrasies, sir." I waited a second. "Unfortunately, Mr. Timm, I overheard you squabbling with your brother while I was in Mrs. Zeller's parlor. The walls are thin…"

He turned red in the face. "What?"

"I was surprised to learn that he's planning on leaving the high school." I spoke rapidly, purposely defiant, violating whatever tacit laws of privacy I believed in. I wanted to annoy now, to goad. Prick my vanity and I'm hell bent on revenge.

Good for me.

Gustave Timm looked lost for a minute. "That's not definite, Miss Ferber…and not for publication. I'm hoping you'll honor that." He sighed. "What you heard was brotherly rivalry. My brother has been shattered by his wife's illness and…and estrangement…and has been paralyzed. I actually took this job at the Lyceum to be near him." His voice rose. "I've come to love Appleton. I have a life with Mildred now. And to *spite* me—it has nothing to do with his failed marriage—he says he wants to leave. He's playing a game and…" He held up both hands.

"Enough. What you heard was private. I don't know why you have to bring it up now."

Because I want to irritate you. "Well, you seem to want to provide a detailed explanation."

He shook his head. "Touché, Miss Ferber. It's a failure I have. My brother Homer is the taciturn one, the tombstone in the graveyard. I'm the chattering magpie, running on and on…"

"I was just curious." I shrugged. "I'm a reporter."

"Surely…"

"This is not news…Yet."

"Homer is *not* leaving Appleton."

"All right, then. But this *is* what the citizens of Appleton will want to know."

"Please."

For some reason Gustave glanced at Houdini. "I've said too much. I'm protective of my brother, even as we do battle."

Houdini looked into the wings. "My brother Theo and I have our problems, I'll be the first to tell you. He's my shadow, you know. He even does his own show under the stage name Hardeen, but it's a pale reflection of mine, and so…well…he runs off to talk about me with his friends…" He frowned. "While I yammer about him to you."

I thought of Fannie. She was my sister and I would defend her, even though we argued. I did love her. She was my blood. I supposed someday, should we cross paths one time too many, especially with her frilly Cinderella posturings, I'd have to kill her. Deputy Moss would fumble with the leg irons…and wither under my tongue-lashing.

"We have to go," I said. Esther had been frowning at my sniping at Theo and Gustave Timm. "I'm headed home. I promised my father a walk."

"I'll walk you both home." Houdini moved toward me.

"Of course not. I've told you before…"

"There's a murderer afoot in Appleton," Houdini said, his tone a little too flippant. Esther and I gasped. Gustave Timm looked at him, befuddled. He sucked in his cheeks. "Oh, Lord,

I'm sorry, that was careless of me. I choose the wrong words. My English is poor…Sometimes I speak…"

"No," I agreed, "you're right. But I walk the streets of Appleton all the time. People know me."

"I only meant…" Houdini's craggy face got soft. "I think of that poor girl. A girl just like you two. Young."

No one knew where to look. Gustave Timm cleared his throat and checked his watch.

"Thank you." I broke the awful silence. "But I can find my way home."

Quietly, tension still in the air, we walked off the stage.

While Gustave locked up the theater, we lingered in front of the marquee that still bore Houdini's name. A life-sized poster of Houdini filled the display case by the entrance, and I noticed Houdini checking his image. At that moment a plum-colored Victoria paused in front of the theater, the two majestic horses neighing noisily, and we turned to see Cyrus P. Powell, reins in hand, staring at us.

Gustave, flummoxed, dropped his keys, but Houdini half-bowed, European-style, ready to speak. Mr. Powell's censorious eyes swept from me to Esther, then to Houdini, and he said through clenched teeth, "A private show at my theater?"

The rich man's voice had a metallic, whistling timbre, so much like nails pulled across a school slate.

But in the next instant, he turned to his horses, and the Victoria moved away.

"He's not happy with me," Gustave mumbled.

"I doubt whether he's happy with himself," I chimed in, and I caught Houdini grinning at me.

Houdini said he was ready for a nap and planned to head back to David Baum's house. Esther was meeting her mother at a friend's two streets over, and began her generous good-byes, which rivaled the farewell scene from some Italian opera. Houdini kissed her hand. I walked with Houdini and Gustave, but Houdini turned off at Oneida Street. Gustave and I continued on, and I purposely made peace with him, the two of us talking animatedly about Mabel Hite's recent performance in *A Knight for a Day*. I thought her acting strained, the famous actress "underplaying the needed comedy."

Gustave's face brightened. "God, yes. You know, I thought the same thing." I smiled at him; we were friends again. He added quickly, "I do think you should convince Sam Ryan to let you do theater reviews. I've read your news pieces. I'm not just saying that."

"I'm lucky if I have a job next week."

He seemed surprised and concerned. "Tell me."

But suddenly Houdini was calling from behind us, returning. "Miss Ferber, let me walk you home."

"I told you, sir, I'm safe in Appleton. This isn't New York's tenderloin district."

"I need to ask you something."

"What?"

"Let's walk. It's beautiful out."

As the three of us walked along, Houdini wove an elaborate question about the differences between European and American audiences, and whether I thought—as someone who went to the theater regularly—he came off as a bumpkin with his rough accent, his boasting, and his faulty grammar. "You *write* for a living. Bess tells me to watch my speech. I just don't know." He looked me in the eye. "When you get famous, sometimes it's hard to step backward to learn what you should have learned..." He faltered. "Sometimes I say *ain't* and sometimes I say *youse*, and I know the audience thinks I'm a fool. In Europe it don't matter. To them I'm a crazy American with my tenement-house gab. But here I notice people laughing. The other night, in my hometown, I said *youse guys*, and I saw some folks shake their heads."

He didn't wait for me to answer nor did he seem to care. His monologue was spirited and amiable...and a little insane.

I started to say something about elocution lessons and what he could do, how they'd given me confidence to speak before audiences, but he spoke over me. I got quiet and listened.

Gustave Timm seemed confused by Houdini. When he turned off at Edwards Street, heading home, he waved goodbye and shook his head, amused. Houdini talked on about his wife Bess and her attempt to correct his grammatical lapses, his egregious blunders; and of his brother's mockery; and of the Russian and Germans and Hungarians and…and…

"Thank you for listening to me," he said. "You've answered my question."

"But…" I started to protest as we turned onto North Street. "Sir, I haven't."

"Oh, but you have." He tipped his hat and bowed. He left me.

I continued on alone, smiling to myself. The international celebrity had walked me home, had asked me for advice. He filled me with wonder, this special soul, and for a moment I felt as if I owned the universe. When I reached my front steps, I turned to look after the departing handcuff king, a very strange man, indeed—but a kind man, a gentleman.

Houdini was no longer in sight.

Down at the intersection of North and Morrison a farm wagon passed, a horse neighed and stomped. A woman called out; a child yelled back. I saw a shadow by a grove of elm trees. I froze. I saw the quick movement of a man. Maybe. But there was no one there. Yet I felt a spasm of terror. In that moment I panicked. I was being followed. I *knew* it. Standing there, I watched the shadows. Nothing moved. No one moved. Nothing. Yet my spine tingled and my heart pounded. There *was* someone there. But *where*?

Chapter Seventeen

When I walked home from the city room the next evening, I spotted Houdini deep in conversation with my father. I stopped, amazed. The two men, these two vagabond Hungarian souls, looked like old, old friends, both dressed in similar at-home suits, Houdini in a gray flannel jacket, my father in black. Twins, brothers out of a grubby shtetl from an unforgiving land. They could be sipping coffee as the sun set on the Danube. I waved but Houdini didn't even notice me until I stepped into the yard.

"Pete, a surprise for you!"

"Well, I guess so. Hello, Mr. Houdini."

"I'm catching a train tomorrow for New York. I wanted to say goodbye."

I pulled up a chair on the porch. Houdini was watching me, eyes narrowed. He fiddled with the sailor's cap in his lap.

"Is everything all right?"

Houdini chuckled. "Ah, a reporter's response. I've come to recognize it—me being interviewed over and over." He acted as though he just thought of something. "I think I left you with a strange impression of me yesterday, walking you back from the theater, my dear Miss Ferber. I always get a little, well, energetic, especially when I'm working on a new stunt, my mind darting all over the place, and that new routine made me nervous. Things always do until I get them right." He sighed. "So I talk too much and I bounce around—I can't sit still. I walk for hours. In Appleton if you walk for hours, you end up in the Fox River or in Little Chute. One place leaves you soaking wet, the other leaves you lost in farm fields." A moment's silence. "I guess I'm doing it again."

I felt there was something he was not saying.

In my brief encounters with him, I'd been struck by his larger-than-life presence, a kind of bluster and electricity that the famous seem to project…a little man who filled up all the space around him. Perversely, now on that porch, he seemed my father's cherished chum, an immigrant stepping out of steerage with a tattered cardboard suitcase under his arm.

My father was talking. "We've been talking about Europe. Mr. Houdini has just visited Budapest. He mentioned a pastry shop on the Váci Utca where I went with my mother as a young boy."

"Your father and I are taking a sentimental journey." He twisted his body in the chair.

"But I remember so little," my father said.

"There are things you can't forget about that beautiful city. You remember the smells in the air, the light in the sky, the way the moon rises over the Buda hills…"

"Sometimes I think I'm making it up."

"It's stamped onto your soul."

Both men lapsed into silence, a sliver of a smile on my father's lips. He was enjoying himself.

Houdini turned to me. "So how was your day of reporting?" An innocent question, tossed out carelessly, but I detected wariness, tension in the throwaway line. I stared out at the catalpa tree, the heavy green boughs dipping to the earth. In the flower boxes on the porch Fannie had planted mignonette and marigolds. For a second the aroma covered me. A wash of images flooded me: the aromas of a city old before the Romans arrived, the stench of the Danube in summer, the eye-watery hint of sulfur, the butter-heavy pastry…

I rattled on about the nonsense I'd written that day—an ambitious account of the popular Fox River Baseball League, with snippets of information on competing teams from Fond du Lac, Green Bay, Oshkosh. The Appleton Badgers. But I stopped.

Houdini was not really listening, though he was staring at me. "I feel there is something you want to tell me, Mr. Houdini."

He shook his head. "Oh no, I just came to say goodbye."

Still, his forehead was creased with worry. What was going on here? I talked about some riverboat excursion on the Fox, all the time watching Houdini's face, but I detected nothing. Houdini asked my father about My Store, which he'd passed in his wanderings down College Avenue; and he said the mishmash of sidewalk display—lamps, stacked tin ware, toys, porcelain figurines, gadgets, spilling boxes—reminded him of the Lower East Side in New York. My father laughed and said, "My wife knows how to sell. I never did." He drew his lips into a line. "America has gone on behind my back."

"Everyone comes to America hungry, Jacob. You got to learn to feed yourself right away."

"But America is hard work, Harry."

"Everybody can breathe here." Houdini stretched out the last word.

"*Jews* can breathe in America." My father stressed the word.

"You know, my father was lost in America, a wanderer until he died." Houdini was still staring at me and not at my father. "A man who simply gave up."

Silence on the porch.

Houdini added, "He never understood America. You gotta know how to invent yourself with all this freedom."

Then Houdini spoke in starts and stops of gossip he'd gleaned from David Baum, from others. Twice he mentioned watching Caleb Stone hauling drunks to the city jail. "The big crime of Appleton," he declared.

All the time he was watching me.

Suddenly I understood. He'd come to talk about Frana's murder. He was here for a reason. I interrupted, "Of course, the city room is still talking of Frana's murder. The police are stymied. Our city editor Matthias Boon has made it his mission to uncover the truth."

Houdini breathed in. "No, *you* want to solve it, Miss Ferber."

"What?"

"You are so much involved with the mystery."

"True but…"

My father stared into space. "Edna?"

"Of course not, Mr. Houdini. But I'm curious. That's natural…I'm a reporter."

Houdini leaned forward and brought his face close to mine. "I'm worried about you." A sidelong glance at my father. His tone became confidential, serious. "I talk a lot but I also listen. David and Theo and I sat up late last night talking of the murder. We are afraid for *you*. You, Jacob's pioneering daughter. You walk alone…" He glanced nervously at my father. "All of my life I've always sensed trouble…danger…and, well, I fear there is something in this town…"

"I don't understand."

He waved his hand in the air. "You are a young girl…"

Next to him my father was getting agitated, a whistling sound invading his breathing. Houdini pulled back and managed a polite smile. "Enough. I'm a foolish man. I take emotions as fact, and I believe darkness has more power than daylight."

I caught my breath. "I'm…I'm…"

"I'm sorry."

My father's voice was raspy. "Pete, is there something you're not telling us?"

I made a joke of it. "Bill, I'm spending my days advising young women to use chiffon velvet instead of panne velvet in the making of a shirtwaist."

Houdini shifted, uncomfortable. "I must go." He watched me, though he shot a concerned look at my father.

Again, silence, Houdini fidgety, my father wrapping his arms around his thin chest. I felt my heart in my mouth, my throat dry, my temples pounding. Houdini had touched a wellspring within me, ill defined and elusive though it was; and I'd been tossed, pell mell, into a vortex of grown-up trouble. Houdini was telling me something. The man with the tremendous heart had delivered a message. But what? I felt overwhelmed, smothered.

Insanely, I wanted to be a little girl again, sitting with Esther at the Volker's Drug Store, nursing a lemon phosphate. Like Kathe, I wanted the old Appleton back.

Houdini checked his gold watch and stood. "I'm sorry. Sometimes I'm a foolish man who speaks unwisely. I must be off."

"Stay for supper." My father reached out, seeking his sleeve. "My wife will insist." But Houdini said he had obligations.

I rose, agitated. A world I didn't understand was spinning around me. What had just happened here?

I sat with my father and tried to think of what to say. Cozy platitudes sprang to mind: Houdini is a wonderful man, no? An interesting man; quite the character, no? An eccentric man. A wildly egoistical man. I tried to encapsulate the jaunty Jewish vaudeville performer, but no words came. Something was gnawing at me. My father was rubbing his neck, so I moved behind his chair and began slowly and methodically massaging his head in the practiced manner I knew so well. Deftly, I pushed my fingers hard into his neck and scalp, rubbing the fragile temples, my father's clammy flesh yielding to my kneading touch, until, at last, I could sense his body relax. His head dipped into his chest, and I knew, for now, the cruel and raw agony had passed. He reached up and touched my hands, his long, slender fingers resting on my wrists, a touch so protective and sure that it always made me want to weep.

When I closed my eyes, I imagined a photograph of Houdini and my father as they huddled together. Fragments of their talk came to me…The old country, the wandering Jews, America, a country in which the landscape went on forever. As I opened my eyes, I was suddenly thrilled that my father had given me a life that was American, that was Jewish, that was mine to do with as I pleased. My father never left the porch and Houdini never stopped moving; but both men were at heart rag-tag yeshiva boys running toward the horizon.

My mother and Fannie turned in from the sidewalk, their arms loaded with packages. At the bottom of the steps they took in the silent tableau of father and daughter, me leaning against him, one hand on his shoulder. My mother hurried past us, shifting the packages in her arms, and said, "Fannie, Ed, we need to get to supper."

"You missed Houdini," my father told her. "He stopped here to say goodbye." But my mother was already walking into the house. I'd caught her eye and I understood how much she resented what I had with my father. At that moment I realized what she'd lost…she didn't know how to handle the space left by an empty marriage. Watching her stiff back, I knew that she struggled in the same darkness that engulfed my father.

"Fannie, dear," my father began.

She spoke over his words. "Something horrible has happened."

I tensed. "Tell me."

Fannie's voice was cutting. "Well, you've managed to make Kathe Schmidt abandon us. For good. She showed up after school this afternoon and said she'll no longer work for us. Never again. I just came from her house, pleading."

"Because of me?"

"Of course."

"Well, that makes no sense."

Fannie drummed her fingers on the porch railing. "After those assaults on her, right in the house. I don't know what you thought you were doing."

"It seems to me that she was having *her* say, too."

"Her poor father accused of murder, and what do you do? You attack her."

"I didn't…"

"Edna, I *heard* you. More than once. I even heard you say, 'Aren't you ashamed of yourself?' Because she was laughing with her friends in the library that afternoon—at Frana's expense. You came at her like—like I don't know what. Edna, aren't *you* ashamed of *yourself?* You practically called her stupid…"

"Well, she *is* stupid."

"I know that, but to say it…"

"She seems to think I'm to blame for Jake Smuddie's leaving her."

"Edna, I *heard* you." A deep sigh. "We all did."

"Fannie, I'm not to blame here."

A flash of anger as she spun around. "And who is? She says you intimidate her with your questions and all-out assault. Here she is, the help. Helping me cut dress patterns or…or…we were going to have Wiener schnitzel tonight, but we're not now. She's here as a worker, not a suspect."

My father broke into our spat, his voice weary. "Must we entertain the neighborhood?"

Exasperated, I cried out, "Fan, why must you take her side?"

She adjusted the bow on her blouse. "Edna, you always believe you're right."

"This time I *am*."

"For God's sake, Ed."

"Fannie, it's not my fault…"

My father, into the squabble. "Could we stop this now?" He half-rose from his seat.

But Fannie was not done. "You don't know what it takes to run this household. You're off—you go out *there*"—she pointed to the street—"and I have to do everything. Do you realize how long it took me to train Kathe?"

"Fan, she's not a circus animal."

Fannie snarled, "Flippancy—that's what you give me."

"You talk like she's a dumb ox who is…"

My father stomped his foot on the floor, and we stopped. He stumbled past Fannie and disappeared into the back of the house.

Fannie spoke through clenched teeth. "See what you do, Edna. You drive him to anger."

I brushed past her into the house, headed to the stairs to my room. "And you drive him to sadness." I looked back at Fannie. "And that's the bigger crime here."

◇◇◇

The war among the Ferbers escalated through supper. Which was, of course, not Wiener schnitzel but a dreary liver and onion dish Fannie half-heartedly threw together. Sometimes the aftermath of our battles was a dark curtain that covered the house for days. The walls bled with recrimination and anger and weeping. One time last year it had gone on, irrationally, for weeks—this was just after I took the job at the *Crescent*. No one was happy with that move…even me. One night, distraught over the screaming match of the two volatile sisters, my mother carried her diary from her bedroom and in a clipped, deadened voice said, "Let me read you everything I've written in my day book for the past three days. Tuesday: 'Stomachache all day, shipping delayed at store. At night Ed and Fan at war.' Wednesday: 'Jacob to doctor at noon. Edna and Fan crying. Fan smashes vase.' Thursday: 'Bad headache. Pain in side. Jacob groaning in his sleep. Edna and Fan tore at each other's hearts. Fire and pain.'" She'd paused. "What shall I write tonight?"

It had done no good: Fan was jealous of me, and I was of her; and each of us watched for a signal to rush to battle.

When my father attempted a few words about Houdini's surprise visit, my mother snapped, "And didn't you ask him to supper, Jacob? Did you leave your manners behind?" Fannie and I muttered at each other. My mother, alarmed by the loss of Kathe Schmidt, blamed me. "Perhaps if you apologize to her, Edna."

"For what?"

"Ed, you were always a bit cruel to her."

"I *talk* to her."

My mother's voice was matter-of-fact. "Sometimes you don't hear the acid in your tongue."

"You talk like I'm a witch." I placed a piece of dark rye bread I'd just buttered onto a dish and announced, "Kathe wouldn't accept an apology from me because I don't believe she can recognize decency if she toppled onto it."

Fannie grumbled, "See, Mother, she…"

"Ed." My mother cleared her throat. "Today I learned a disturbing bit of news." She glanced at Fannie, who nodded. "Some townspeople mentioned that you actually paid a visit to Jake Smuddie's home to see him. His father told people."

"I'm a reporter."

"A young lady does not make such a visit, unannounced, unescorted. Or, I suppose, even invited. Ed, think of your reputation in this town. People *talk*. Yes, you have a job to do, but this murder seems to have pushed you beyond the line of respectable behavior and conduct and…"

"He wasn't home."

"And had he been?"

"I knew he wasn't home."

"Then why did you go there?"

"I'm a reporter."

Fannie was frustrated. "If you use that sentence one more time…"

My mother pushed some dishes around, bit her lip. "You were also seen talking with him at the gazebo in the park, the two of you, at twilight, talking, alone."

I waited. "Yes?"

Fannie raised her voice. "She doesn't understand, Mother."

"Oh, I understand. Of course I do. You're assuming my conduct is…improper."

"Well, it is," Fannie insisted.

"And yours isn't?" I shot back.

Fannie mock laughed. "Mine? How is that possible?"

"I'm talking about your baseless accusations—that's the real questionable conduct here."

"Your name keeps coming up," my mother said. "I don't know what to say to folks anymore. I'm out of excuses." Again the deadpan voice, weary, broken.

"You don't realize, Edna, how people are gossiping about you," Fannie added.

My mother sighed. "You're my daughter and…"

A fist crashed down on the table. Dishes shook. A plate slid to the floor, smashed. Water sloshed out of a glass onto the crisp white linen cloth. My father half-rose from his chair. "Have you all lost your minds?" He sat down, folded his arms, and looked as though he were in prayer.

Silence in the room, but not peace: the Ferber women glowered like tempestuous Macbeth witches on an Appleton heath.

My mother turned on him, her eyes cold. "Jacob, I'm trying to guard the reputation of our daughter. People are talking. What they're saying is not *nice*. So, yes, maybe I have lost my mind. Someone in this family *has* to. You sit all day and…" She stopped, breathed in. "I slave all day in that hell hole of a store, making a penny here, a nickel there, pleading the change from dull farmers' wives who look at me as though I'm gypping them of their first born. And I come home to this…and now this…" She raised a hand, palm up. "The doctor's visits, the medicines, the…the silences, the dead air of this place."

My father spoke in a reedy voice. "I understand."

"Do you? Do you really? What do you understand? A silence so loud I can't hear myself think."

"I don't bother anyone."

"And yet you bother everyone. This is a house without walls. Tissue paper. The sound of the bank at our backs, hands out. The empty change purse."

"I worked…"

She shook her head, bitterness lacing her words. "You worked at failing a family. And it wasn't the blindness"— holding onto the word as if it held an awful power—"it's the death of something inside."

"Julia, not now. Don't accuse…"

"Yes, I accuse you."

"Julia, stop."

Her laugh was sardonic. "I sit here and listen to Ed and Fan ripping their love to pieces, night after night, and I hear you say 'Stop!' And then again, 'Stop!' As though you can use that word as a hammer. Or 'Peace'—that utterly unreal word." She started to shake. "I have no peace in my life."

Silence. The ticking of the hall clock.

"I've failed you," he said, quietly.

I waited for my mother to soften her words, to soothe, as she often—usually—did when they had their altercations, my mother relaxing, apologetic. Her hand would reach out to touch her husband's hand or face. Instead, she said something I'd never heard her say before.

"Yes, I'm afraid you have."

Later, everyone hiding in the far corners of the house, I approached my father's chair. "It's chilly out here."

"It's warmer than inside."

"I'm sorry."

"No, I'm sorry. You and Fan should not be here to witness one more sad skirmish of a marriage."

"It's all right, Father."

"Well"—a pause—"no, it isn't."

"But…"

"Pete, let's take a walk."

Finally, something to enjoy. I wrapped a woolen scarf around his neck. "Night chills," I warned, "and wind from the river."

We left the yard. I glanced back at the upstairs window to see my mother there, a shadow looking down on us. While I watched, she disappeared into the room. We strolled on North, down Morrison, over to College, past the Masonic Temple, one of our familiar rambles. On summer nights we'd walk as far as the river and sit on a bench under the leafy sycamores; in winter, we ambled on ice-slicked roads through the Lawrence University grounds. Tonight we turned at the *Crescent* office, headed down the largely deserted street toward the Lyceum. For the longest time we walked in silence, my arm holding my father's elbow, my body leaning against his. A leisurely walk, a meditation. An exquisite treasure, I always thought. Even tonight, when the air in the Ferber household was poisonous and heavy.

My father broke the silence. "Don't judge your mother by her anger."

I was anxious to talk. "She accuses you of…of letting down the family."

"Well, I have."

I wanted to cry out, You're ill. You're blind. You're…you're a poet, a gentle man in a lion's den of fiercely demanding women, myself included. But I didn't. Instead, I snuggled closer to him, reassuring. I could smell the sweet talcum of the soap he bathed in daily, an aroma I recalled from childhood. For a moment I shut my eyes, dizzy.

"And you and Fannie will always be devoted to each other, bound by love, but each of you is cut from steel. You need to be apart from each other."

"Since I joined the *Crescent*…"

"It's what you have to do. You know, Edna, when you took the job last year, something shifted in the house. I noticed it. Fan can't understand you. She looks at the four walls of the house and says to herself: 'This is where a girl belongs.'"

"And I look at the four walls of the house and say, 'What's on the other side?'"

"Exactly." A quick laugh. "You got the same fever Houdini has, you know."

"What?"

"You want to move through walls."

"Father, I don't like to see you hurt or caught in the middle of these shouting matches."

Again, a ripple of laughter. "You two have the same fight over and over, and it's always as though it's brand new."

I peered into the subterranean windows of the *Crescent* office. A light gleamed. Someone was working. Perhaps Mac? I shuddered and surveyed the street, expecting to see the mysterious man watching me. But my father and I were alone.

He read my mind. "You're determined to find Frana Lempke's killer, Ed." A declarative statement, headlined.

"What?"

"I do listen. And the talk with Mr. Houdini was telling."

There was so much I wanted to tell him now, but I had trouble sifting through the whirl of thoughts. Images of Matthias Boon at the office—his criticism, his coldness, his diminution of my assignment sheet. I had no future at the newspaper. Even Sam Ryan, a kindly old man, found my writing overly effusive, flowery. He was losing faith in me. I wanted to be an actress. I wanted to leave Appleton and study elocution. I felt I was being followed. Houdini made me feel special. Houdini was *not* telling me something…

I was haunted by Frana's death. "The investigation drags on. The police do nothing."

"How do you know that?"

"Well, I don't. But it's been a week."

"They wouldn't tell you, Pete."

"Bill, I'm just asking questions."

"I repeat—we do have a police force."

"Yes, we do."

"But you feel you can help." Was that wonder in his voice?

"I'm a reporter." God, how often and cavalierly I hurl that sentence around. Surely, should I die now, it would be etched on my gravestone and some merry prankster would pass by and draw a question mark in chalk over the period.

"But you're not happy being a reporter." My father spoke into the darkness.

"What?" Now I stopped.

"At least not at the *Crescent*. I've sensed a change in you."

"The atmosphere there is different now."

"How?"

"You know, things change. The new editor, Matthias Boon…"

"You like to write?" he interrupted.

"Yes."

"Then be a writer. A novelist. Books. Stories. You have it. I think of the times you've read to me from your reporter's pad. The way you describe people you meet. Those snippets of overheard conversation. Write."

"I can't do that."

I saw him smile in the darkness. "Ferber women don't use that line." He waited a bit. "Mr. Houdini likes you."

"I know he does. I'm a curiosity to him."

"Not true. You're more than that."

"I know."

"He says you have 'a lightning-flash imagination mixed with a wide-eyed wonder about the world around you.'"

"He said that?"

"But he's worried about you."

"I know. I don't understand that."

His voice rose. "I do. It's because he knows you want to solve this murder."

I blurted out, "It'll prove something to me, Father." A stupid line. With all the coolness and dismissal at the *Crescent* office, with all the battles raging in the house of Ferber, somehow I *needed*—what? I searched for a word. Definition. I needed to define myself. Frana's murder had changed everything.

My father was talking. "The murderer is not a drummer staying for a few days at the Sherman House."

"Why, Bill?"

"I've listened to the stories you and the others tell. Frana was an ambitious girl, pretty everyone says, a head filled with silly notions, a girl who wanted something to change in her life. There's nothing wrong with that. She was like you in some ways. But she came from a strict home where the men are the task-masters—her father, her uncle. Maybe her brothers. She didn't know how to escape that world. It seems to me that Frana would only have listened—and planned that foolish escapade—with someone who represented similar authority."

"An older man?"

She knows someone who lives across from a theater in New York.

"Yes, certainly not a footballer boy like Jake Smuddie. But someone she saw as stable, a community figure, someone people trusted."

"Some man who *lives* in Appleton." I got excited. Maybe someone with roots in Appleton.

"Yes." A pause. "And that's a scary thought. That's why I worry about you." Tension in his voice. "Like Houdini, I hear something in your voice. I heard it when you talked to Kathe. I'm afraid someone might hear you and think you *know* something."

"That murderer is among us?"

"I can't win, can I?" He smiled. "But, yes, I think so. You know, that flight through that unused storeroom at the high school—the *idea* of it—is telling, no? Someone, but not Frana, thought that up."

"So the murderer..."

My father shuddered. "We all know him. And that terrifies me."

That night I lay in my hot bed, unable to sleep. The talk with my father had unsettled me, and I wrestled with bits and pieces of it: my job, the murder, my sister—a trio of weights that pressed me to the ground. I was at a crossroads and that notion frightened me. Just that afternoon Matthias Boon, walking past me with an armload of copy, glanced down at me while I was idly typing my copy. A smug look, as though he had a secret he knew I'd not like. And Fannie, sleeping across the hallway, had glowered at me before bedtime, a look that suggested the war would continue on the morrow. And the murder: my father's cryptic words. The passageway as a clue...to something. Trust. Authority. A stalwart citizen of the placid town.

Though I drifted off, I suffered a nightmarish rest, images of the Fox River overflowing its banks, floods washing over Appleton. And there, glistening and gigantic, stood Jake Smuddie in his football togs, a bulwark against the raging river. Herr Professor stood nearby wagging a finger at me. Miss Hepplewhyte and Mr. McCaslin and Principal Jones and Homer Timm surrounded me. I woke in a sweat and struggled to fall back to sleep.

I dreamed of the Deputy Sheriff Amos Moss sneaking back into the high school where he'd once been a student. Everyone had gone to Ryan High School. I dreamed I took refuge in my own house, but the house had been moved back to Ottumwa, Iowa, that hateful, coal-mining hamlet. Drunken revelers followed me home: "Oy yoy, sheeny. Run! Go on, run!" I couldn't find a hiding place. "Christ killer." Everywhere I ran in the hundreds of rooms—each one empty of furniture, each one a coffin-like box—there was no refuge. Finally I located my family, a frozen Sunday-best photograph of Jacob, Julia, and Fannie lined up and staring bleakly into the photographer's lens. Where am I? I begged. I'm not in the picture. And no one answered. Why am I not in the picture? I woke again, gasping for air, and sat up. One thought knocked me back into my wet pillow. My home was behind enemy lines.

But what did that mean?

Chapter Eighteen

The next day I was restless. At the city room I snapped at Miss Ivy, apologized, and the woman nodded, though occasionally she glanced my way, a puzzled look on her face. Matthias Boon, in and out of the office—"Chief of Police Stone has been talking to a drummer who's back in town and yammered about the murder in a drunken stupor"—had edited my article on baseball down to an innocuous paragraph, which, I thought, made me sound like an idiot. A good part of the time I stared straight ahead, vacantly; and one time I spotted Sam Ryan peering at me, eyes narrowed. I tried to busy myself with a rewrite of a Milwaukee story: Lafollette and the wars at the state capital. Nothing like my own wars, I told myself.

Byron Beverage walked in, a grin on his face. "Well, I saw your Harry Houdini getting on the train an hour ago. The most famous man to ever come out of Appleton had uncombed hair, a poorly-tied cravat, and, I swear, dried shaving cream on his left cheek."

I stayed quiet, typing with my two fingers.

I waited for someone to comment on Houdini, but Miss Ivy started to ask her brother about an overdue account, some advertising from the Fox River Electric Car Company. "Again, they're two weeks late," she complained. "It throws everything off."

Sam rustled some papers. Every month they conducted the same conversation. Like clockwork. Within a day or two, Maxwell Pellum from the streetcar line would rush in, dropping shiny quarters on Miss Ivy's desk, get a receipt, and leave. He never apologized. A routine. Like me and Fannie, warriors in muslin and gingham.

I treated Esther to an afternoon coffee and a powdered dough-nut at the Elm Tree Bakery, and she nonchalantly informed me her father had decided she was to marry. She shared the news so calmly it took me a second to understand how important this was. "Who?" I was flabbergasted. "Esther, this is a bolt out of the blue."

She sighed. "He's chosen Leo Reiner. You don't know him. He's from Kenosha."

"Do *you* know him?"

"I've met him."

"And?"

"He's built like an ice house and will be bald at thirty."

"And you're actually going to marry him?" Grim, flat out.

"Well, in two years, yes." She waited. "Well, I have to." She had to? Of course, she did. Esther's father, Rabbi Mendel Leitner, a redoubtable Old World cleric, believed in the East European tradition of a father choosing his children's mates. Esther's older sister, now saddled with a gaggle of colicky babies, had quietly acquiesced to her father's dictates. Esther, vivacious American girl with her own Garibaldi-styled dresses, tennis rackets, and Gibson girl face, had no choice but to comply.

"Slavery." My severe declaration.

"Please, Edna." Esther, I sensed, had her own reservations but would never voice them. After all, she was *not* me. She was a small-town girl who wanted a grand home on Prospect Street—with electricity and an Alaska Opelite refrigerator. She wanted a dozen children in a crowded kitchen. She wanted to watch yeasty dough rising in a crock settled into a warm corner of the pantry. She was a girl who would define her life by the High Holy Days and the keeping of two sets of dishes.

"Esther..."

She twisted in her chair. "Be happy for me, Edna."

A long pause. "I am."

But I saw Esther's lips tremble. I hurried to change the subject, mentioning Kathe's abrupt leave-taking from the Ferber household.

"Yes," Esther acknowledged, "I heard all about it from Kathe. We're still friendly."

"Why is she so hostile to me?"

Esther broke into a big grin. "Edna, sometimes you don't see yourself as others do."

"And what does that mean? I seem to have heard that before—and recently."

Esther waved her hand in the air. "*You* know you can be a little harsh with people…"

I broke in. "The girl accused me of interfering with her already failed romance with Jake Smuddie."

"Well, you know Kathe is not so clever."

"Putting it mildly."

"But she *can* pick up how much contempt you have for her. And—now don't get angry here, Edna—she thinks you have an infatuation with Jake Smuddie."

I fumed. "He left *her* and she practically named him the murderer."

"She's feeling hurt…and deserted."

"Conditions she's brought upon herself." I tapped a finger on the table. "More than once she's suggested she's glad Frana is dead, as though death opened the doors for Jake to rediscover her massively-concealed charms."

Esther shrugged her shoulders and took a big bite of the warm cinnamon-dusted doughnut. "You have to accept that Kathe is now your sworn enemy."

"She's chosen me because she *needs* an enemy now."

"And you're the girl reporter."

I whispered, "I'm starting to hate that expression."

Esther's eyes twinkled. "Why? You use it all the time."

"So Kathe has been chatting with you?" A hint of betrayal. The two pretty girls in cahoots.

"We met at Kamp's. I was buying bon bons. You know, we talked about Frana, and I think she's sorry more than you give her credit for. Edna, nobody wants their friends killed."

"Are you sure?" Bitingly.

Esther bravely made eye contact. "Which is why people have trouble liking you, Edna."

"Houdini likes me."

"That's because he knows how to escape." She said the words so innocently. We looked at each other, eyes bright, and we both started to laugh out loud. We laughed for a long time.

For a moment I wondered whether Esther had heard the story of Frana's pregnancy. I wanted to tell her but I thought of Jake's sobbing, the mournful way he said Frana's name. I kept still.

"Seriously," Esther was saying, "Kathe told me something I didn't know. Frana was having some real trouble at the high school. Kathe didn't know what. She'd been called into Mr. Timm's office lots of times and reprimanded. Once, passing by, she thought she heard Frana crying out of control. When she asked Frana about it, Frana only said that she was scared of Mr. Timm. Like we all were, you know. But he was always calling her into his office on some stupid little pretense. And she didn't like the way he treated her. He singled her out."

"What does that mean?"

"I don't know." She deliberated. "I guess Frana's uncle blamed the school for Frana's behavior. You know, all those fantasies she had. I heard that when Mr. Powell sent her father a letter telling Frana to stop pestering the actors at the Lyceum, the uncle waved the letter in front of Mr. Timm and blamed the teachers for putting ideas in her head."

"That's ridiculous."

"So Mr. Timm felt he had to yell at her."

"What did Mr. Timm say to her?"

"She wouldn't tell Kathe. But Kathe believed Mr. Timm had it in for her."

"That makes no sense." I took a bite of my doughnut. "Are you sure it was a disciplinary problem?"

"What else could it be?"

"Mr. Timm is nobody's friend, Esther. He hates the students. God knows what makes that man tick. He…" I paused. "Frana probably tried to smile her way out of…" Another pause. "Oh, my God. You don't think…" My eyes got wide. "Is it possible…"

"What?"

"Could he have…"

Esther gulped. "For God's sake, Edna, he's a scary, humorless…"

"He's a man to trust." As I said the words, I remembered my father's words. "Yes, a severe man, but who knows what sweet talk a man can muster up."

"Well, I don't believe it." Flat out, clipped. "It's impossible."

"Well, neither do I, frankly. But who knows."

Early on, I'd considered the men at the high school, but those dull, plodding men, locked into the routines of the school, seemed so far from Frana's fantasy world. Part of me never trusted Mr. McCaslin because he always seemed to be performing. He was always darting off to Milwaukee. Principal Jones, the grieving widower, seemed too…too sad. But Homer Timm. He told his brother he was headed back East. Escaping. It was all so…impossible. Dismissible. But the idea took over, grew; and then, in a lightning flash, it made bizarre sense. Homer Timm? The lonely man away from his family. My father's words came to me: The key to the murder is in that mysterious passageway.

"I have to go."

"Where?"

"Nowhere."

"Well, you're in a hurry to get there," Esther said. "And you're making no sense now."

"Lately I've been very good at that."

Late afternoon the high school was nearly deserted, the cacophony of student voices gone from the hard-polished halls. I passed a few straggling students rehearsing a skit in one classroom, and

Principal Jones was writing at his desk. He looked up, puzzled. "Miss Ferber, may I help you?" At his side Miss Hepplewhyte looked curious, but I waved and mumbled something about a follow-up story on Houdini.

As I walked past, I glanced over my shoulder. I saw Miss Hepplewhyte eying me suspiciously. No matter. Miss Hepplewhyte viewed the world with distrust. It gave her purpose in a universe cluttered with rosy-cheeked schoolchildren.

I turned the corner, headed toward the auditorium where I'd spent so many delightful hours rehearsing plays and my oratory. I'd won first place in the state competition my last year at the school and had returned home at midnight from Madison to a massive bonfire and my protesting body carried high on footballers' shoulders, one of them being Jake Smuddie's. Those were intoxicating years at Ryan, and I roamed the hallways as the Close and Personal Editor for the *Clarion*.

I skirted past the library where Miss Dunne was berating a student worker. The auditorium was eerily quiet. Most of the vast room was dark, though here and there gaslight flickered. I paused in front of the three stairs that led to the landing and the janitor's storeroom. As a student, I scurried up and down while working on scenery, spouting lines, laughing and chatting with friends. Sometimes a student would rush up there for a pail or broom. No one lingered there. No one discovered that secret storeroom. Except the murderer.

A murderer who knew the school intimately.

I remembered an episode in high school when the football team hid on that landing, some sort of practical joke. I tried to remember: Was Jake Smuddie there?

I stepped onto the dimly-lit stairs but backed down; I needed light. I found a lantern on a shelf, struck a match and lit it, and the swaying lantern reminded me of how nervous I was. At the top of the landing I stepped into the janitor's storeroom and surveyed the orderly display of August Schmidt's domain: brooms and brushes and pails and wash rags and soap, everything neat and tidy, a careful man's prideful organization.

A patina of dust lay on the surfaces now. Mr. Schmidt had abandoned this room, of course. Bending down, I examined the latched panel. Partially blocked by a small table covered with paint cans, it was unobtrusive. I slid the table over. Simply by undoing the small wooden latch, I was able to push open the door, exposing the unused storeroom with the discarded furniture. It was, I told myself, just a door in a wall. Nothing more. How simple! Scarcely hidden. Actually, not hidden at all. There was no Edgar Allen Poe intrigue here, no need for M. Auguste Dupin's ratiocinative process. Certainly no locked chamber of horrors. No, it was simply that no one cared. No mystery.

Stooping a bit, I walked inside the musty, secret room. I placed the lantern on the dusty desk and looked around. I turned the knob of the outside door, opened it a crack, and for a brief second peered into the final hallway of Frana Lempke. I feared Miss Hepplewhyte, marching through on military surveillance, might spot me peering out that door; but no one was there. The hallway was quiet. How easy it was to spy on students passing by! I shut the door and heard it latch, locking. Caleb Stone and Amos Moss had investigated the forgotten room. Or had they? How thoroughly, these two inexperienced marshals? I doubted whether they'd read Wilkie Collins' *The Moonstone*, as I had. Twice. Or Sir Arthur Conan Doyle. Or, I realized, Israel Zangwell's thrilling *Big Bow Mystery*, with that dreaded locked-door intrigue. There was always something left behind. I'd learned that from those dark gothic writers.

I looked.

Fergus Hume's *The Mystery of the Hansom Cab*. What was the mystery of the locked room? I *owned* that gripping detective romance. Perhaps I'd read it again. A literary roadmap to a solution.

Back in the janitor's storeroom, the panel shut behind me and latched, the table slid back in place, the lantern suddenly went out, and I yelped as the small room was plunged into darkness. No matter. I was near the stairs. For a moment I stood there, quiet. I could hear someone in the hallway. Homer Timm was humming a tune. No, he was singing. Worse, he seemed to be having a good time.

Ida, sweet as apple cider
Sweeter than all I know.
Come out in the silvery moonlight,
Of love we'll whisper, so soft now.

God! That dour man was enjoying himself.

Slowly, I stepped onto the top stair but I stumbled, knocking the lantern against the wall. The noise echoed in the space. I fell to my knees and then, breathless, I sat on the top step, regaining my composure. As I balanced myself to stand, my fingers brushed a piece of paper, so tiny I almost missed it, but I wrapped my fingers around it. I slipped down the stairs, and in the light I found myself staring at a cigar label, dusty and torn. A Grand Avenue cigar, a common enough brand, I knew, for my father had once smoked it—until blindness robbed him of the pleasure. I tucked it into the pocket of my dress. Moving, I tore the hem of my long dress, which had got caught on a jagged piece of molding. I frowned. I hated sewing and I knew I couldn't ask Fannie to accommodate me. Not, at least, for a few more days.

I replaced the lantern and followed what I assumed was the path the murderer and Frana had taken, moving around the edge of the stage and toward the back door that led to small wooded copse where students sometimes studied on warm days. In fact, I read a good part of *Les Misérables* in the shade of one of the sycamores there.

Frana and friend had followed this route without being seen. Someone knew the auditorium would be empty then.

I opened the door and stepped out into sunlight, disoriented. I reached in my pocket and extracted the cigar wrapping and fingered it. Probably every other man in Appleton smoked Grand Avenues, a popular Milwaukee cigar, save the pipe and cigarette smokers. Many teachers at the high school did, and even the principal. Maybe even August Schmidt. And Homer Timm. I'd seen him with such a cigar, the tip of one often visible in his breast pocket. I thought of him singing that awful tune in the hallway…

"Miss Ferber!"

I screamed, spun around. There I was, face to face with Homer Timm, and for a second I thought I'd imagined it—conjured him up with my demonic thoughts. But no, the man stood there, feet away, with one of those loathsome cigars actually planted between his teeth.

"You startled me," I stammered.

"I stepped out to enjoy the afternoon and have a smoke. I didn't expect to see you, Miss Ferber, emerging like a moth into this abundant light."

"I was just being. . ." I almost said *girl reporter* but thought the words too lame and questionable.

Homer Timm puffed on his cigar, but he never took his eyes off me. He spotted the cigar wrapper in my hand. "What's that, Miss Ferber? Evidence?"

"Evidence?"

A wry grin. "Are you still doing Caleb Stone's job?"

"I thought I'd trace the route of the…you know…" I faltered. His steely eyes, unblinking, alarmed me.

"A young girl getting too nosy, perhaps." He puffed on the cigar.

"I was curious."

"And what did you discover?"

"Nothing." I tucked the cigar wrapping back into my pocket.

"A cigar wrapping?"

I pointed behind me. "I found it at the top of the stairs."

"I wonder how it got there." He stepped close.

I backed up. "I have no idea."

"But you have a suspicion?"

"Not really."

"You don't lie very well, Miss Ferber. Usually you're so forthright."

"Well, I need to…" I looked past him toward the woods. Beyond that grove of trees lay Lovers Lane. No one was in sight.

"You seem nervous."

I looked him in the face. "You're making me nervous, sir."

"I'm just here having a smoke." He puffed on the cigar. "What did you learn today, Miss Ferber?"

"Learn?"

"This is a school, and I recall you as an exceptional student. Not in mathematics, of course; but in Speech, the power of which you seem to have lost. And in Composition, as in reporting what you see. You are a reporter."

"Nothing," I blurted out.

He took another step forward, and I didn't like what I saw. There was about him a ferocity. No, that was too intense, I thought. Wrong word. No, it was an edginess—sinister at that—trying now to mask itself as innocent banter. I closed my eyes and saw lightning flashes.

I started to move away.

"Stay a moment." He looked over my shoulder.

"No, I…"

"We need to talk. I think you have the wrong idea…"

"I have *no* idea." That sounded dumb even to me.

"You seem to know something."

"No."

"Stay." His voice grew more insistent.

"I'm expected…"

As I started to move, he reached out and actually touched the sleeve of my dress, a quick gesture that alarmed more than it stopped me.

I ran past him, smashing through some hedges, my dress catching on the briars, and kept running. I thought he might follow me, but when I paused, breathing hard, gasping, he was nowhere to be seen.

◇◇◇

I nearly toppled down the five cement steps of the *Crescent* office, where Sam Ryan, sitting by himself at his desk, looked up, bewildered. "Miss Ferber, for God's sake. You look like you fell into a bramble bush."

I checked myself in the small mirror behind Miss Ivy's desk. I saw a wild-eyed girl, hair undone from its combs, my velveteen box hat lopsided, and a smear of grime across my chin. Worse, I'd torn the hem of my dress, which trailed after me like an unraveling ball of string. I was trembling.

Concerned, Sam rose and poured me a glass of water and motioned for me to sit. "Tell me what happened." I sank into a chair—it happened to be the absent Matthias Boon's chair—and I gulped the water. Images flooded me: that hideous Homer Timm approaching me, his fingers grasping the sleeve of my dress. My new dress, I thought, the fabric shipped from Chicago. A gift from one of my cousins. Now I would have to burn it in the basement furnace.

Sam drew up a chair and the two of us sat—the old shriveled man and the young shivering girl who always wanted to please him—so close that I could see a shadowy yellow cast in his watery eyes. Wildly, I thought, Sam will be dead within a year or two.

"Tell me," he repeated.

Slowly, sipping the water, I talked of my trip to the high school—Sam frowned at that—after my talk with Esther. Of Homer Timm's undue interest in Frana, her visits to his office, the cigar wrapper, his being an authority, a man of trust. I speculated but what did I really *know*? Sam looked unhappy. But then I was talking, building the story: I wove a picture of terror and fear and surprise; I presented Homer Timm as a man who had something to hide.

Sam listened closely. "Miss Ferber, he should not have scared you like that, but it doesn't mean he's a murderer. Nothing you say…"

"Haven't you heard me?"

Sam suddenly looked over my shoulder, his eyes wide..

A voice behind me, loud, booming. "I have."

I swiveled to see Mac standing in the doorway of the printing room, just standing there, his face purple with anger. I screamed and thought, Lord, I do more screaming than a damsel tied to a railroad track in a penny-ante nickelodeon reel.

Mac approached me. "I heard what you say," he roared in a thick whiskey voice. "I know something is wrong with him. I smell it like a dead animal."

"I don't know…"

Sam held up his hand and smiled. "You have not been aware of it, dear Miss Ferber, but Mac has been worrying about you moving through the Appleton streets by yourself, especially at night. More so after the murder, to be sure. You may not have noticed but at times he's been following you. Guarding you, as it were."

I looked at the hulking, simple man, now grinning with embarrassment. "There's a killer out there," he said, matter-of-factly.

Sam beamed. "Mac, I'm afraid your secret is out."

"Why didn't you tell me?"

"How would you have reacted?"

"I'd have been furious. I don't need protection."

"There you go. Well, Mac's an old-fashioned guy who's taken a liking to you."

Confused, I was hesitant to look at the big man filling the doorway.

"Miss Ferber, my apologies." Mac bowed. "I ain't mean no harm. But you travel in places where women ain't supposed go. And at night."

I was ready to say something but stopped. All right, play chivalric knight, if you must. Stand in the rain until your armor gets rusty.

Mac was looking at Sam Ryan. "One night at Mrs. Zeller's I hear Homer Timm slipping out the door, quiet, on tiptoe, so no one hears. I catch sight of him, sneaking out. Up to no good, I know. So I follow him. He walks and walks. I seen you walking home from the theater by yourself. He watched you from the shadows. He spies on his brother. He walks around the high school. He even walked past the house of that dead girl Frana. I follow him, not trusting such a man." He looked at me. "A couple times, lately, he stood by your father's house. He watches you. Your friend, the pretty girl. He's a dangerous man, that one. Up to no good. A shadow in the streets. Some nights when I see you about, sooner or later, he's nearby."

Suddenly I was flooded with frightening images: my footfall tracked, shadows in the woods, a menacing silhouette against a cast-iron-gray sky, the dark Homer Timm in wraparound cloak, sheltered behind thick cedars, the hand that reaches out, touches the young girl's neck…

I looked at Mac. "Thank you. But why didn't you say anything?"

"Say what? I follow a man who sometimes walks at night? He ain't do nothing but walk."

"But he spies…"

"But nothing. He walks and walks, and then he returns to Mrs. Zeller's."

"But I don't like the way he accosted you today at the high school, Miss Ferber," Sam added. "That was scary. Maybe he is the murderer, maybe not. But his behavior toward you needs to be addressed."

I winced. Perhaps I'd overstated the facts, embellishing grandly, Homer Timm as ogre writ large. But it was too late now.

Mac was talking. "I think he is the murderer."

"What?" From Sam.

"I've met murderers."

For some reason the line from the tramp printer struck me as amusing. Then I saw Sam's quizzical look.

Sam went on. "You and I need to talk to him now. At the high school. He has some explaining to do. He didn't act like a gentleman."

"He's ain't no gentleman." Mac frowned. "I don't trust the man. You, Sam, he can push over like an old chair." Sam did not like that. "And you, Miss Ferber, he can break your neck like a baby robin caught in the jaws of an eagle."

Well, thank you. Another graphic image of my demise.

Sam looked up at the tall man. "Mac, you got a paper to print. Miss Ferber and I…"

Mac's thick beefy fist crashed to the table. "I'm going."

Sam and I both nodded.

Chapter Nineteen

I felt a bit foolish as my army of two protectors moved with me down College Avenue, across streets and onto the high school lot. We were a curious trio, me with my tattered dress flopping in the breeze, my hat slightly askew; Sam, so ancient, shuffling with old-man steps; and the mighty Mac, whose long legs kept moving him yards ahead, anxious as he was, so he had to periodically pause, waiting for the lesser mortals to catch up. At the entrance to the high school Mac stopped, nervous. He seemed unsure of himself, like some errant bad boy summoned to the principal's office.

Miss Hepplewhyte, startled by the trio of interlopers, was in the process of locking up the school. She announced that everyone was gone, Principal Jones a while back, and Homer Timm—"He looked like a man frightened by a horse"—had bustled by her, rushing out in a hurry, without saying goodbye. No, she said, he didn't say where he was headed. Hadn't we *heard* what she'd just said. He spoke not a word of goodbye as he left.

We looked at one another, and I suggested he'd returned to the rooming house or, perhaps, he was hiding at the Lyceum, sheltered by his brother.

Homer, indeed, was at the Lyceum, sitting in a front office with Gustave and Mildred. Sitting behind Gustave, however, was Cyrus P. Powell, who'd obviously been interrupted in some discussion with Gustave and Mildred. His face set, lips razor-thin, he held a sheaf of papers. Facing the doorway, Homer spotted me, jumped up, alarmed, and pushed past us into the deserted lobby. He stumbled, crashing into a wall, but then stood against the glass display case that still contained the full-sized portrait of Harry Houdini, menacing in chains and locks. Mac planted himself in front of Homer as Gustave appeared, his face puzzled.

"Miss Ferber." Gustave greeted me, and nodded at the others. "What's going on? Homer stumbles in here all agitated. He's been telling me some wild story." He walked toward Homer, who looked both satanic (I thought) and frightened (I hoped), but Mac's big body blocked him. "He says he may have frightened you." He never took his eyes off Homer.

I gasped. "He did."

Looking both peevish and furious, Mildred Dunne stood in the doorway, one hand holding a brochure, a refreshing photograph of Niagara Falls on the cover. Her eyes were icy. This was not a woman comfortable with interruption. Her father's fortune had made her a tad imperious.

"My brother?" Gustave asked. He shook his head. "That seems impossible. Homer may be a little severe, but he's a gentle soul."

Homer was frozen against the display case, and I feared he'd smash the glass. Behind him, Houdini fixed us all in that penetrating stare, the eyes hard, and Homer looked like a scrawny schoolboy held in place by the class bully,

Mr. Powell walked out of the office and announced in his pebbles-on-a-tin-roof voice, "This is madness, all of it. I'm in a meeting with Gustave, and Mildred Dunne flounces in to wave Niagara Falls brochures at him. And just when I tell her to *leave*, Homer flies in, a maniac. Has everyone lost their minds? I have businesses to run."

Sam Ryan ignored Mr. Powell. "Mr. Timm," he addressed Homer, "Miss Ferber says you were less than gallant at the high school. You *alarmed* her, sir. To the point where we thought it best to talk to you about your behavior."

Homer moved but Mac's hand held him pinned to the display case. I waited for breaking glass, Houdini's cardboard image crashing down on Homer.

Gustave stood next to Mac. "I don't understand this. Homer rushed in here, a little crazy, saying Miss Ferber seemed to be suggesting something about the murder of that poor little girl."

"I never accused him," I insisted.

Gustave actually grinned. "Homer?" As though the idea were preposterous.

Mildred Dunne's free hand grasped the doorjamb, her knuckles white.

I breathed in. "Your brother tried to hold me there. And I wonder why."

Mr. Powell approached Homer, ready to speak, but thought better of it.

Gustave, eyebrows arched, "Miss Ferber, this is hardly the stuff of court testimony. My brother said you startled him coming out of that doorway, and you…What was that all about a cigar wrapper?"

Almost on cue Homer extracted a cigar from his breast pocket, waved it in the air. "I smoke what most Wisconsin men smoke." He'd found his voice, tough and sure now. "I apologize for startling you, and I certainly didn't want to keep you from leaving. You seemed…hysterical…and…"

"Sir, I have never been hysterical in my life."

"I only mean…"

"I'm not imagining things. I was following the path taken by the murderer of Frana."

Gustave squinted. "Why would you do that?"

"Why not? The answer to the murder is in the idea of that locked storeroom." I heard echoes of my father's voice.

"What?" From Mr. Powell. He moved closer to us.

"Think about it, Mr. Timm." I addressed Homer. "Your conduct just moments ago did lend itself to suspicion. Wouldn't you agree? Suddenly you spot a reporter at the very door where the murderer and Frana emerged, and you act peculiar."

"Peculiar isn't guilt."

"But peculiar seems alien to your normal behavior."

"Well, thank you."

"I wasn't intending it as compliment." I was emboldened. "So far as suspects go, Mr. Timm, you have to admit that you are near the top of the list."

More confident now, Homer shifted his position to the left, and all eyes focused on the poster of Houdini. Homer followed our eyes and seemed uncomfortable next to the imposing photograph. He sucked in his cheeks and glanced at Gustave. "Indulge me, please. Explain your nonsense. Tell me. To me, an innocent man."

I suddenly was reluctant to accuse, but staring at the brothers, I went on. "Here's what I know or, at least, suspect. Frana was seeing an older man, someone obviously familiar with the layout of the high school. That storeroom, though unused, wasn't so difficult to spot or maneuver. Lord, it's just a room, not a medieval vault. The sports teams and student actors lounged around in that hallway, up and down those stairs, as you know. In and out of the janitor's room. The cigar wrapping on the landing is nothing, admittedly. That could be years old, in fact, or from yesterday; or even from Amos Moss or August Schmidt. I mention it only because it seemed to *bother* you, got *you* agitated."

"I told you. You startled me."

"I gather you called Frana into your office often."

"That's my job, Miss Ferber. Frana flaunted rules. Of course, I talked to her."

I faltered. "But maybe things were said."

"Yes, reprimands, not…not enticement…"

I ignored that. "Frana was seeing an older man who made her promises, a man who gained her trust, someone she met in some position of authority. Someone who used her naiveté to…to seduce…"

"Good God," Homer breathed in, blanching.

"Frana was carrying some man's baby…"

Mildred gasped and Sam Ryan *tsk*ed. My remarks were unseemly but necessary.

"I'm not naming you a murderer, Mr. Timm."

"But you're coming mighty close to doing so," Gustave spoke in defense of his brother. "Really, Miss Ferber."

Mildred echoed, "Really."

I had been watching Homer's face as I outlined the pitiful, meager evidence, and something of his bluster seemed to dissipate, the color draining from his cheeks. For a second he closed his eyes, his shoulders sagging, and he lost energy. He looked *beaten*. A whipped child on a playground, slapped down one too many times. I feared he might slip to the floor.

"What?" I asked him.

He shook his head and started to tremble. Gustave whispered, "Homer."

Mac had stepped back from Homer but now he rested a long arm on the man's shoulder, stabilizing him. Homer's eyes were vacant, wide with fright.

What had I done?

Silence in the room.

I felt faint, dizzy. As I stared at Homer, he seemed far away, seen through a telescope, a man stuck against a shimmering black background; then, as I watched, everything seemed to reverse itself, like an hourglass upturned and plunked down before me. His tiny distant face loomed large and ballooned, closer and closer, up against mine.

Then everything cleared. I found myself staring at Homer, who hadn't moved. Everyone was silently watching me, all of us bunched together in that lobby, Houdini's eyes watching us. A clock tick-tocked on the wall, a heartbeat. Sam expressed concern. "Miss Ferber, are you all right? You look like you've seen a ghost."

"I've made a terrible mistake." I spoke into the dry space.

Everyone waited.

Cyrus P. Powell scowled.

I turned to look at Sam, then at Mac. Then at Gustave Timm. I said, "Mr. Timm, why did you kill Frana Lempke?"

Pandemonium. Mac stepped back and knocked into Mildred Dunne, who'd started to rush toward Gustave. She fell back into the doorway. Sam belched and apologized. Homer gasped. Only Gustave seemed not to have heard me clearly. "What did you say?"

My voice was hoarse. "I've been accusing the wrong brother."

Sam leaned into me. "Miss Ferber, be careful here."

In a stronger voice, "Suddenly it's clear to me."

I held up my hand. I spoke to Homer. "I'm sorry, sir. I truly am. But it seems to me that you are still partly to blame here, at least for covering up for your brother."

Homer looked at his brother, then back at me. He closed his eyes.

"I thought so."

Gustave suddenly moved, backing toward the stage door, his eyes white-rimmed, wild. Mac stepped behind him. Gustave froze. "You're simply accusing men willy-nilly, Miss Ferber. After you're through lambasting me, will you move on to, say, Mr. Ryan here? How about Mad Otto the Prophet, screaming Biblical quotations?"

Leaning against the doorjamb, Mildred was clutching the Niagara Falls brochure so tightly it crumpled in her hand.

"It suddenly makes sense to me. Of course, it wasn't Homer Timm. He's *married*. Everyone knows that Homer Timm has a wife and children back East. Frana knew that, too. So if she was seeing an older man, especially a man who, as she said over and over, planned to *marry* her, would take her back East to marry her, she wouldn't listen to the attentions of Homer Timm, a married man. Gustave, now, you are notoriously unmarried."

Mildred snapped, "Are you aware, Miss Ferber, that Gustave and I are to be married this September?"

I ran my tongue into my cheek. "But you're not married yet."

Gustave scoffed. "And on the basis of that you accuse me?" He looked at Cyrus P. Powell. "Why not Mr. Powell? He's unmarried."

Powell grunted. "Hardly a crime."

"Other things point to you, sir." I looked into Gustave's eyes. "A second ago it came to me when I was thinking about Frana wanting to be an actress. You might have promised her *that* life. She couldn't stay away from the Lyceum, true, but you made a point of telling me that you'd discouraged her a number of times. You said she often came with Kathe Schmidt. Well, it just hit me. Kathe told me she'd been here *once*, a visit that so unsettled her she wouldn't go again with Frana. Yet you said she came a number of times. I'm thinking that Frana came alone, pleaded with you. A gorgeous girl, and attractive to you, Mr. Timm. Prettiness means a lot to you. The way you flirted with my friend Esther that time we stopped in at Houdini's rehearsal, telling her she should be an actress. Outrageous."

"Miss Ferber."

"Let me finish my thought," I insisted, fiercely. "I came away from that evening angry, thinking you shallow. I think you have a penchant for pretty girls, and Frana was certainly that." I glanced at Mildred, who'd turned pale. "Alone—no Kathe with her—you flattered and eventually seduced her, promised her escape. That unbelievable tale of the man with the New York apartment. You're the ideal older man. In theater. A young girl's dream come true."

"But you have no proof." He was looking at Mildred.

"True, but I always thought it curious that you and Homer Timm didn't live together. Then I understood the tension between you two, the dislike. Two brothers ending up in Appleton, both coming out of the East, yet not living together. Homer chose Mrs. Zeller's rooming house; you chose a solitary cottage by the river, out on the Flats, isolated, in the shadows of the mills. Homer would have difficulty conducting an illicit affair at the rooming house, especially under the eagle eye of Mrs. Zeller. You, Gustave Timm, had privacy galore."

"Nonsense!"

"Miss Ferber," Mildred interrupted, "Gustave and I are together constantly. I think I'd have known if he…he wandered…"

"And just how would I have arranged to meet that young girl in that storeroom? Lord, the day before I was in Milwaukee. You can check that. I was negotiating a contract. I got back late at night. And the next day she's missing. No one got near her, as you know. Her uncle was a watchdog."

I started to feel faint again.

Gustave spoke to Sam Ryan. "This is your reporter, sir? This foolish young girl who spins funny tales to sully men's names, first my brother, then me."

Mildred swallowed a sob.

Sam cleared his throat. "Miss Ferber, you do seem a little hasty here. Perhaps you need to reflect..."

"Stop!"

We all jumped.

Homer Timm spoke in a softer voice, "Just stop."

"Stop indeed!" Gustave echoed his brother.

"No, Gustave." Homer's voice was grave. "I can't do this anymore."

"Homer." Gustave warned him.

"Enough of this. A girl is dead, and I believed you when you said you had nothing to do with her murder. But now I don't." Homer looked at me. "A young student, Miss Ferber. I shut my eyes to something horrible, and now it's too late."

Homer adjusted the front of his frock coat, smoothed the edges of his moustache. "I can't go on protecting Gustave." Gustave lurched toward his brother, his face flushed with anger, but Mac grabbed the wiggling Gustave, one beefy palm on the squirming man's shoulder. "I believed Gustave when he said he had nothing to do with the girl's death. But I wondered. He swore to me. He said he had a new life. He was in love with... with Mildred. He was getting married." Homer glanced at Mildred. "I never understood what that was all about. I never *believed* it."

"Homer, I'm warning you..." Gustave's voice broke.

Homer rushed his words. "You see, Gustave had to leave home back East because he'd had an incident with a fourteen-year-old girl, accusations, an arrest that was squelched, someone paid off, promises to leave town. Our mother wrote me, pleaded with me. I wanted nothing to do with it. There were other episodes along the way, covered up, ignored. Each time he said he'd reformed. He learned about the job at the Lyceum, applied, got it, I suppose, because of me. I *had* to. He's my brother. Cyrus hired him."

Mr. Powell broke in. "Homer, you lied to me."

"No, no. I said he'd been in some trouble and…"

The man stomped his foot, furious. "An outright lie."

Homer closed his eyes for a second. "I was so afraid. I *watched* him. I'd seen that girl at the Lyceum, I'd seen other young girls, and I'd seen Gustave flirting, flattering, and I worried. I *warned* him. When she was in my office, I tried to ask her questions, but she never said anything. At night I'd leave the rooming house, sneak up to his home, watch"—Mac made a clicking sound, nodded triumphantly at me—"but I saw nothing most of those nights. I just walked and walked. Every so often I spotted him walking. I was going crazy. I couldn't sleep, so I followed him, afraid of what he might do. There were nights he wasn't home, and I searched for him. I didn't trust him. But I couldn't be everywhere. When Frana died I asked him, and he said no. He may have had liaisons with young girls way back when, but he would never *kill* them, he said. And that made sense to me. It did."

Gustave twisted his body and looked toward the stage door. Mac tightened the grip. "I wasn't around. How would I…"

Homer held up his hand. "No more, Gustave. No more. You scare me. I watched you. You walked the streets and I didn't know why. One night my brother followed you, Miss Ferber, as you walked home. I was there. Afraid."

Mac spoke up. "I was there, too."

Homer went on. "I didn't want to believe murder but I started to suspect. All the yammer about actresses and Broadway—it sounded so Gustave. When I saw Miss Ferber coming out of the back door of the high school, I felt she'd get to the bottom of it. I was afraid something was going to happen to *her*. You were close," Homer said to me now. "I didn't *want* it to be my brother. Up until that moment I believed him. I'd even hoped this charade of getting married was real. But somehow, with you standing there, I thought—oh God, no! It might happen again."

"Gustave." Mildred Dunne's voice broke.

Homer looked at his brother. "Now I'm sorry. A young girl got strangled…"

"I didn't do it."

"Yes, you did. That afternoon, after the hysteria at the high school when I told you a girl had disappeared and no one knew how, there was something about the way you looked. You knew something. I asked you about that afternoon. I said I'd seen you strolling by the fountain near the high school. I was lying. Of course, I didn't see you, but you said you were meeting Mildred at the end of the school day. Still, I told myself—no, no. He can't kill anyone."

Silence.

Homer's voice trembled. "It's over, Gustave."

Mildred spoke up in a small voice, breathless. "Gustave, tell them he's mad. Tell them."

Gustave faced her, but kept quiet. He looked like a little boy, terrified. At that moment I wondered how Gustave had found the courage to…I stopped, out of breath.

I needed more information.

"Wait," I said. "Miss Dunne, did Frana stop at the library the day before she disappeared? Perhaps with her class?"

Mildred didn't answer.

"I'm assuming she did."

"So what?" A frigid glare.

"Gustave was in Milwaukee. I would hazard a guess that *you* communicated with Frana that afternoon, perhaps slipped her a note from Gustave. You knew of Frana's…predicament. Gustave had no other way to reach her. You were ready with a letter."

Mildred faltered, pale. "No." She searched for an explanation. "It's not what you think it is. Yes, I had Gustave write a note, but a note telling her to *stop* her foolishness. She was hounding poor Gustave, hanging around him, moonstruck, wild-eyed. She made lurid *accusations* about him. To *me*. I told him to write a letter telling her to stop the nonsense. A letter that would threaten to involve the police."

"Why didn't you tell the Chief of Police this?" I kept my face blank.

"Because we thought to say anything would be incriminating. It would look bad, such a note a day before the murder."

Gustave spoke. "I would look guilty of something."

I had enough. "Miss Dunne, just what…"

I stopped. Gustave stretched out his hand toward me, not belligerently but in surrender.

Silence in the room. No one moved. The image of Houdini's eyes, hypnotic, pinned us all in place.

Then Gustave spoke, his voice resigned. "Leave Mildred out of this, please. For God's sake, Miss Ferber." He bit his lip. "It was *her* fault, really. Frana's. She pursued me. Actress this, actress that. And she was so pretty, so delicate. I couldn't stop thinking about her. They do that to me, you know. It's not my fault. It was her fault. She *threw* herself at me. One night she came to my home, and one thing led to another. I thought—all right, a little liaison, a European affair. I thought Frana would marry that dumb lummox she talked about, the football player. She brought up marriage, which surprised me, so I said, yes, of course. It was just talk. She kept saying, look at *me*. Mildred is rich but I'm real *pretty*. I'm…"

He swallowed. "I thought she'd go away. And then she said let's go to New York. The stage. My connections." He laughed. "What connections? I don't know a soul. I avoided her. I *pleaded* with her. But she understood me, and she flattered me. She had a way about her, so soft but so…so iron-like. Frana…so beautiful…so…so fragile…such a woman." He closed his eyes.

"But why did it go so wrong?" Sam Ryan asked.

Gustave waved him off. "She was carrying a child. I said to keep it quiet, for God's sake. But she couldn't do that. Everything was spinning out of control. I made her promise to keep my name a secret, but I couldn't trust her. She kept asking if I'd told Mildred yet. Then she told me her family knew, and they were going crazy. They locked her up. She couldn't sneak out at night the way she'd been doing. She insisted I *visit* her father."

"How did you know about the secret storeroom?"

"I stumbled on it. I was bored, waiting for Mildred one afternoon, watching the students rehearse onstage. All the pretty girls. Mr. McCaslin asked me to get a screwdriver from the janitor's room. It was not well lit, so I tripped, falling into a small table. I saw the latch. It intrigued me. Another day I checked it out. Well, there it was, a secret space that opened onto a busy hallway with a simple twist of the knob. I got excited, thrilled. I used to slip inside, crack open the hallway door, and I'd spy on girls, unseen. The only person I told about it was Frana, who thought it stupid. Once, just as I closed the panel and latched it, the janitor walked in, seemed surprised to see me standing there. I reached for a broom and he just nodded."

Gustave paused, drew a shaky breath. "Then they locked up Frana at home, the crazy uncle in control, and I panicked. One night, before they barred the window, she slipped out of her house. That night I said we couldn't get married, and if she was having a baby, she should say it was her football boy. She went crazy. She threatened to tell her family about me, tell everyone I was the one."

He glanced at Mildred, whose eyes were moist and half-closed. "I knew what I had to do, but I didn't know how to contact her. I'd told Mildred how Frana was driving me crazy, the flirtations, following me around. She said we needed to write her a note, tell her in writing to stop. Threaten her with the police. But I wrote a different letter, sealed it, and Mildred slipped it to her that afternoon. I was in Milwaukee."

"Gustave." Mildred's voice was flat. He wouldn't look at her.

"I planned the escape. I told Frana to write that letter supposedly from her uncle, slip it onto the secretary's desk the next morning, destroy my letter, and meet me that afternoon around two, watch for the door to open. We'd run away. Late that morning I stopped at Homer's office, dropped off a note for Mildred, and managed to drift in with the students until I got down to the auditorium. I had to hide in that hot, brutal room for hours, waiting for two o'clock. I'd closed the panel latch but stuck a piece of wood so I could spring it open. And then Frana was there, all excited. We ran off. She was laughing so hard. 'You love me, not her,' she kept saying. She actually thought we were getting on a train to New York."

He paused and seemed lost in thought. When he spoke again, his voice was a whisper. "I got crazy and grabbed her. The next thing I knew she was lying there, dead." He twisted his body again, a hand brushing the stage door, but Mac tightened his hold on him. Gustave flinched. "You know, I had no choice. She chased after me."

Something was wrong. I felt it to my marrow. Gustave's long confession seemed rehearsed, a performance. His last lines, delivered in a whisper, struck me as false. Now he turned to face Mildred. She was staring at him, her expression one of anger mingled with disgust. She stood there, monumental, in that doorway, her fingers gripping the doorjamb. He gave her a thin smile.

"Miss Dunne," I began, now seeing it. "This is not the whole story. You saw your plans for a longed-for marriage sabotaged by a foolish little girl. Perhaps this weak man mentioned that Frana expected marriage, that she was carrying his child. A scandal, your name bandied about town. Perhaps that witness who saw a young girl running off with a man also saw you and Gustave returning. He said a couple. Perhaps you helped plan…"

Sam Ryan spoke up. "Miss Ferber, perhaps we'd best not go there."

"But…"

"Miss Dunne is a member of an old Appleton family and…"

Mildred's face turned scarlet as she sputtered, "How dare you?"

"I dare."

Sam interrupted me. "Miss Ferber, stop this now."

Mildred Dunne's hand tightened on the doorjamb.

"Who had the most to lose?" I asked the men. "Mildred."

Gustave was looking at me, his gaze unfocused.

I went on. "I keep thinking of the witness who saw that man and woman walking back. At one point the man was leaning against a tree, and the woman pushed him. Perhaps the man was bothered by what…"

Sam, wishing away the unthinkable: "He said the woman was laughing loudly."

"That doesn't defeat my argument."

And he thundered. "Miss Ferber, please. Aren't you ashamed of yourself?"

Quiet in the lobby. The line stunned me, not because it was comeuppance but it made me recall Fannie's hurling the same remark at me. I'd said those words to Kathe, and Fannie, attacking me, had said, "Aren't *you* ashamed of *yourself?*"

In a rush of images, I recalled Kathe's conversation. I'd asked her why she wasn't with Frana that afternoon and she'd told me she was in the library. She'd described a boisterous scene, the clown Johnny Marcus joking about Frana's captivity, the other students chiming in, adding to the joke, even Kathe, disloyal, barking her laughter.

"You left the library that afternoon, Miss Dunne," I said.

She didn't answer, but I could see her face twist, her eyes question.

"Miss Ferber, stop." From Sam.

"Kathe talked of all that noise. You famously demand silence there. You condemn those who whisper. You must not have been there. Where were you?"

She sputtered. "I…"

I raised my voice. "You never leave the library unattended. Riots will follow, laughter, tomfoolery."

A small voice, laced with fear. "A meeting. Mr. Jones called a meeting…I had to stop in his office…a second."

"I guess if we question the principal about this meeting you had at two in the afternoon he'd deny it. I hazard a guess…"

Mildred began to speak but her words were garbled, thick. We all waited. Slowly, that one fierce hand still gripping the doorjamb, she looked from me to Sam to Mac. When her eyes caught Gustave's, they hardened. She looked ready to lash out, but then the hand slipped from the doorjamb, fluttered around her face, and her head started to roll back and forth, a doll's head with the wiring snapped.

"Stop her," she mumbled so low I thought I hadn't heard it. She started to sob in short, hiccoughy gasps, and then closed her eyes. "Gustave…backed off…unable. And she was standing in front of me, taunting. 'Why are you here? He loves me, not you.' Laughing, foolish, her hands on her belly, mocking me." She shot me a sharp look. "I slapped her. The next thing I knew she was lying there at my feet." Her voice swelled, hysterical. "It wasn't supposed to happen. Finally I was going to be…happy." A deep wail escaped from the back of her throat, a trapped animal's cry. "Wrong, all of it. All…Why? I was promised…Why?"

Suddenly she started to rock against the doorjamb, arms flailing, head bobbing. She still spoke but the sounds she made were dark noise. She hugged her chest, seemed ready to topple. That awful moaning unbroken now, she disappeared back into the office, and I watched her drop into a chair, her arms still wrapped around her chest, her body rocking, rocking, rocking.

When I turned my eyes away from Mildred Dunne, I expected to see the men staring into the room at the distraught woman, the sad woman who had just confessed to the unthinkable. I expected someone to go to her, someone to summon Chief Stone. But no: the men were all staring at me, and the look in their eyes was one of reproach and disapproval. Sam, with a face I'd never seen before, was shaking his head back and forth.

In the other room Mildred Dunne was beating her fists against her chest. Her careful pompadour had unraveled; long strands of hair covered her face like a veil.

At that moment Homer sobbed so loudly we all turned toward him. He covered his face with his hands and slowly sank to the floor, his legs stretched out before him. We watched as he crumpled up, but my eye caught the magnificent poster of Houdini in the display case. Powerful, fierce, resolute, brilliant,

Houdini's muscular physique dominated that space. And under it lay a shattered man, loose-jawed, a man in pieces.

Gustave was mumbling something to Sam Ryan. "No one understands. She was so beautiful. No one understands…beautiful girls have a special power, a…lure, a control over men that cripples, corrupts. Temptation."

"You killed beauty." My verdict was plain.

Gustave sneered, his hatred palpable. "There is no way you can ever understand, Miss Ferber. Not a chance in hell."

Chapter Twenty

I sat on the front porch with my father. The end of June had been balmy, with warm, serene days and cool drifting nights; but the first days of July were unbearably hot, more like August dog days, the air static and dry, the leaves wilting. The late afternoon sun was shrill and orange in the sky. For a while neither of us spoke. It had been over three weeks since that awful day at the Lyceum. What immediately followed had left me frustrated and angry. Gustave Timm had been arrested, of course, but it took both Chief Stone and Deputy Moss an hour to grapple with Mildred Dunne. She'd vacillated between periods of shrieking hysteria and chilly stupor. Carted off indecorously in the police wagon, her parents summoned, she was seen by the family doctor, declared to be in a state of nervous collapse, and, within days, quietly delivered to the Women's Asylum in Dubuque, Iowa, where, Chief Stone confided to me, the doctors predicted she'd spend the rest of her life.

Meanwhile, Gustave Timm was charged with murder, confessing to plotting and carrying out Frana's death. His brother Homer resigned his position, and the splashy front-page accounts in the *Crescent* and the *Post*—and in the Milwaukee papers—recounted Gustave's admission. What was missing was any mention of Mildred Dunne's real role—those grasping hands choking the hapless Frana—but, instead, a brief note that Gustave's intended bride, Mildred Dunne, school librarian, had suffered a complete breakdown and was now under a physician's care out of state.

I bristled at the lie. Chief Stone didn't sympathize with me, though he admitted, "Fact is, sounds to me like Gustave told her about it and she went into action."

But a genteel lady of the town could not be prosecuted. It just wasn't done.

I whispered back, "If I'd been caught with a gun in my hand, I'd certainly be taken away."

He'd laughed. "And there'd be a crowd of angry citizens ready to lynch you, too."

Within the week, the Lyceum closed its doors, canceling a revival of *Ten Nights in a Barroom*, as Cyrus P. Powell announced the building was for sale. Privately he'd told Chief Stone that he'd been planning on removing Gustave Timm from his post.

"A man I didn't trust," he'd reportedly said.

The day after the arrest, at the *Crescent* office, I listened as Sam Ryan and Matthias Boon concocted the front-page story. Not only was the truth squelched, but there was no mention of my role in solving the crime. I, who cracked the mystery. Somehow, filtered through Matthias Boon's autocratic lens, diligent police work had solved the case.

Sam, still shaken, suggested that it was unsuitable for a young girl like me to be so prominent a part of such a sordid story, girl reporter or not. Murder, seduction, abandonment. I fumed. He seemed sheepish and hesitant. Civil War veteran, this man; old-fashioned, man of his time, a Midwestern gentleman—all that prehistoric claptrap that insisted that only men had province on the front pages of a newspaper, especially in a murder investigation.

"Mr. Ryan, you know the truth…"

"I'm doing it for you, Miss Ferber."

I'd gotten testy. "I can take care of myself."

Matthias Boon, sitting nearby, smoking his pipe, had a complacent look on his broad face. "Would you ruin your chance for marriage, Miss Ferber?"

"Marriage has nothing to do with it."

"We were thinking of you."

"I doubt that."

Matthias Boon was nonplused. "Our readership would frown on such reportage."

"I doubt that."

Sam tried to be kind. "Miss Ferber, Appleton is not ready for the New Woman."

"But you hired me."

"To do society reporting, to describe luncheons, to record property transfers, not to be at the center of a sordid murder."

"The *Crescent* mentioned earlier that I helped find the body."

The men looked at each other. "That was a mistake. We had comments on that." A heartbeat of silence. "Letters, in fact. The Women's Temperance League thought it indecorous. To mention an unmarried woman in such a story."

Matthias Boon clicked his tongue. "You're just lucky you weren't the next victim."

"Then my name would have been on the front page of the paper."

"That would have been a difficult piece for me to write."

I sucked in my cheeks. "You'd have found the words."

I sat patiently as Boon read his copy aloud. Then I erupted. "And you accuse me of being a fiction writer, Mr. Boon."

Sam glared at me. "You have to understand the way things are in Appleton, Miss Ferber."

"I understand duplicity."

"Enough." Sam turned away.

"I'm sorry," I continued, "it's not enough. I got Mildred Dunne to confess to the actual murder."

Sam paused, chose his words carefully. "She was hysterical, Miss Ferber. You heard her. It was a lot of babble. You can't seriously…"

"This is wrong. An injustice. Yes, Gustave was in on the murder but she…"

"Stop!" he yelled.

Matthias Boon, a sliver of a smile on his face. "Yes, stop, Miss Ferber."

Both men turned to the fiction they were assembling, ignoring me. They began to squabble over some wording, Boon insisting on heightening the melodrama. Sam wanted to commend Homer's role—the brother doing the right thing—but Boon pooh-poohed that idea, informing Sam that he knew how to write copy. The anger grew, and Boon stormed away. Sam stared at his retreating back and I knew at that moment how much Sam disliked the strutting rooster. But it gave me little satisfaction now.

"I can't work here any longer," I said into the silence.

"What did you say?" Sam turned to me.

"I can't stay in a place that celebrates a lie."

Sam's face turned red. "Miss Ferber, please."

I started to gather my belongings.

Sam watched me closely, mumbling that perhaps I needed a vacation—take two or three weeks, think about it, rest, go shopping in Milwaukee—but I drew on my gloves, adjusted my hat, and for the last time began climbing those dreaded five steps to street level.

I looked back into the city room. "No."

Three weeks became ancient history, the sensationalism and the surprise giving way to shrugged shoulders, shaking heads, and the passage of days. Weeds grew around the gravestone of Frana and her unborn baby. Mildred's mother was heard telling a customer at Pettibone's that she'd never approved of Gustave, that she thought him a shady man who simply wanted into a rich family. Everyone had a similar story to tell. Nobody, it seemed, had trusted him. After all, he was from out of state. Back East. Heads nodded. But by then everyone was getting ready for the Fourth of July parade, patriotic bunting already being hung on College Avenue, a grandstand being erected by the fountain, and boys stockpiling fireworks. Folks congratulated Chief Stone for saving the Fourth of July. Life, they said, was getting back to normal.

I no longer knew what that meant. Too much had happened. I sat with my father in the early heat, sweat on my brow. He looked drained.

"Hot, Pete."

"Like August, Bill."

"We should walk by the river."

"Too hot."

I looked at him and my heart raced. He looked so withered now, so pale. The shadow of death hung around him. I had to look away.

I had news to tell him and I didn't know whether it was good news or bad. When I'd delivered the news of my resignation three week back, news that startled my family, my mother seemed happy, though my father just shook his head. I welcomed the time away from the city room. Then, just last week, I found a note from Matthias Boon inserted into the front door, informing me that I'd been fired. That baffled. Had he forgotten that I'd quit? Had anyone listened to me? But I realized Boon probably needed to assert his feeble authority one last time. When I read the note to my father, he smiled. "Some men like to have the last word."

That afternoon I'd met Miss Ivy on College Avenue and she'd whispered that the bickering between Mr. Boon and her brother had escalated since my departure. "Sam seems a different man these days. Unhappy with the paper." Then she leaned in. "Boon's days with the paper are numbered."

She told me that Mac and Boon battled over a misplaced piece of writing; and the pugnacious Boon had pushed Mac. The tramp printer, already moody since my departure, had exploded, hurling Boon into the chicken-wire enclosure surrounding Sam's desk. Since then Boon avoided Mac and refused to return to Mrs. Zeller's rooming house, renting rooms at the Sherman House. Miss Ivy ended, "He's a bunch of nerves, my dear."

That afternoon I'd walked home with a smile on my face, and was immediately greeted by an excited family. "Ed, Ed, a letter from Mr. Houdini," my mother called as I walked into the front yard. I took the letter from her. The outside of the thick creamy envelope was splashy with his name and picture: "HARRY HOUDINI! The ONLY Undisputed King of Handcuffs and Monarch of Leg Shackles." Sitting in the parlor, my family around me, I opened the envelope. The letterhead covered the top of the first page and announced that he was world famous. To the left were five snapshots of his legendary escapes. A dazzling display of boasting.

I read the letter aloud, modulating my voice and leaning toward my father. David Baum had sent clippings from the *Post* and *Crescent*, the story of Gustave Timm's arrest. Houdini's note, written in a tight, cramped script, sent greetings from New York, hours before he left for Europe. I read out loud: "'Strange, though your name is nowhere mentioned in the articles, I sense your presence, dare I say your resolution, in the matter.'"

I looked up, pleased, and continued. "'I have to make a confession, and it embarrasses me. I must tell you that I began to distrust that theater manager. You remember how I told you I always sense danger? Gustave was too friendly with the young girls; and the night I walked you home, I had become nervous. That scene on the stage with your friend Esther bothered me. I had no idea what was going on, but the man talked too often of the beautiful girls who passed by when we strolled College Avenue; and that night, with his fawning attention to your pretty young friend Esther, I sensed something wrong. Even Cyrus P. Powell had hinted that brother Homer whispered about dark family secrets. I felt uncomfortable with Gustave. He could be dangerous. I might have acted a little odd that night, rushing alongside you, but I didn't want *him* walking you home *alone*. I wanted to see you to your door, safe and sound. You know, I can escape handcuffs but sometimes I can't escape the worry and confusion that floods me. You are safe now, and that is all.'"

My mother interrupted, "My, my, he senses a man is a murderer, and he says nothing."

"He's not exactly saying that, Mother."

"What *is* he saying?"

Something slipped out of the envelope onto the floor. I picked up a worn handcuff key wrapped in a piece of paper. Houdini had written: "A key for you, Miss Ferber, though you don't really need it." I tightened my fingers around it, this talisman of good fortune. My eyes moist, I hid it in the pocket of my dress.

Stubbornly, I read the rest of the letter in silence, while my mother and sister debated Houdini's moral character, his lapse of judgment. When I was through, I folded the letter, placed it in the envelope, and laid it on the table. My father was nodding his head.

"Bill, what do you think?"

"Pete, I think his letter is an apology to you."

I sat with my father, and I was nervous. I cleared my throat.

"It feels like it'll shower," my father said.

I looked out across the yard. Yes, the air felt heavy, and at the horizon the slate-gray sky had turned a pale white. I heard cracking, and suddenly there was a flash of lightning in the sky. We waited for the downpour that would drench the heat of that long day.

"What is it, Pete?"

"What?"

"You've been trying to tell me something all night."

I saw the first fat drops of rain splatter on the railing, and the wind blew a mist onto the porch. "We're gonna get wet."

"I've been wet before."

"Your clothes will be ruined."

"Edna." He raised his voice.

Inside the house Fannie and my mother were moving a large oak sideboard. A grand piece, heavy rococo with frilly lattice-work, it was always too large for the long narrow room. For a month it had been wedged by the piano, and now, again, my mother had decided she wanted it near the hallway arch. So the two women, chattering and bickering, were sliding it across the polished walnut floor. Fannie wanted to sell it. My mother said no. "When I die, you can do what you will with my possessions."

Fannie whined, "I only said…"

"I know what you said."

"It clashes with the wing chair."

My mother, furious. "So does the shawl on your back."

On and on, some verbal game they played, a cat-and-mouse skirmish that excluded my father and me. Glancing through the window at them, I felt the isolation.

"Bill…It's nothing."

My father was not to be assuaged. "It isn't your resignation from the *Crescent*, I know, though that's left you stranded. It isn't the murder of Frana, because that's finally justice. And it isn't even the letter from Houdini, which bothered you…"

I was surprised. "How did you know that?"

"I'm your father. I know everything." He chuckled. "Houdini is a good man, but I think his arrogance bothered you. And you were annoyed that he sensed Gustave was untrustworthy and didn't act on it. True?"

I nodded. "True. Somehow the letter suggested that he sensed all along who killed Frana."

"No, not true. What he sensed was a weakness in a man," my father said, completely without irony.

"Which led to murder."

"He didn't see the whole story. But you're bothered because you sense a weakness, too, in Houdini."

That surprised me. "What?"

"He didn't come through for you. Though he did…in a way. The mystery of the latched doorway. Even walking you home that night. I think Houdini gave you much more than a glimpse into his frailty. He let you understand things about yourself… your dreams of a world out there. You'll carry him around for some time, Edna. The thing with Gustave, well, he did what he knew how to do."

"Is that a weakness?"

"Edna, all around you are weak men."

"What are you saying?"

"I'm saying you get impatient with weak men."

"No."

"And that includes me." He paused. "It's your mother's legacy to you."

The rain started, full blown now, gusts of heavy pelting rain against the earth. The spray covered us.

My mother called from inside. "Get in here, you fools. Would you catch your death out there?"

Neither of us moved.

I hurried to say, "I got a telegram today from Henry Campbell at the *Milwaukee Journal*. He's offered me a position as a reporter. In Milwaukee. He liked my work with the *Crescent*." A rush of words, choked and heavy.

My father sat up. "Well, that's good, Pete."

Was it? Milwaukee was one hundred miles away. I'd have to leave home, build a life on my own, a world removed from my mother, my sister Fannie…and my father. Who sat with me now. Who walked with me through the quiet Appleton streets. Who relied on me when the Pain struck. Who let me be his sight. Who singled me out.

Inside Fannie and my mother were arguing, not over the sideboard now, but a wall sampler that had fallen during the arranging of furniture. Their voices were rising and I expected, within minutes, full-pitched battle.

My father sat dying, sheltered from the rain but not from what assailed him.

He was listening to the squabble; already the pain was coming to his temples. I closed my eyes. How could I leave him to this? How? I knew he would be dead within a few years, and I'd be in Milwaukee. The thought pierced me like an icicle to the heart. My lips trembled.

Leave? Impossible.

My mother rapped on the window and motioned, Get in here. My father and I, clammy with rain now, sat still, not speaking.

I suddenly thought of Jake Smuddie. He'd left town after the arrest of Gustave. He'd told a friend he was going to California, and his father supposedly had implored Chief Stone to fetch him back. When Caleb Stone refused, telling him Jake was a man and responsible for his own life, Herr Professor Smuddie had stormed away and cursed the good sheriff in rapid-fire German. Now I pictured this boy I always liked, out there on the Pacific Coast, the footballer on the white sand. All right. That was all right. That was good.

My father was speaking. "I never saw the world, Edna."

"What?"

"I planned to. I *started* to, coming to America. Everyone plans to. America gave me this porch. And I can't even see that."

The rapping at the window. My mother, furious now.

"I can't leave the family." I choked out the words.

"Of course you can. You already have."

"But I love…"

Jacob Ferber raised his hands, palms out, and I watched his long, slender fingers getting wet with rain, the sleeves of his jacket soggy. He turned his body to face me. He cleared his throat, and he was smiling.

"Go."

To receive a free catalog of Poisoned Pen Press titles, please contact us in one of the following ways:

Phone: 1-800-421-3976
Facsimile: 1-480-949-1707
Email: info@poisonedpenpress.com
Website: www.poisonedpenpress.com

Poisoned Pen Press
6962 E. First Ave. Ste. 103
Scottsdale, AZ 85251